BEWITCHED BY THE DJINN

THE BEWITCHING HOUR

MARY FRAME

For everyone who still believes in magic, even when life has lost it's spark.

Bound by a curse—and maybe some chemistry!

Bennet is on a mission to find his runaway sister. She's ditched her royal wedding and fled to the mortal world, leaving Bennet to clean up the mess before their family name goes up in enchanted flames. But when he tracks her down, she flips the script, trapping him in a cursed lamp.

Enter Cassie, a no-nonsense New Orleans witch juggling a wild family, a mountain of bills, and a knack for locating lost things. When she stumbles across Bennet's lamp, she unleashes not just a very cranky—and attractive—djinn, but also a world of trouble.

Beneath Cassie's tough exterior is a loyal and selfless heart, and Bennet can't help but admire her resourcefulness and strength, even if she looks at him like he's the devil himself. And while Bennet is a spoiled prince lost in the mortal world, his courage in leaving his home to rescue his sister and save his people shows Cassie there's far more to him than just good looks and bad manners.

To break the curse binding them against their will, they'll need to track down Bennet's sister, dodge two realms' worth of family drama, and sever a connection that's growing stronger —and hotter—by the minute.

CHAPTER

ONE

I'm haggling with Ernie over the price of a seventeenth-century music box when an antique lamp in the glass case under my elbows starts singing.

I glance down, skin prickling.

What the hell?

The lamp keeps singing, a siren song winding its way through my veins, the melody pounding a drumbeat in my blood.

Mine.

My limbs freeze. I can't drag my eyes away from the lamp. This isn't how my magic works. I have to set the intention first. I need an image, a clue, something the object touched or was near. Only then does the magic engage, like a well-trained bloodhound.

But this?

This lamp is calling to me out of nowhere. No prep, no plan. Just raw, uninvited, full-volume magic.

What does it mean?

". . . and I'm not selling for less than that. I may as well toss it in the garbage." Ernie's gravelly voice breaks through my flustered shock.

I breathe slowly in and out through my nose. *Play it cool, Cassie.* "Can I see this lamp?" I tap on the counter with a finger, super calm, like I'm not ready to punch through the glass and grab it.

Ernie arches one of his caterpillar eyebrows. "Are we done with the music box already?"

"No, I just want to see this too."

"Really?" He frowns so hard his salt-and-pepper mustache twitches.

On the surface, this is a basic Victorian-style lamp you could find in any dusty antique shop from here to Poughkeepsie. But Ernie doesn't know what I know.

He doesn't have a single drop of magic in his blood, poor guy. Just your normal copper, iron, and forceful opinions.

"Let me see it, Ernie." I wave him along before the siren song turns into a scream.

"All right, all right, where'd I put the damn keys." He scratches his chin—gray bristles rasping like sandpaper—then rummages behind the counter. "Moira! Where are the keys to the case?"

A voice screeches from the back, "In the drawer!"

"I looked in the drawer, they're not in the drawer!"

"Are you looking in the one next to the one on the right? It should be on the left!"

Their domestic drama is usually the highlight of my week. But today? I'm one eye twitch away from smashing the case with a decorative ashtray.

I need. That. Lamp.

"Ah—here we go." Ernie holds up a key and squints at it like he's trying to decipher ancient runes. After approximately four million years, he sticks it into the lock and pulls the lamp out with all the reverence of someone passing over a microwaved burrito.

He plops it in front of me.

I pick it up as casually as I can, though my insides are doing cartwheels. My hands tingle instantly. This thing is stuffed with magic. Overflowing with it.

It looks unassuming enough. A dual-light Victorian lamp with faded yellow glass and hand-painted roses curling along the domes. Dusty. Delicate. Harmless looking.

But it's like it's alive. The energy filling it is almost human. But that's impossible.

My fingers wrap around the bronze base, and I'm not entirely sure I can put it back down. It hums in my grip.

I have to have it.

It's *mine.*

I shake my head, trying to jostle the word loose.

What is wrong with me?

Focus. I need to play it cool, or Ernie's going to charge me an arm, a leg, and my future firstborn. I need enough left over from this music box sale to buy groceries and chip away at Jackie's latest ER bill.

I tap the side of the lamp, feigning mild interest. "When did it come in?" I was here last week and it wasn't, I'm sure of it.

"Yesterday."

I can't drag my eyes away from it. "Who brought it in?"

He clears his throat. "Why does that matter?"

I guess it doesn't. "How much?"

He shrugs. "One hundred."

"I'll give you fifty."

"Seventy-five."

I frown. "Sixty."

"Seventy," he fires.

A shrill voice calls from the back, "Dammit, let the girl have it, Ernie! Stop being such a cheap bastard!"

"No one asked you!" he shouts over his shoulder. Then he scowls at me, but it's half-hearted. He waves a hand. "Fine. You want the music box still?"

Oh, right. I had nearly forgotten why I was here, to get the music box for my client for less than a grand so I can turn a neat profit. "Yes."

"I'll give you both, music box and the lamp, for seven hundred."

Bless you, Moira.

That's what I was willing to pay for the music box anyway. I'd been trying to talk him down to five bills, but if he's throwing in the lamp? "Deal."

We shake on it.

Ten minutes later I'm walking home with my bag of goods, winding through the quieter arteries in the French Quarter, right off Chartres. Even here, blocks from the noise and chaos of Bourbon Street, art galleries and bars are opening their doors, blues and jazz music spilling out onto the darkening street. The sky looms above, a swollen gray slab of clouds.

A balcony overhead is draped with fake spiderwebs. A giant skeleton leans out over the street, wearing a pirate hat and eye patch.

Once upon a time, Halloween was my favorite holiday. Now, it's just another line item in a budget already screaming for mercy. *Find costumes for two tiny humans who change their mind hourly.*

I quicken my pace, cutting through a gathering of people reading a menu outside of a restaurant.

After dinner I'll get a chance to take a closer look at the lamp. It will be late, but it's not like I sleep anyway.

I should talk to Mimi about it. She's been around the

magical block so many times she's worn a groove into it. But . . . I am not sure I can share it yet. The thought makes me physically ill.

Why? What is wrong with me?

I need to understand why it's calling to me. The urge to yank it out of my bag and plop down on the dirty sidewalk for a look is nearly overwhelming.

Footsteps echo behind me. Slow. Then faster.

I glance back, my grip tightening on the bag. My other hand slips into my pocket, fingers closing around the key fob with the pepper spray.

The wind picks up, sending an empty Pat O'Brien's hurricane cup skittering across the pavement like a drunken ghost crab. No one's there.

I hug my sweater tighter and keep moving, a little faster now. Only two blocks from home.

The footsteps return. Closer.

Okay. *Nope.*

I spin around, pepper spray in hand.

Nothing. The street is empty.

First the lamp sings to me like a magical Disney trap, now I'm getting phantom stalked?

Unlike my brother Kevin, our own little ghost whisperer, I don't do the dead. Thank the stars my magic's limited to finding things. Or being found by them, apparently.

I stretch out my senses, sending a ripple of magic down the street like a fog, sweeping across sidewalks, up lampposts, curling around the buildings.

Come out, come out, wherever you are.

There are people inside the buildings, inanimate objects littering every corner, but not a soul is in my immediate vicinity out here on the street.

Except there is something.

A shadow?

But not a shadow. It's alive. But not human.

I try to get a read on it, wrap around the shape of it in my mind, but it's slippery. Wrong. Not a person. Not an animal. More of a magical echo of something. A shadow with teeth.

The hairs on my arms stand up. Cold trickles down my spine.

Leave. Now.

The instinct is sharp and certain, and I don't question it. I learned long ago to trust my gut. My grip tightens on the pepper spray, and I clutch my bag like it's a shield.

Then I turn and run.

The scent of cayenne and black pepper envelops me as I slam the door shut and engage the lock.

It's Monday, which means Mimi is making red beans and rice. It apparently also means I'm losing my damn mind.

I gaze through the peephole, breath sawing in and out.

The narrow alley between our building and the one next door is empty, aside from the uneven cobblestones, the opposing brick wall, a half-dead ficus in a chipped blue pot, and a sagging jack-o'-lantern Kevin brought home from school.

I would bet money I was followed the entire sprint home. Was it a ghost? I have never sensed one like it, if it was. The hex bags should keep them out.

I set my keys on the heavy wooden Bombe table in the entry and then tiptoe in the direction of the stairs, willing the sounds from the simmering stove to cover my steps and the slight rustle of the bag in my arms.

"Hey, Cassie," Mimi calls as I pass the open doorway of the kitchen.

Dammit.

I shift my purchases behind my back. "Hey, Mimi."

"What's in the bag?" Her focus remains on the food, not even glancing at me.

Mimi is like a steel cable. She looks like she'd snap in half with a strong breeze, but she's tough as old leather—weathered, unyielding, impossible to wear down.

"Nothing important."

"Lie." She points her wooden spoon in my direction like a tiny wizard casting a truth spell.

That spoon has seen some things. We've had it since Uncle Jeb died—possibly longer. It's cracked, stained, and looks like it should be in a museum next to the Rosetta stone, but Mimi swears it makes everything taste better and won't listen to my concerns about things like bacteria. She refuses to part with anything that still works, which includes the battered Dutch oven simmering on the stove, her ancient floral slippers, and the bright blue silk robe wrapped around her that she bought in 1967.

Normally I wouldn't even attempt to lie to Mimi, but I'm not ready to share until I figure out more about what is going on. Not because I have an unhealthy obsession with it. Nope. Not at all.

She'll just worry unnecessarily. I'm sure it's no biggie anyway, a lamp that calls to me, strange malignant shadows, me losing my mind. Nothing to see here.

"I'll show you later."

"Another lie?" Her piercing gaze finally strikes me. "Now I'm curious. What do you have in there?"

Ugh. I should have thought of a good cover story before coming home so I wouldn't set off the lie-dar. Something true-ish. It's impossible to get away with anything when she's around.

I stride toward the stairs. "We'll talk later," I yell over a shoulder. Retreat is always the best option in these situations.

"You can't run from me." Her words drift up the stairs.

"But I sure can try," I murmur.

Thank the stars she doesn't have super hearing.

I peek in on Jackie, napping in the armchair tucked into the corner of her room, a book splayed open on her lap. The floor is its usual war zone of discarded clothes, fuzzy socks, and a rainbow of tangled hair ties. Her desk is drowning in papers and empty tea mugs, beneath them an ancient, wheezing computer blinking like it's holding on by sheer willpower.

Online school was the only option this year. She's missed too many days to keep up in person.

At least she's resting.

I linger in the doorway a few extra seconds to make sure her chest is rising and falling, then pad down the hall.

The sound of running water echoes from the Jack-and-Jill bathroom that connects Jackie's room to Kevin's. I knock lightly.

"Dinner's almost ready," I call.

"Okay!" he yells back over the spray.

I continue deeper into the house, climbing the second staircase—the one that creaks less—up to the third floor, to my room and the office.

The house is too big for only the four of us. It made sense when Mom and Dad were here, when there were enough hands to keep things running. But they've been gone over three years, and now . . .

The ceilings are tall, the windows drafty, and every room is painted in some vibrant color or wallpapered with patterns older than Methuselah. It's beautiful in that eccentric, lived-in way, like a house that's seen too many Mardi Gras parades and refuses to tone it down.

No mortgage to pay, thank the heavens, only taxes, utilities, and an endless list of repairs sucking the life out of me one busted pipe at a time. I could sell. But that would mean declaring them legally dead. And even if it's true, I'm not ready to let go of that last thread.

I push open the heavy door to my office and it thumps into something solid.

I squeeze through the doorway, sidestepping Kevin's chaos. His sports bag is behind the door, his mitt and ball have taken over the recliner, his backpack has exploded across the chaise, and his bat is leaning against my desk.

I weave through the mess and collapse into the desk chair, a mahogany Victorian number upholstered in red velvet. It creaks ominously under me but doesn't give. Dad loved this stuff. The rest of us mocked him for it. Who willingly fills a house with furniture that could double as medieval torture devices?

But here it is. Still here. Still heavy. Still uncomfortable as hell.

I glance at the bag under the desk. The lamp is inside. Waiting.

My fingers tingle.

I could take a quick peek. Just for a minute.

I reach for the bag, barely grazing the edge, when Kevin clomps in wrapped in a towel, damp hair sticking up like he wrestled the shower and lost.

"I couldn't shower. The water's cold."

It takes a second for the words to compute. "What?"

"The shower won't get warm."

"Maybe the water heater needs to be re-lit." It's an ancient beast that lives in the basement.

"Mimi already tried. She said it's busted."

I throw up my hands. "Of course it is."

Because why wouldn't the water heater die today? It only completes the disaster aesthetic: molding floorboards, a leaky roof, a flickering electric system. Now we've added freezing showers to the growing list of things for Cassie to stress about.

I was hoping things would hold on long enough to pay off the more urgent bills. But no, clearly the water heater had other plans. It wanted to die dramatically. Along with everything else around here.

I drag myself up from the velvet seat with a creak and a groan, shoving the bag deeper under the desk like I can bury my curiosity along with it.

"Come on. You can take a bath tonight, after dinner," I tell Kevin. "We'll heat water on the stove like it's 1892."

While Kevin gets dressed, I retreat to the kitchen. "How was Jackie today?" I ask Mimi before she can even open her mouth.

A classic defensive maneuver. Cut her off at the pass. If I keep her focused on our biggest concern, maybe she won't remember to interrogate me about my earlier trip to Ernie's or the mysterious bags I swore were "nothing important." Pay no attention to the witch behind the curtain.

Thankfully, it works. For now.

"She slept off and on." Mimi heaves a skillet of cornbread from the oven.

My stomach growls. I lean against the counter and rub my head. "That's good."

She slides a bread knife from the block. "Headache?"

"Always."

She frowns. "You work too much. You need to take a break. Go out with your friends, let your hair down. Maybe get laid."

My mouth pops open. "Mimi!"

"What?" She shrugs. "You're young."

"I'm twenty-eight." Going on forty-five, but still, not exactly a babe in the woods.

"Do you know what I was up to when I was your age?" She lifts her brows.

I wince. "Do I want to know?"

"Let's just say, I made sure I lived it up before I settled down with your uncle, bless his soul. And you should too. Will you set the table?"

I nod, anything to save me from the path this conversation is taking. I grab the bowls from the cabinet, silverware from the drawer, and head to the thick wood table in the connected dining area. It's the kind of table that could survive a hurricane, or be used to summon a demon, depending on how you arrange the candles.

I set a spoon on a bright red placemat, and the utensil immediately twitches sideways, clattering to the floor.

I lift a brow at Mimi.

She waves an oven mitt in the air like she's swatting away a fly. "One of Kevin's visitors. It's an active one. Harmless, though. Had to be, if they made it past the wards."

"They better be," I mutter, bending to retrieve the spoon. "We paid an arm and a leg for those hex bags. And suffered through two weeks of Richard to get them."

Every doorway and window now has a charm bag—herbs, crystals, stitched symbols, all spelled to keep out the nasty spirits. Though friendly ghosts can waltz right in and help themselves to the cornbread, apparently.

I hold the spoon up. "Okay, ghosty. Kevin's just a kid. Be patient. His gifts are new and unstable. No acting out."

The lights flicker in response.

Hopefully that was agreement and not foreshadowing. We do not have time or money for another poltergeist incident. The last one almost ate the washing machine. To spirits, Kevin is a flare shining through the dark fog, brilliant, burning, and impossible to keep away from.

"Anyway." I turn back to Mimi. "I bought the music box from Ernie. Got enough to make a partial payment for Jackie's last ER visit. That should keep collections off us for another month."

She pauses midslice, knife hovering in the air. "Cassie—"

"I'll figure it out, Mimi. No worrying." I walk over and rest a hand on her tense shoulder. "I got a call from someone hunting for some specific Marie Laveau items. They're willing to spend a small fortune. I'm meeting them next week. We'll be okay."

She keeps cutting cornbread, tossing the pieces into a shallow, towel-lined bowl. "Are you going to tell me what else you brought home that has you all twitchy and telling lies?" Mimi asks, not even looking at me. The question is casual. The tone is not.

"I don't know yet."

She pauses, then glances at me over her shoulder. "The truth. Finally. Was that so painful?"

"I am in a lot of existential anguish, I'll have you know."

She snorts. "Is there anything more you can tell me?" she asks, while attempting to evil eye me into submission.

I wave a hand at her. "Hey, quit with the stink eye. I will tell you as soon as I have anything to share."

"What does that even—?"

"You only won because you cheated!" Jackie shuffles into the kitchen, glaring at Kevin.

"I didn't cheat. I'm just better than you," Kevin declares, flexing one of his scrawny arms like a bodybuilder.

Jackie tosses her messy dark hair back. "Yeah, right. You wish."

I pull out a chair for her. "Let me fix your hair. What was it this time?" They're always in a competition about something or other.

She sinks into the seat, and I start smoothing her hair into a braid. Her arms have gotten too weak to manage it herself lately. Small things like this hit the hardest.

Kevin plops into the chair beside her. "We did five rounds of rock-paper-scissors and I won every time."

"You used magic."

He gives her a pointed glare. "My magic doesn't work that way. What's a ghost gonna do? Read your mind and flash me the answer? They're dead, not psychic."

"Help Mimi with the food," I tell him, jerking my chin toward the counter.

He hops up and grabs an oven mitt.

Jackie tilts her head toward him without turning. "How do you know they aren't psychic? They could be sticking their ghost hands in my head or something."

"There are no ghosts here," Kevin insists. "Richard's hex bags took care of it."

The lights flicker.

We all freeze, eyes on the ceiling.

Then . . . nothing. The bulbs steady.

I blow out a breath, more worried about the ancient electrical system than a haunting, honestly.

The cabinet next to the fridge creaks open and slams shut.

Jackie points. "No ghosts, huh? That was basically a confession."

Mimi sets cornbread on the table.

Kevin's face goes slack for a few seconds. "No. He's just letting us know he's here."

"What does he want?" Jackie asks.

I tie off the braid with a hair tie from my wrist.

Kevin grabs the pot of rice and beans, placing it next to the cornbread. "What everyone wants. To be heard."

He's only eleven, but he's already carried more than most adults. He grew up fast when Jackie got sick, and faster still when Mom and Dad disappeared.

He'll always be my baby brother, no matter how wise he gets or how fast he grows. He's already taller than me, which is like a personal betrayal.

Our parents had me young—twenty and wild-hearted—so by the time I hit high school, they were still young enough to start over. Jackie came when I was fifteen. Kevin the year after.

I grab the serving spoons and we dig in, taking turns ladling beans and rice into our bowls.

"How was school today?" Mimi asks.

"Boring." Jackie stabs at her food. "I hate online school."

"Sucks to suck," Kevin grins.

She shoves his shoulder.

"Hey. Hands to yourself." I point at her with my fork. "Did you get your work done?"

"Yes."

"Did you eat lunch?"

Jackie rolls her eyes. "Yes, I ate half my sandwich and a whole yogurt. Ask Mimi. And before you go down your checklist, I drank water, I took my vitamins, I even did my breathing exercises. Can we not do the inquisition tonight?"

Am I that predictable? "Fine. Kevin." I turn to him. "How was *your* day?"

He launches into a play-by-play of his latest baseball triumph. I pay attention, sort of, but keep half an eye on Jackie, making sure she eats more than a spoonful.

And I try very, very hard not to think about the lamp hidden upstairs. It's waiting, humming, calling, even from three stories over my head.

We finish eating, and I help Kevin boil water and carry it upstairs for a lukewarm bath. Then it's homework, getting ready for bed, and making sure the house is locked once everyone is tucked away.

By the time I escape and shut myself in my office, it's almost nine and I'm so exhausted my bones are aching. I don't think I've had a full night's sleep since Mom and Dad disappeared. I'm always half awake, all night long, waiting for another catastrophe.

And now I can't possibly sleep until I get my hands on the lamp and at least attempt to figure out what's in it.

I stumble over Kevin's bat on my way around the desk—again—and mutter a curse as I prop it back up and then reach down, yanking the bag from Ernie's out from beneath.

Electricity zings up my arm the moment my fingers connect with the smooth yellow surface.

I set it in front of me, one hand gripping either side of the bronze base. Then I shut my eyes and take a deep breath, weaving my magic around it and pushing it through the gap at the top.

Why is it so compelling?

It can't possibly be a person, but the sensation won't stop. My magic circles and pools around it, trying to determine the shape and substance.

It's a condensed ball of pure bright energy. A dense, seething knot of life, coiled tight like a spring, waiting to unspool.

I shake my head. I must be losing it. Lack of sleep. Stress. Stress does crazy things to your body. I had a weird rash on my arm last month and I've skipped my period twice this year. Maybe my magic is broken.

I take another deep breath, draw on my magic again, and poke at the circle.

It crackles and then blazes out of the lamp, rushing through the top and exploding like a firecracker above my head.

I fall back in the chair, blinking through the remnants of the flash, a silhouette outlined against the glow in front of me.

"What the—?"

My heart drops into my toes.

There's a man standing on the other side of my desk.

CHAPTER

THREE

Without thinking, I grab the nearest object—a paperweight shaped like a star—and chuck it at his head.

It hits him square in the forehead with a satisfying thunk, bounces off, and he catches it midair. He raises an eyebrow, then sets it gently on the desk. "Was that strictly necessary?"

"It felt appropriate." I narrow my eyes. "Are you a ghost? Were you haunting the lamp?"

"Excuse me? A ghost?"

He has an accent. British maybe. Or New Zealand or something.

The hex bags aren't working. They're defective. No way Kevin's friendly neighborhood ghost could materialize, hold physical objects, and speak coherently without some serious mojo. Mojo that should be hindered by Richard's hex bags. Even if the ghost has no malicious intent, the bags prevent a manifestation of this strength, theoretically.

I got conned.

I am going to kill Richard. Slowly and with something extra painful, like a cheese grater.

I smack the top of the desk and then point at the spook. "I am calling Richard and getting my money back. Those hex bags were supposed to keep creatures like you out of here."

"What? Creatures? I don't—who? Hex bags?" He glances around the room. "Where am I?"

I speak slowly. "You're in my house. You don't belong here. Go toward the light."

"Light?" His brow furrows.

I've never seen a ghost like this.

Sure, when we had the poltergeist infestation, there were all kinds of bursts of activity, knickknacks falling off shelves, doors slamming, appliances turning on and off, and all that. I caught glimpses of shadows and movement, but never like this.

He's clearly formed. Tall, easily over six feet, with broad shoulders filling out a supple black leather jacket. His features are all angles and contrasts: thick pink lips against a sharply cut jaw, tousled honey-blond hair half-falling into his eyes. His clothes are strange, like he just stepped out of *Bridgerton*—linen pants tucked into well-worn boots, soft and supple.

The clothes, the accent . . . where is this guy from?

I don't know whether to be terrified, or turned on. Maybe a little bit of both.

"Do you see a glowing tunnel? Feel a warm sensation? Light pulling at your soul? Anything?" I gesture vaguely upward.

"There is no light except for those sconces," he nods to the wall, "which appear as though they need to be dusted and are not very bright."

"So you're a judgy ghost. Got it. Maybe instead you should be seeking a dark door full of hellfire."

He takes a few deep breaths, closing his eyes for a second and then opening them again. "Who are you? Where am I?"

The words are resonant. He pins me with an intense gaze, almost like he's willing me to answer him.

I almost laugh. Is he trying to compel me? Cute.

None of this makes sense. Ghosts don't need to breathe and gather themselves. They aren't bossy. They're an annoyance, the leftover energy from life, no longer grounded in a body.

I walk around the desk toward him, keeping my steps measured. "You look so real."

"I *am* real."

The paperweight bounced off him. He touched it. He must be solid.

He breathes in deeply, leaning toward me. The scents of jasmine and cedar brush against my senses, along with the heat of his body.

He's warm.

Not a ghost.

Not a ghost that is now reaching for me with both hands.

With a gasp, I jump out of his reach. "You're real."

He shakes his head, dazed for a second before focusing on me once again. His hands clench at his side. "As I said."

My eyes alight on Kevin's bat. Perfect. I pick it up. "I am not above violence. Just so we're clear."

"You freed me. Why are you now threatening me with a stick?"

"You jumped out of a lamp. I didn't free anything." I lift the bat higher in an attempt to appear more menacing.

He lifts his hands. "I will leave peacefully."

Is his lip twitching? Is he mocking me? "Hell yes you will."

"I did not intend to intrude on your evening, I assure you. I assume I can go out this way. Shall I?" He jerks his head toward the door.

"Wait!" The kids are sleeping on the floor below us, which

he will have to pass to get to the door. This place can be a maze if you don't know the way out and I can't risk him accidently wandering where he doesn't belong.

We stare at each other for a few long, silent seconds. I think I'm going into shock.

"Yes?" he asks.

"I'll show you to the front door."

We move through the house in silence, my whispered directions guiding him through the maze of creaky stairs and shadowed hallways.

I want to ask him questions.

Why was he in the lamp? What is he? A genie? I can't believe genies are a thing, but maybe it's not that outrageous. I have magic. There are witches and psychics and vampires. A genie can't be that much of a stretch, can it?

When we pass the kids' rooms, his steps falter.

"Keep walking." I jab the bat into his back.

He shoots me an exasperated look over his shoulder, but keeps moving. Down the last staircase, past the quiet kitchen, to the heavy front door.

I unlock it and shove it open. "Out you go."

He pauses on the threshold. "You know, most people offer tea."

"Most people don't pop out of antique lamps in the middle of the night."

Questions throttle me, like who is he and how did he get in the lamp and what the hell is going on? But it's better if he leaves. I don't know him. I can't trust him. I have a family to take care of.

He steps outside, and I slam the door behind him, throwing the locks. I hit the switch, plunging the porch into darkness, then lean against the door, letting out a long, shaky breath.

What just happened?

And what about the lamp, the object that has divided my attention all night? Now it's silent. No siren calls coming from within the house.

Instead, curiosity gnaws at me, drawing me not to the lamp, but to the entity that was inside it. I glance through the peephole.

He's staring back at the door, a frown tilting his lips. He rubs a spot on his chest.

I jerk away, heart lurching. He can't see me. It's not possible. But then, slowly, he turns and walks away, hand to his temple. He disappears down the alley, into the dark and out of sight.

I stay frozen, counting to ten before finally exhaling.

It's over. We're safe.

I turn away, picking up an empty bag of chips from the table and a dirty sock off the couch, my brain spinning in overdrive. Should've asked for a wish. Or twelve. I snort at the thought. *Dear genie, grant me hot water, pay all my bills, cure my sister, oh, and do something about world peace.*

Too late now.

I make it halfway up the stairs when pain lances through my middle, sharp and sudden, like something's ripping me apart from the inside.

CHAPTER

FOUR

I'm dying. This is it.

The pain is intense, nauseating, overwhelming. It rips through me and I crumple into a ball on the stairs, clutching my stomach, desperately trying to breathe through it.

I should have known the day would end like this. It started with an early morning after Jackie had been up all night. Taking Kevin to school, dropping a check off for taxes that I hope doesn't bounce, then hunting down the music box for my client. Then the weirdness of the lamp calling to me, being chased by the strange shadow, the broken water heater, and the goddamn full-grown man that popped out of a freaking Victorian lamp like Temu's very own Robin Williams. Now, I'm being stabbed to death by a thousand tiny ninjas that mysteriously appeared in my belly.

"Cassie." Mimi's voice cuts through the haze of pain. Her palm settles on my shoulder, the warmth seeping through the cold. "Are you okay?

The pain—so intense only seconds ago—vanishes as

quickly as it came, rushing out of me like water down a drain. What. The. Actual. Fuck?

I unwind from where I've coiled against the wall in the fetal position, my muscles stiff. "Mimi?"

She's sitting next to me on the stairs, her face tight with concern, brows drawn. "What happened?"

I would like to know that myself. I stretch my arms up carefully, but the pain is gone. "I don't know, but that sucked."

"We need to talk." Her tone is sharp. No room for argument.

I nod. "Yes. But not here. I don't want to wake the kids. Let's go up to my office." I push myself up, using the banister for support, my legs shaky.

Once we're upstairs, alone, I recount what happened at Ernie's, and then after. The lamp, sitting innocuously on my desk, no longer calls to me. It's only an object again—unassuming and silent.

She eyes me, face wreathed in concern. "How do you feel now?"

"Fine. Exhausted. That's my normal state, though." I wrinkle my nose. "I am kind of hungry." Which is weird because I had seconds of Mimi's red beans and rice and that always fills me up for a day and a half. Tendrils of anxiety, confusion, and fear weave around me, but after the day I've had, I wouldn't expect any less.

"I have heard stories of—"

My office door slams open with so much force, it hits the wall.

Kevin stands in the doorway, breathing heavy. "It's Jackie. Come quick." Then he bolts out of sight.

My mind races through a whirlwind of possibilities as we charge through the house, following Kevin's frantic footsteps. *What if she fell? What if she stopped breathing?* The thought makes my heart lurch. She's done that before. Stopped breathing, lips turning blue, and I almost had a heart attack trying to help her get air in her lungs. What if it's something worse this time? *What if she's gone?*

We round the corner and burst into the front room, and there, at the center of it all, is the lamp man. He's crouched next to Jackie, his hand on her back, and her face is a ghastly, splotchy red. A cold spike of fear jabs through me.

"What are you doing to her?" My voice is harsh, a growl rising in my throat. I should've grabbed the bat. Why the hell didn't I grab the bat?

Jackie breaks through my spiraling panic. "I let him in. He helped me." The words are barely audible, her voice ragged as she breaks into a violent coughing fit.

"Remember, slow, deep breaths." His tone is calm, reassuring.

A cool breeze sweeps through the room, rustling the curtains. Rain patters against the windowsill. It's open, not broken.

She let him in. My stomach twists.

I drop to my knees beside her, hands trembling as I rub her back. "Are you okay? What happened?"

Mimi hands Jackie a glass of water.

She takes a few thirsty gulps, wiping her mouth with her arm. "Thank you. I'm sorry, I just choked a little."

"On what?"

"I don't know. Air." She shrugs. "I tried to swallow and then I just . . . couldn't breathe anymore."

I stifle a whimper, then point at lamp man. "That doesn't explain him."

"I needed help, but I couldn't yell or anything. Then I saw him outside, so I let him in. He got me sitting upright and breathing again. Then Kevin came in here." She shrugs again.

"Why are you still here?" I ask, still pointing at lamp man. My voice shakes, just a little.

He rubs his head. "Jackie needed assistance. I could not leave her alone, not until air was flowing freely into her lungs again. Besides, I can't leave. I tried."

"What?" I stand, the urge to pace growing. The shock of his reappearance and the relief that Jackie is okay all churns into an emotional maelstrom vibrating through my limbs. "What does that mean? That doesn't make sense."

"I know," he says, his tone almost apologetic.

What the hell is happening? Why can't he leave? My thoughts are all jagged edges, none of them fitting together. "Explain yourself."

Jackie places a hand on my arm. "You don't want him to leave."

"Um, yes. Yes, I do, actually."

Jackie purses her lips, biting back whatever words she's struggling to find. Then she shrugs.

The lamp man pats her back. "It's fine. I'll go out the way I came in." And without another word he ducks through the window, his movements smooth and assured, like he leaps through windows in a single bound every day.

I stride forward and slide the window shut, locking it in place. But it doesn't bring the relief I expected.

Turning, I face Jackie, my stomach twisting into tight knots. "What were you thinking?" My words are sharper than I intend, the fear spilling into my voice. I'm trying so hard to hold it together, but cracks spread beneath the surface.

Jackie's face is pale but determined. "He seemed lonely."

"Lonely?" I throw my hands up in frustration. "That's your brilliant reason?"

Her chin juts out in defiance. "He was sitting out there in the rain, all alone."

I blow out a breath. "When a strange man is outside your house, you don't let him in." Even if you're choking. Dammit, that's the fear talking.

"I'm not stupid." She crosses her arms tightly over her chest. "He's connected to you."

I blink. My brain stumbles to catch up. "What? What do you mean? How is he connected to me?"

Before she can respond, the searing pain rips through me again. My vision goes white, and I crumple to the floor, my knees giving way as the world spins out of control.

The last thing that reaches through the agony, before everything goes black, is Jackie's frantic voice. "Cassie!"

CHAPTER

FIVE

When the pain finally ebbs, rolling out of my body like a receding tide, I blink, trying to focus.

Four faces loom above me.

Jackie sits on the floor beside me, dark smudges under her eyes, her face drawn with the weight of long nights and exhaustion.

Lamp man stands nearby, his mouth pressed into a thin, tense line, his gaze too intense to hold for long.

Mimi's gaping at the man, her mouth open. I can't blame her. He's not hard to look at. There's something about the way he stands, his presence. It's magnetic.

Kevin stands opposite him, his face wide-eyed and worried. "You almost died."

I push myself up, slowly, my breath still unsteady. "I didn't almost die."

Kevin jerks a thumb toward the lamp man. "He almost died too."

"What? Why?" The questions burst out of me before I can stop them, panic flaring in my chest.

Jackie's hand cradles my arm, steadying me as I stand. "Every time he goes too far away, you both feel the pain. I told you. You're connected."

Mimi's eyes widen. "Yes. This is what I was trying to tell you when we were upstairs. I've heard of something like this—it's a curse. A binding curse. If someone is bound to an object, whoever frees them, they sort of take over the binding."

"Take over the binding?" My voice is tight, the words not quite making sense.

Mimi nods. "It's possible you're bound to each other now, instead of him being bound to the lamp."

"A lamp?" Kevin's voice rises in disbelief. "He was bound to a lamp, like a genie?"

"Can you grant wishes?" Jackie's eyes gleam as she looks up at the lamp man.

He frowns. "I do not know of this *genie*. I am djinn. I do not grant wishes."

"Lame," Jackie mutters.

Kevin glances at Mimi. "Is he lying?"

"He's telling the truth."

I raise my hand. "Wait. What the hell is a djinn? And can we circle back to this whole binding thing?" I turn my attention to Jackie. "And how do you know we're connected?

Jackie sways on her feet, her shoulders slumping. "I don't know. It's just there, like this thing."

"What thing?"

Her mouth opens like she's going to answer but then she pales and her eyes flutter closed, her legs buckling beneath her.

"Jackie!" Before I can so much as take a step, lamp man reaches her first.

He catches her before she hits the floor and scoops her into his arms. Her head lolls against his chest, face pale, lashes dark against her skin.

"I'm okay." She lifts a hand.

"You are not okay."

She shifts to meet my eyes. "I'll be fine after I sleep."

I bite my lip, torn between wanting to rip her out of lamp man's arms and appreciating his lightning-quick speed.

This isn't the first time she's passed out, or nearly passed out. She's right. She does need to sleep.

"I can take her upstairs," lamp man says.

Before I can formulate a response, Mimi is herding Kevin, Jackie, and her savior toward the stairs. "That's mighty kind of you. I'll show you her room. Thank you." She squints at me. "We'll meet you in the kitchen in a minute. Make some tea."

I clench my teeth and nod. "Fine."

I head toward the kitchen, every footstep a drumbeat of guilt and frustration and worry and confusion. I fill the kettle with water and set it on the stove. My hands move automatically—mugs, tea bags, honey—but my thoughts are stuck upstairs.

Jackie's pale face won't leave my mind. She's been running on empty for weeks, and now this.

And lamp man . . . he was just there. Steady. Fast. Careful.

The kettle begins to hiss. I lift it off the heat before it screams.

I line up three mugs and drop a chamomile tea bag into each one. The old yellow one with the happy face and chipped handle for Mimi because she loves that dumb thing. The one with a dancing banana for me. And the dainty one with moon and stars for our guest. I don't know what kind of tea a djinn drinks, but he's earned one tonight.

I reach for a spoon and he's standing in the doorway of the kitchen.

"Holy crap on a cracker!" The spoon goes flying, clattering

to the ground. "Could you warn me before sneaking up like that?"

"I apologize." He studies me with unnerving intensity, his sharp gaze flicking over my face like he's searching for something.

I cross my arms over my chest. "What?"

"Are they your children?"

A startled laugh bursts from me. "Kevin and Jackie? They're my siblings. I would've had to be pregnant at fourteen." I scrunch my nose. "Which, I guess, is technically possible, but no. Why?"

His head tilts, considering me. "You all smell alike."

"We smell alike?"

Great. Djinn apparently have an extra strong sense of smell. And here I am, unshowered, probably reeking of New Orleans: fried food, stale beer, and sewer. Lovely.

But if it bothers him, he doesn't show it. In fact, there's something about the way he looks at me—like I'm a puzzle he wants to figure out. Like I intrigue him. And damn it, that's distracting.

"What is wrong with her?"

"There's nothing wrong with her." The words snap out.

He doesn't flinch. "I don't mean—I know there is nothing *wrong* with her. But she is sick. She was as light as a feather." He pauses, studying me with those too-sharp eyes. "What is it?"

I give him my back and pour the water into the mugs. "We don't know."

It's a horrible thing, the not knowing. Test after test with no definitive conclusion. Watching someone you love suffer while doctors poke and prod and shrug their shoulders. At least if you know what the monster is, you can figure out how to fight it. The not knowing is pure hell.

Jackie's pain comes in waves, sometimes so deep it settles into her bones, leaving her barely able to move. Other times, her stomach rejects anything she eats. Then there's the exhaustion, the weakness, the migraines—

"Come on." I pick up two mugs and head to the dining table, the wood smooth and familiar beneath my fingers. He lowers himself into the chair across from me, his movements fluid but careful, like someone used to measuring a room before letting his guard down.

"So." I slide a mug over to him and rest my elbows on the table. "How did you get bound to the lamp, exactly?"

He doesn't answer right away. Instead, his gaze drifts around, taking in every detail of the chaos of our daily lives: the cluttered countertops, the colorful tile backsplash Mom picked out before she was gone, the stack of Kevin's comic books shoved into the fruit bowl.

My cheeks heat slightly. It's clean, sure, but there's an undeniable messiness to a house with kids. And now some ancient genie-man is judging my kitchen.

Then his attention snags on something across the room. His brows dip, lips pressing into a faint frown.

I follow his gaze. He's staring at the microwave.

I blink. Look back at him. He's still staring.

"Hey, weirdo." I snap my fingers in front of his face. "Why are you glaring at my microwave?"

"Micro-wave?" he echoes, pronouncing it like a foreign word.

I resist the urge to laugh. "Oh. Right. You probably don't have those in your magical lamp world."

His frown deepens, but before he can answer, Mimi strides into the room. "What did I miss?"

"Our friend here was just about to explain things."

Mimi arches a brow. "Without so much as an introduction?

You were raised better."

I lift a hand in his direction. "Mimi, he's an intruder!"

She grabs her mug from the counter and joins us at the table, sitting beside me. "Uh-huh. An intruder you conjured with your secretive bagged item." She nudges me with her elbow, voice teasing. "And a handsome one at that."

I press my lips together. I will not comment. She can't be serious.

She points at me. "This stubborn child is my dear niece Cassie Broussard. And you can call me Aunt Mimi."

Bennet inclines his head slightly. "Bennet Ashford. A pleasure, madam."

Mimi grins. "So formal."

"Now that we've been properly introduced." I clear my throat. "The lamp. How were you bound to it? Where are you from? Why are you here?"

He meets my gaze, and for a second, there's heat there, sharp enough to make me inhale a fraction deeper. "I'm from a place called Aetheria."

Mimi's brows knit together. "Is that in California?"

His expression is blank. "I do not know of this California."

Mimi leans forward, resting her elbows on the table. "So where is Aetheria?"

His expression doesn't change. "Beyond the veil. Another realm."

I stare at him.

He has got to be shitting me.

Mimi turns to me, picking up her mug and blowing on her tea. "Well, he's not lying, but he might be crazy. He believes it."

Bennet's eyes narrow slightly. "Are you a truthsayer?"

Mimi shrugs. "I can tell when someone lies. I haven't heard that term used before. It's just my magic."

His gaze sharpens. "And the boy, Kevin. He is a spirit speaker."

I straighten. "How do you know that?"

"I heard him and Jackie speaking while I was outside." He picks up his mug and sniffs the contents.

They were inside. He was outside. Add supernatural hearing to the list of his abilities.

He fidgets with one of the bright red placemats. "And what about Jackie?"

Mimi shakes her head. "She doesn't have magic."

Bennet hums, thoughtful. Then, suddenly, his gaze zooms back to me. "And you. Your magic expelled me from the lamp."

"I can find things, sense them, that sort of thing." He doesn't need to know more than that.

He nods, as if filing the information away.

"And you?" I tilt my head. "You obviously have some magic too."

"All djinn have magic. I have more than most."

Not good. If he has so much power, what could he do to us? Fear licks up my spine, but it almost immediately dissipates. I should be afraid. But I'm not. Why? No time to ponder it. Back to the topic at hand. "How did you get bound to the lamp?"

"My sister."

I blink. "Your sister?"

His sharp gaze meets mine. "Yes. Why does that surprise you?"

"I don't know. I guess I thought maybe you crossed realms for," I wave a hand, "world domination? Organ harvesting? To fuse with your shadow self?"

Bennet's frown deepens. "Shadow self?"

I shrug. "Happened on *Superman & Lois*."

His expression remains blank.

"Oh, right. No microwaves. No television."

"This is the first time I've ever left my home in Aetheria." A muscle in his jaw tics.

Guilt stirs in my chest. The first time he ever leaves home, and he ends up trapped in a lamp, only to be released by a strange lady with a baseball bat, then tossed out into the rain? Yeah. Rough day. But I shove the guilt aside. My own life is a mess, and now, apparently, I have to deal with this too.

"And I am not here to harvest or dominate anyone. I came here to find my sister. She did not wish to be found. We argued and she bound me to the lamp." His voice is even, robotic almost.

"How did she do it?"

He rubs the back of his neck. "With her magic."

I fight the urge to smack my forehead. "No kidding. Do you remember what she did? How she did it?"

He shakes his head. "No. I was trying to convince her to return to Aetheria. The next thing I knew, I was here. And you were threatening me with your stick."

Mimi snorts.

"It was a bat," I correct.

He rocks back in his seat.

"I threatened you with a bat. Not a stick. It's for baseball."

Bennet's brow furrows.

I groan. "Never mind."

"We need to find her and get her to release this," he gestures between us, "curse. Then I can return with her to Aetheria."

Mimi fidgets in her seat. "Say we do find your sister. If she did this to you, what makes you think she'll fix it?"

"She must. She will. Once she hears reason. If you help me find her, I will leave. I will return with her to Aetheria. In the meantime, we are bound together until this is resolved—it is in both of our best interests to locate Helen."

"Why is your sister here? I assume your kind doesn't cross the veil often." If djinn were popping into our world with any kind of regularity, I would have heard about it at some point.

He shifts in his chair, leaning closer. "You are correct. We aren't supposed to. Helen ran away from her wedding. It has been planned since birth. My family is important in Aetheria. My parents are gone." His hand lifts, touching the center of his chest.

There's a bulge there, under his shirt. What is it?

He continues speaking. "It was always expected that Helen would make a good match for our people. She's known this her whole life. The wedding is set to take place next week. At least, I think so. I don't know how long I was in the lamp."

"The shopkeeper I bought it from just got it in yesterday."

Bennet nods, absorbing the information.

I rub my forehead, my thoughts sluggish with exhaustion. "So let me get this straight. Your sister is somewhere in New Orleans, and you have a week or less to find her. Meanwhile, you and I are stuck together because I released you like some kind of genie?"

Bennet gives me a flat look. "That is the second time you have referred to me as 'genie.' What does this term mean?"

I wave a hand. "It's a magical being stuck in a lamp. Whoever rubs the lamp releases the genie and then the genie must grant them three wishes, anything they want." I glance at Mimi. "Do I at least get three wishes?"

She shakes her head. "I wouldn't test it. In every story, bad things happen. Hell, sometimes something bad things happen with each wish."

"What kind of bad things?" Bennet asks.

Mimi drums her fingers on the table. "Like the man who wished for riches and eternal youth, and then his wife won the lottery, died, and left him a fortune. He was alone for eternity.

A lifetime of luxury, but it was hollow and lonely. Or the woman who wished for endless love, only to have her partner become so obsessed, he killed her. And then there's the story of the man who wished for power, but it twisted him. He became a tyrant, unable to stop himself. His wish stripped him of his humanity, and he was left a monster."

"So he became a politician?"

She considers that. "Most likely."

Bennet leans his elbows on the table. "I am most certainly not this 'genie.' If I were at my full power, or if Helen were here, there is quite a bit of we could accomplish with our magic, but it would not be something someone could compel from us. Djinn don't pull miracles out of thin air. We channel. Transform. Influence what's already there."

"So what kind of magic do you have?" Mimi asks.

"Our power is elemental. Tied to the land. Fire, wind, stone, sea—each of us is born with an affinity, a source that shapes us. In Aetheria, that connection is strong, and so the magic is abundant. Here, it's more distant. Muted. But it's the same current."

Fascinating. "So it's the same magic just watered down?"

He inclines his head. "Essentially. Magic is not confined to one realm or the other." Then his lips purse. "But I suppose it is possible one of my kind came to your realm, perhaps inspired these genie stories. The kind of power you describe though, especially on this side of the veil? Nothing short of the Ring of Solomon would be powerful enough."

"What is the Ring of Solomon?" Mimi asks.

"One of our own legends. A powerful ring given to King Solomon by the gods. With it, he was able to bind and command djinn. They were forced to obey his every command, build him temples, go to war for him, even die for him."

"One ring to rule them all," I intone.

Mimi rolls her eyes, then turns to Bennet. "Myths often come from twisted kernels of truth. So with the Ring of Solomon, djinn are bound and forced to do someone's bidding, like genies in our stories are bound to lamps and forced to grant three wishes."

I bite my lip. "So then how are we bound together?"

Mimi shrugs. "Maybe the lamp has some kind of Ring of Solomon-ish power, or Helen has possession of the real thing and when she cast her spell, it caused the binding?"

Bennet lifts his hand. "No. The ring is only a story told to scare djinn children into behaving. Even if it were true, Helen would never do that. She would never hurt or imprison someone intentionally."

Maybe she would if it meant escaping an arranged marriage. "Okay." I snap my fingers. "New plan. Maybe we should destroy the lamp?"

"No," Mimi says immediately. "Not until we know more. Binding curses are tricky. If we destroy the vessel, you could be stuck like this forever."

I turn back to Bennet. "Do you have any idea where Helen might be?"

"No."

I slump over and suppress the urge to bang my head onto the table. "Fantastic."

"Normally I could track her with my magic," he says slowly. "But I'm unable to access it." His fists tighten. "I haven't been able to use any of my power since you expelled me from the lamp."

I lift my head, studying him. Aha. He *was* trying to compel me before, when I first released him, but he couldn't because his magic is gone.

"Do you think she's still in New Orleans?" I ask.

His mouth firms into a thin line. "I don't know."

I sigh, running a hand through my hair. "So you know absolutely nothing."

His jaw tics. "I may not know much about your world, but I will find my sister. She's the only one who can fix this. She created the curse, she can break it. Then you can move on with your life, and I shall move on with mine."

Poor Helen. Trapped in an arranged marriage, she finds an escape route, only to be hunted down and dragged back by her brother, who apparently has little sympathy for unwilling brides.

"Have they heard of consent in Aetheria?"

Whoops.

Bennet's mouth pops open.

I lift a hand. "Sorry. It's none of my business." What is my business is getting rid of this curse so I can get rid of this djinn and move on with my life, such as it is.

"Helen did consent to the marriage. She has known for years about it. It is how things are done in my world, to unite kingdoms and keep our people safe. She never told me she didn't want to marry Lord Wallace, and if she had, I would have—" He scrubs his hand through his hair. "It doesn't matter. What matters is that we need to find her to fix this."

Okay, so maybe he's not quite the long arm of Aetheria's patriarchy. But does that change anything? I'm too exhausted to deal with any of this right now.

Mimi reaches over, squeezing my hand. "We should all get some rest. The problems will still be here in the morning." She points at Bennet. "If you hurt anyone in this house, I will kill you."

Bennet meets her gaze, serious. "I promise I will not harm you or your family."

Mimi holds his stare a second longer before nodding. "He's

telling the truth, Cass." She pushes up from the table, moving stiffly.

I move to help her, but she shoos me away. "I've got it. Tonight, we sleep. Tomorrow, we figure out our next move." She glances at Bennet. "Come on, I'll show you where you can sleep."

CHAPTER

SIX

I'm dragged from fitful slumber by the unmistakable sound of mischief.

Kevin and Jackie sneak by my bedroom, except they are as good at walking quietly as a horde of stampeding elephants. No to mention they keep shushing each other to be quiet.

"Do you think he's in the office?" Kevin's whisper is always louder than his normal speaking voice.

Jackie is only a decibel under him. "Duh, Cassie left the key in the lock."

"So he's stuck in there?"

"I guess."

"What if he has to pee?"

The words sink in and I lurch up in bed. My door is cracked open. I left it that way so I would wake if our overnight guest made any moves, although if he got far enough away, apparently I would be overcome with violent agony, so that in and of itself is a decent alarm system.

I just didn't want him creeping around our house while everyone was asleep. Despite Mimi's assurances that he spoke true, there are too many ways to sneak around her lie-detection abilities. I know, I've done it myself.

I heave myself out of bed and into the doorway.

Sure enough, Jackie and Kevin are outside the door to my office, Kevin with one hand on the knob.

"Hey."

They both jump, turning guilty eyes my way.

The scent of syrup and bacon drifts from downstairs. "Smells like breakfast is ready. Go wash up."

They trudge past me toward the stairs. "The water's still cold," Kevin tosses over his shoulder.

Shit. "Cold showers are good for you." Or so I've heard.

I'll call someone later. I'll figure out how to pay for it later too. My to-do list stacks up in my mind like a mountain of bricks.

Take care of this Bennet guy and help find his sister so I can get him out of my house, call someone about the water heater, work an actual job that pays money for said water heater . . . It won't be enough to solve all the other catastrophes, known and unknown, but it's a start.

Once the kids are out of earshot, I pad over to the office door and hesitate before turning the key.

Maybe locking him in was excessive, but he agreed to the confinement, which went a long way toward easing my concerns about a strange man in my home. A strange man from another dimension, no less.

I knock gently and then push open the door.

Bennet is splayed out on the couch, his legs hanging over the edge. His broad shoulders are too wide and his legs are too long for the blanket tossed over him, exposing the soles of his feet and the upper part of his chest. His bare chest.

A slender chain hangs around his neck, a delicate gold ring dangling from the end of it. Whose ring is that? A wife's?

A lover's? He didn't mention leaving behind a family in Aetheria, but then why would he? Although, if he were married she would have the ring on her finger and not around his neck.

Also . . . is he completely naked?

I glance around the room and finally land on his clothes, folded in a neat pile on the chair in the corner.

My attention drifts back to Bennet.

He's all long limbs and lean muscles. His dark blond hair is rumpled from sleep, one strand hanging over his forehead and making my fingers itch to push it back. His face is soft with sleep, contrasting with the strong jawline covered in stubble.

I need to wake him, but I can't get my feet to move.

This would be a lot easier if he looked like a hobgoblin instead of an Adonis.

He shifts on the narrow sofa and the blanket slips down to his waist.

My mouth goes dry. His chest is scrumptious. Like if someone wanted me to conjure up the most perfectly put-together man, muscled but not too bulky, broad shouldered, narrow hipped, and . . . *oh my.*

I guess interdimensional travelers are also victims of morning wood. I can't drag my eyes away from the obvious bulge under the blanket.

Stop gawking.

I clear my throat loudly and knock on the open door with more force.

With a strangled yelp, Bennet leaps off the couch, blanket puddling at his feet.

Holy giant banana.

Flames lick up my body.

He grabs the blanket from the floor and covers himself, but not before I've gotten an eyeful and then some. Adonis is almost an insult compared to his masculine perfection. He's big and hard and holy hell.

Now he's the one brandishing a stick.

Bennet glances around. "I do not have a stick."

"Uh." Did I say that out loud? I smack a hand over my mouth.

My mind is blank. Why did I come in here? What day is this? Who am I? I shut my eyes. I can't think.

Embarrassment and arousal blend inside me into a murky and annoying cocktail.

I clamp down my rising desire and concentrate all my energy on the bevy of problems swamping my life. An immediate arousal killer.

Once I'm ninety percent sure I won't say anything incriminating, I remove my hand and open my eyes. "I wanted to see if you're hungry."

Do genies eat?

His stomach growls loudly in response. "Yes. I haven't eaten since . . . I don't remember."

Guilt knots in my stomach. I hadn't even thought to offer him food last night. I'd been too preoccupied with Jackie, my family, and the danger he might pose to even consider it.

I twitch a hand toward the hall. "There's food downstairs. You can use the same bathroom you used last night if you need to," I wave a hand at his clothes, "get dressed or whatever."

Before locking him in my office last night, he used the bathroom attached to my room to take care of whatever djinn need to do before bed. I didn't ask questions, even though I am intensely curious. Do magical creatures have to pee? Their anatomy is clearly human enough. If anything, maybe a little more enhanced.

"Do you have any other clothes?" I ask.

He shakes his head.

Another problem to deal with. I blow out a breath. "Maybe I can find something that will fit you." Dad's clothes are still in the closet, neatly hanging or folded in the dresser like they're just waiting for him to come home. A ghost of a hope I haven't let go of, no matter how ridiculous it is after three years. He wasn't quite as tall as Bennet, but it will have to be good enough.

I swallow the lump rising in my throat. "Did you bring any money from Aetheria?"

Bennet stares down at his feet. "No. I didn't think I would be here long enough to need it. And if I did, I could use my magic to manifest whatever I required."

A pang of loss flutters through me. But it's not mine.

I blink, thrown off-balance.

What was that?

This isn't the first time emotions have fluttered through me that don't belong. Last night, I kept catching these echoes that didn't quite fit. The hunger even after the large meal, the excess fear and confusion. Sure, some of that was mine, but there was just more. I chalked it up to exhaustion and one hell of a crazy day, but now, if we're connected, does that mean—

"Can you feel what I'm feeling?"

He bites his lip. "Maybe a little."

"A little? *A little?*" My voice squeaks. "What does that mean, exactly?"

He winces. "I noticed it last night but wasn't certain. I was overwhelmed. I thought I could block it, so it would be a nonissue."

So the connection isn't only physical. It runs deeper than that. "Were you going to say something or were you just gonna pretend not to notice that you can feel everything I am feeling?"

His eyes dart to the side. "I was planning on telling you."

I point at him. "Liar." I don't need to be a truthsayer to figure that one out.

His cheeks flush. "I'm sorry. But it's not like it matters. You don't hide what you are thinking."

"Who cares if I'm honest? I don't like you knowing how I feel. It's invasive." What if he can tell how attractive I find him? I want the floor to swallow me whole. "How do I stop it?"

"You can block it with your mind, by forming your mental shields."

"Mental shields? How does that work?"

He frowns. "You protect your thoughts and emotions from intrusion with an imagined object. It's all in your head."

"Great. How do I do that?"

"I can show you." He sits back on the couch, the blankets covering him from the waist down.

I have to force my gaze to stay on his face.

He gestures for me to sit beside him. "I can help you through the connection itself. If you are amenable? It will be better if we are touching. Stronger."

"How does that work? I thought you didn't have access to your magic."

"This does not require channeling magic. It's simply connecting to something that exists between us. The bond itself has the energy we can tap into."

Hmmm. This is a bad idea.

But leaving an emotional channel wide open between us is worse. Maybe I should make him put some clothes on, but I'm not sure I want to wait.

I walk further into the room and lower myself onto the couch beside him, my hands clenched in my lap.

Bennet sets his hand on his knee, palm up.

I stare at it like it's going to sprout fangs and bite me.

"Would you like me to take your hand instead?" he asks.

"No."

I appreciate that he's letting me set the pace, but *what the fuck* doesn't even begin to describe it.

"This is all just very weird," I mutter.

"Yes."

"I guess for you too."

Considering he's in a whole other dimension surrounded by strangers who haven't exactly been rolling out the red carpet, it's probably been worse for him.

Flustered—and hating that he can probably sense that too —I place my hand on top of his.

His palm is big, fingers long, warm, and dry. The moment our skin touches, a charge surges between us, like static but deeper, a low hum under my skin. I jolt, but his grip tightens ever so slightly, grounding me.

And then another sensation rushes in.

Heat. Arousal.

Not mine.

I don't think it's mine.

I haven't been this turned on in years. I take a deep breath.

It's only the bond. It has to be. An unnatural, forced connection. That's why it's so intense, so overwhelming.

How do I know what's mine or his? Do they amplify each other?

What would it be like to sleep with someone when you could sense their arousal, have it feed into your own?

My face burns. Nope. Not going there.

"Close your eyes," he instructs.

"Why?"

"It will help you concentrate."

I hesitate, then comply.

The air between us is thick, charged. I drag in a breath and force myself to pay attention.

"Concentrate on your breathing. In and out."

I follow his voice, deep and soothing, letting it guide me. The buzz of energy is still under my skin, but I push past it.

"Now," he continues, "imagine there's a wall around your mind. It can be made of whatever you like, whatever is strongest for you. Iron, stone, or brick."

I need something impenetrable. Thick steel. Heavy, gray, molded around my thoughts like a vault.

"Good," he says softly. "You don't need to hold it down with force. That will only exhaust you. Instead, envision a latch. A locking mechanism that secures it effortlessly."

In my mind, I form four latches—one on each side of the steel casing—and click them into place.

That's better.

"Excellent." There's approval in his tone. "I can't feel you anymore. Now, you can choose to keep them locked or release them whenever you want."

"Why would I release them?"

He tilts his head. "I'm not sure. Perhaps if you wanted to share something with me in private."

I snort. "Not likely, buddy."

His lips press together, his eyes sparkling with a glimmer of amusement before he draws his hand away.

The absence is immediate.

"So. Food." I push to my feet.

"Yes," he agrees, though his gaze lingers on me a moment too long.

I turn sharply on my heel. "Right. Food."

Pull yourself together, woman.

One touch of his hand and a charged look and suddenly my brain cells run off and I can only speak in caveman sentences.

"I'll get you some clothes."

I head over to Mom and Dad's room.

I've avoided this space for the better part of three years. Most of it is still exactly the way they left it. Mom's favorite throw folded neatly on the chair by the window, Dad's reading glasses tucked beside the bed. There's no dust. Mimi must be keeping it clean, like part of her believes they'll walk through the door any day now.

The air smells like lavender and cedar. Familiar. It shoots me right in the chest.

I move quickly, avoiding their bed, their pictures, the memories. Straight to the closet. Jeans, shirt, an old pair of sweats, sneakers that look like they've barely been worn. I don't think. I just grab and go.

I leave the clothes at the bathroom door before heading downstairs. My mind tries to take me back, to when my parents were here, to what they would do about this situation, but I shake the thoughts away. They aren't here. They aren't coming back. I'm on my own, and I need to figure this out myself.

We need to find his sister, and soon.

I reach the kitchen right as Mimi and Kevin are getting ready to leave.

"I'll be back in a bit." Mimi slings her purse over her shoulder.

Kevin frowns at his shoelaces, struggling with a stubborn knot. "Ugh, come on," he mutters.

I crouch to help, making quick work of it before squeezing his shoulder. "All set, kiddo."

"Thanks." He straightens, grabbing his backpack from the floor. "Bye, Jackie!"

Jackie doesn't even glance up from the table. "Bye."

Mimi glances between us like she has more to say, but instead, she waves. "See you later."

Then they're gone.

Bennet strides into the kitchen, dressed in a white T-shirt and a pair of Dad's jeans that are a couple inches too short. He should look ridiculous, but somehow he's still hot.

Drat.

"Good morning, Miss Jackie."

She lifts a hand from where she's sitting at the table, idly pushing scrambled eggs around her plate with her fork. Her wrists are as delicate as bird wings, and her cheekbones are sharper than they should be.

My stomach tightens. She needs to eat, but I know better than to push too hard.

"Have a seat," I tell Bennet, gesturing toward an empty chair before heading to the stove where the food is keeping warm. "Do you like pancakes?"

"Cakes?"

"Pancakes," Jackie corrects. "They aren't actual cake."

His brow furrows. "I am not familiar with this pan-cake."

Jackie lets out a soft laugh. "What do you eat in your world?"

Mimi must have given her some of the details of last night's conversation. I grab a plate and fill it with a couple of pancakes, scrambled eggs, bacon, and leftover beans before setting it in front of him.

"It depends," Bennet says, cutting into the pancakes with precise, practiced movements. "To break our fast, we might have bread and cheese. Or pork and kippers with eggs."

"Kippers?" Jackie asks, wrinkling her nose.

"It's a type of fish."

She makes a face. "For breakfast? Ew. No thanks."

I walk back to the stove, making up my own plate. "People put salmon on bagels sometimes."

"People are cringe," she says.

I can't argue that.

Bennet lifts a bite of pancake to his mouth, chewing thoughtfully. His brows rise slightly. "Hmm."

"Good, right?" Jackie grins. "Way better than fish."

"It's not bad," he admits before taking another bite.

I settle next to Jackie, watching as she continues to poke at her food instead of eating it. "How's your stomach?"

She shrugs. "It's fine."

It's not fine.

The way she says it, the way she avoids my eyes, it's an old dance. One we've been doing for too long. Me fretting and fussing, Jackie pretending she's okay so I don't worry, and me worrying anyway.

"Did you sleep okay?"

"Yes."

Her eye twitches. She's lying.

I take a few bites, but my appetite wanes as I watch her struggle through small forkfuls.

After another couple of minutes, she sets her fork down. "I have to log in for school."

Frustration tightens my throat. "Okay. I'll take your plate. Go ahead."

As soon as she's gone, Bennet sets his fork down and lowers his voice. "How long has she been ill?"

I rub my temple. "It started before our parents disappeared."

Bennet stills. "Disappeared?"

"Yep." I shove a piece of bacon in my mouth.

He frowns like he wants to ask more, but I don't want to talk about my parents. Not now. Maybe not ever.

Time for a subject change. "Tell me about your sister."

He wipes his mouth with his napkin. "What would you like to know?"

"I'm not sure exactly. Something that might help us find

her." An object or image that I can use to focus my magic would be nice. "Do you have any of her belongings? Maybe an item she's touched?"

"Only the lamp. I am not sure if she actually touched it though or only used magic on it."

I straighten. "There's only one way to find out."

CHAPTER

SEVEN

"So before you will share this brilliant idea with me, I must be forced into manual labor?" Bennet swipes at the pot in the sink, his grip on the sponge uncertain.

I set two more plates and a cup in front of him. "If you think doing a few dishes is manual labor, you should try cleaning Kevin and Jackie's bathroom." I shudder. "That place is like the seventh circle of hell, complete with a rarely flushed toilet, mystery fluids stuck to the mirror, and toothpaste on the ceiling. How does anyone get toothpaste on the ceiling?"

"I assume that is a rhetorical question."

Judging by his weak attempt at scraping the food from the plate, he probably hasn't lifted a finger his whole life. "Do you not clean in Aetheria?"

"I have servants. And magic." He says it so matter-of-factly. "I've never had need to subject myself to menial tasks."

I snort. "And they wonder why we say 'eat the rich.'"

His head snaps toward me, alarm flickering across his features. "What does that mean?"

I sigh. "You wouldn't understand." I don't give him a chance to press further. "What did you do in Aetheria exactly?"

"What do you mean?"

I wave a hand vaguely. "Like, day to day. What did you do with your time?"

Bennet picks up a wet plate and dries it, a little too methodically, like he's considering his answer. "I have many important duties and responsibilities to the crown."

"Uh-huh. Such as?"

"Training with the guards in the morning, then meeting with dignitaries from neighboring kingdoms to manage disputes and hash out trade agreements and whatnot."

"Oh. Sounds important. You must be a whizz at economics."

The plate in his hand freezes a moment, his eyes glued to it. "Not exactly. We have ministers and advisory councils to write the agreements."

"So that makes you the big ideas guy, and leaves the minions to hash it out?"

He turns the plate over without meeting my gaze. "Uncle sets the agenda. In consultation with his ministers."

I lean a hip against the counter. "So you're there to ease the way. Get the right people in the room, get them talking?"

That must be the most fascinating plate in his universe, because his eyes haven't met mine once. "Actually . . ."

This conversation is like wringing water from granite. "So, how big is Aetheria? How many kingdoms are there?"

He finally sets the plate down. "I'm not sure how large it is in relation to the mortal realm. We are told stories of how our lands were once mirror images of the other, and connected, but Aetheria is shaped and formed by the connection between its magic and its people. It grows and contracts with the balance of power."

"So it's, like, alive?"

He rinses out a cup. "In a sense. All things are alive. The land responds to magic the way plants respond to sunlight. Strong magic makes the land flourish. When it wanes, or is corrupted, it withers. That's part of why borders shift."

I squint. "Are you saying Aetheria can literally change shape?"

He nods. "It has, in the past. The old maps don't always match the new ones. Right now, Aetheria is divided into four regions. Each has its own culture, courts, and ruling families. Sometimes allies, sometimes rivals."

I need a map or something. "You keep calling this the 'mortal realm.' Does that mean you are immortal?"

"We are not immortal, per se, because we age and can be killed, but we do live longer than you."

"How much longer?" I cross my arms over my chest.

"Some djinn have been rumored to live five hundred years."

My jaw drops. "Five hundred years?"

"Our magic shields us from common illness. And we have healers for injury, sometimes even death if caught quickly enough. But war, assassination, misuse of power . . . none of us are invincible." His gaze drops to his hands, his lips turning down.

Without thought, I reach over and put a hand on his tense shoulder. "Your parents?"

His fingers tighten around a spoon. "Yes. Helen and I were raised by our uncle after our parents—" He stops himself, his hand lifting to the ring hidden under his shirt.

Did the ring belong to one of his parents? He touches it almost every time his parents are mentioned. Well. Now I'm an asshole.

"I didn't quite realize how useless I have been with my meetings and attempts at overseeing menial matters in my kingdom. Helen is the one expected to lead. I am merely the spare. Our uncle keeps me sheltered, away from real responsibility. I know little about this land, and the truth is that I barely know my own."

I soften. "It's okay. You can't change the past, but you can move forward and do better."

He blinks, like the idea has never occurred to him.

"Growth and all that." I shrug. "The rough bits shape us. What doesn't kill you makes you stronger, etcetera."

He stares at me.

I clear my throat. "So, why is magic so muted here, in the mortal world?"

"No one knows for sure. Some believe the two realms were once one and magic bled freely for all. Some say the gods severed the realms to protect both sides from each other. Others say your world chose progress over power, and ours, the reverse."

"Hmm." I wish I could get my hands on an Aetherian history book, to compare to our histories.

I turn away to put a plate in the cupboard, only to turn back and catch him staring. The moment our eyes meet, he looks down, hands submerged in the sudsy water, unmoving.

"Are you done yet?" I nudge him aside. "Here, let me do that."

A few minutes later, we finish putting away the dishes and head back to the office.

Bennet perches on the chair near the fireplace, probably avoiding the uncomfortable couch that was his bed last night.

"Okay." I grab the lamp and turn it over in my hands. "I may be able to use this to find her."

His posture straightens. "How?"

I take a steadying breath and shut my eyes, reaching for my magic. I can stretch over the surface of the lamp, seek any remnants of its prior handler.

I frown. Or maybe not.

There's nothing there. Is my magic . . . gone?

No. Not possible. My magic is a part of me, like my leg. It can't run off without me noticing. I take another breath and try again.

I can't get to it. It's like grasping for smoke. It's there, I can almost make out the shape of it, but I can't seize it like I normally do.

Bennet's voice gets louder as he shifts closer. "What are you doing?" His voice is strained.

I ignore him, grinding my teeth and trying one more time.

"Cassie."

His tone makes me groan in frustration. "Apparently, I'm doing nothing because it's not working. It worked yesterday. This can't be happening."

Panic curls at the edges of my mind. My ability to sense objects, to track them, that's my job. My livelihood. And now, all of a sudden, it's just gone?

I snap my eyes open. How do I get it back?

Bennet's brow furrows. "We are connected, and my magic is not working either." His fingers flex against the armrest. "Maybe once we find Helen and fix this, whatever this is, our magic will return."

And yet he doesn't appear convinced.

I set the lamp down. "Why do you have that face on your face?"

"What do you mean?"

"You don't seem like you believe it."

Bennet rubs his chin. "Perhaps Helen can break this curse. But . . ."

"But?"

"There is an old story, of twins who were born without magic. At least, that's what everyone thought. Until one day, they were cornered by a giant. They would have died, but their combined fear for each other caused their magic to snap into place. They fought off the giant with their power, and it didn't come from one or the other. It came from both."

I put my hands on my hips. "Are you saying that teamwork can make the dream work?"

Bennet frowns. "It's more than just working together. It's intention shared at a deep level. A bond forged in trust. That's how they awakened their gift, not by demanding it or commanding each other, but by moving as one."

"And you think we could do this too? Move as one?" My face heats. *Don't think about sex, don't think about sex.*

"I think if we're going to use our magic, we have to stop pulling in different directions."

Except isn't that what we're already doing? He wants to find his sister as much as I do. I rake a hand through my hair. Whatever. We need to fix this. Quickly. "Maybe I can find someone else with magic to help track her."

"That seems logical. Maybe we could start our search with the shop where you purchased the lamp. Perhaps the shop-keeper can apprise us of where she went?"

I raise an eyebrow. "Hey. That's actually a really good idea." Why didn't I think of that?

The tense line of his shoulders drops an inch.

"It'll all be okay," I say, mostly to reassure him, and somewhat to reassure myself.

⚱

Ernie squints past me, his wrinkled brow furrowing as he watches Bennet across the store. Bennet is staring at a bright pink, 1980s-style flashlight, his mouth agape like he's just discovered fire.

Ernie finally looks back at me. "What do you want to know exactly?"

I sigh. "Don't get all weird on me, Ernie. I don't care how much you gave her or anything—I'm not here to check if you're stiffing me." I jerk a thumb toward Bennet. "The seller was his sister."

Ernie grunts, his gaze drifting back to Bennet, who has now picked up the flashlight and is inspecting it with the kind of intense focus usually reserved for bomb defusal.

"Anyway, we just want to find her, that's all. There's some pressing family business. Their grandma is really sick, and we need to let her know before it's too late." Who can resist a sick grandma story? Everyone loves old people.

Ernie scratches the side of his nose. "I didn't get much from her, other than her name and the name of her friend."

"Friend?" That's news. Bennet never mentioned her having someone else with her. I put a pin in it. I will have to ask Bennet later.

His thumb hits the flashlight switch. The beam of light flicks on, and Bennet jerks back as if it just attacked him.

Ernie snorts. "Yeah. Delores something or other."

"Did she put an address in the logbook when you made the exchange?"

Ernie always makes people sign the logbook—it's how he ropes people into his email list.

"Lemme check," he mutters, shuffling toward an old metal filing cabinet. He slides open the middle drawer, stares down into it for a second, then lifts his head. "Moira! Where'd you put the logbook?"

A voice calls from the back, muffled and exasperated. "It's in the filing cabinet!"

"I know that, but it ain't here."

"Are you looking in the middle drawer?"

"Of course I'm looking in the middle drawer!"

"Well, you'd lose your ass if it wasn't attached to you!"

Ernie grumbles under his breath and slams the middle drawer shut. He yanks open the top one, peers inside, then does the same to the bottom before finally extracting the logbook—a battered spiral notebook that was probably black once but is now a faded, scuffed mess.

He flips through the pages, his frown deepening. "Hmph." He flips back a few more entries, muttering to himself. "That's strange. It's not here anymore. I could've sworn she filled this out. I watched her do it."

Great. She probably used magic to erase it.

"Did she mention where she was staying while she's in town? Anything at all?"

Ernie shakes his head. "Nope. She had that friend with her, and I remember them talking about getting dinner, but they didn't say where. Other than that, we only discussed the transaction."

"Are you sure neither of them said anything about sight-seeing? Maybe they talked to each other and you overheard?"

"Nope."

Behind me, an object clatters to the ground.

"Oops," Bennet says.

I turn around. The flashlight rolls across the floor, smacking into a shelf.

I pinch the bridge of my nose and take a deep breath. "I'll pay for that."

Ernie shrugs, already moving on, while I fish out a ten-dollar bill I can't afford to part with.

We exit the shop, leaving behind the musty scent of dust, wax, and old cigar smoke. I pick up my pace, the uneven sidewalk forcing me to navigate carefully. Bennet follows half a step behind.

"Where are we going?" he asks.

"I don't know yet. Who is Delores?" I slow down so he can walk beside me.

"Delores? She is my sister's lady's maid. A companion."

"Why didn't you tell me about her before?"

He shrugs. "I didn't think it was relevant."

"Because she's a servant?" I move out of the way of a stroller coming in the opposite direction.

Bennet follows my steps. "No, because she and Helen are always together."

We weave through a cluster of tourists gathered around a guide, who's dramatically gesturing toward the old Ursuline Convent and rattling off a spiel about voodoo, witches, and ghosts in New Orleans.

I'm halfway up the block when I stop short. Bennet's footsteps are no longer behind me. I spin around.

He's with the tour group, staring at the tourists, his eyes narrowed, brow furrowed.

It's like wrangling a toddler. I stomp back toward him.

"What are the little boxes?" His attention is fixed on a couple of tourists holding up their phones.

I follow his gaze. "Phones. They take pictures."

"Phones?"

I pause. "You don't have phones in Aetheria." Right. Mystical land of magic, not technology.

"I do not know what that means."

Oh, boy. Where to even begin?

I motion toward the steps outside St. Mary's Church. "Come on. We're gonna need to sit for this."

EIGHT

I tug out my cell phone and unlock it. "Here. This is a cell phone. It's like a—" *mini-computer in your pocket.* Except if he doesn't know what a cell phone is, he sure as hell doesn't know what a computer is. "—a multifunctional device. I can send messages to people, like Kevin and Mimi, and it will appear on their cell phone almost immediately."

His brows pop up. "Truly?"

I open the messenger app and show him my latest conversation with Kevin, which is mostly me texting him repeatedly and him responding with *ok* every five messages.

Bennet squints at the screen. "You can communicate with others this way?"

"Yep."

I flip open the camera app, switch to the front-facing camera, and snap a quick selfie. When I tap the image, my face fills the screen, a cloud of dark messy hair, brown eyes, awkward grin, squinting in the sunlight. Beside me, Bennet stares into the camera with intense concentration, his frown deepening, green eyes sharp against the bright daylight.

He plucks the phone from my hand. "Remarkable," he breathes.

I guess I'd be astonished too if I'd never seen a phone before.

"What else can it do?" He turns it over, then gives it a little shake, like he's expecting something to rattle loose inside.

I snatch it back. "Don't hurt it. I can't afford a new one."

We spend a few minutes while I give him a crash course in modern technology. I show him ebooks, the calculator app, and the wonder of the internet, though I struggle to explain how it all works when he asks.

"There's, like, radio waves or something. And satellites. It's all very complicated."

"It's like magic." His eyes are fixated on the screen.

"It's like science." *And I was never good at science.* History, literature, sociology, those were my jam. I was going to apply for my masters in art history when everything went to shit.

He gestures at my phone. "Can you use this magic science to find Helen?"

"No. Well, maybe if I were some kind of hacker who could break into security cameras and use facial recognition to scan for her or whatever."

He stares at me, brow furrowing. "You say that as if it is possible."

"Technically, it *is* possible. But I have no idea how to do it."

"This place is strange," he mutters, shaking his head.

He's so completely out of place. A flicker of sympathy ignites in my chest. It must be hard, being away from every-thing you know, dumped into a world where even the simplest things don't make sense.

I can't imagine being dropped in the middle of Aetheria with nothing more than the clothes on my back, in a land of magic that literally changes the landscape. No cell phones, heating pads, or coffee makers? I might die.

"Tell me more about Aetheria?" I ask. "How is it different from here?"

He rubs his chin. The bristles are longer than yesterday. I should find him a razor, but the stubble suits him. Gives him a roguish look. If we kissed, the stubble would brush the delicate skin of my face and—okay, definitely investing in a razor.

"This town is similar to ones in Aetheria, but Aetheria is less noisy and crowded. Not as large. We have more nature, forests, mountains, rivers." He waves a hand. "And there are no cell phones." He tilts his head at a passing car. "No growling metal beasts roaming the streets."

I smirk. "We call those cars."

"And there are no poles with strings hanging between them." He squints up at a power line. "All this technology is a magic killer. With all this machinery, no wonder it's harder to find magic here, to draw from the land with all this artifice in the way. I am not sure your cell phone would work in my world."

"How do people get around in Aetheria?" I ask.

He stretches his long legs out in front of him, crossing them at the ankles. "They walk, mostly. Some people can move short distances with their magic, depending on their powers and strength. We also have horses."

I tilt my head toward him. "Do a lot of people have magic in Aetheria?"

He shifts on the concrete step. "Yes, but most have minor abilities of little significance."

Okay, Judgy McJudgerson. I cross my arms. "What's considered 'little significance'?"

"Like what you do, locating objects."

I grimace. "Ouch."

He frowns. "Did that cause you pain?"

"Only to my ego."

His expression shifts, like he's struggling to understand why that would bother me. "I didn't mean to imply—"

"It's fine, *Your Highness.*"

He presses his lips together, then continues, "People can manipulate time to a small extent, seconds into the past or future, manifest small objects, heal minor wounds, things like that."

"And you can do all that, plus travel through dimensions and curse people into lamps?"

One broad shoulder lifts in a half shrug. "Some of it. I'm not a healer. Healers use water magic, and my affinity is more for earth and fire. I can open portals to other realms, and wield fire as a weapon."

"And Helen?"

"She's stronger than I am," he says without bitterness. "She is more attuned to fire than I am. She can summon greater force, hold power longer, and shape it with more precision."

I tuck my phone into my pocket. My magic may be on the fritz, and I definitely don't have the technical know-how to hack into any security feeds, but there *is* another option. If Helen's as powerful as Bennet claims, she should be leaving behind a magical footprint, a signature that can be tracked by someone with the right abilities.

I push myself to my feet, wiping my hands on my jeans. "Come on."

Bennet follows as I start down the street, weaving through the throngs of tourists. A street performer plays jazz on the corner, the warm brass notes rolling over the sound of distant chatter.

"Where are we going?" he asks.

"There are people who can track power shifts. If your sister has been using a lot of magic, they might be able to pick up her trail."

"Like you do?"

"Sort of. I don't track magic specifically, I track objects and people. I can sense things in my immediate surroundings, that sort of thing."

He catches the hesitation in my voice. "Are there people you cannot track?"

"Only my parents."

"Why—?"

I wave him off. "It's not important. This way. We're nearly there."

He studies me for a moment before falling into step beside me. "Who is this person who can track magic? Are they a mortal?"

We take another turn, the street narrowing. The neon buzz of a beer sign flickers from a bar nearby, and the scent of incense drifts from a shop selling tarot cards and crystals.

"Not entirely," I say.

Bennet glances at me, suspicious. "What kind of being are they?"

I stop in front of a black and white sign hanging above a heavy wooden door. Words in an elegant script stand out starkly against the dark background.

Boutique du Vampyre.

His brows furrow. "Vampyre?"

I grin. "Welcome to New Orleans."

The small store is cluttered with shelves and displays, leaving only a few narrow aisles to navigate. A pair of twenty-something blondes, dressed in black and dripping with silver jewelry, browse the selection: books on witchcraft, black and purple candles, decorative coffins meant to be hung on walls, bat earrings, vervain necklaces, and clothing—mostly black, with excessive amounts of lace and leather.

I ignore the merchandise and head straight for the bearded guy behind the counter. He wears thick, black-framed glasses and a studded choker, his nose buried in a book titled *Initiation into Witchcraft*.

"Hi there. I need to know where the vamp is this week." I keep my voice low.

Bennet steps up beside me, his attention drawn to a grotesque blue demon head sculpture mounted on the wall behind the clerk.

Without removing his eyes from his book, the clerk plucks a card from a stack on the counter and slides it toward me. "Fritzel's. Courtyard in the back. Tell him Dracula sent you."

"No, I'm not looking for the tourist attraction." I lower my voice further. "I need to find the white vamp."

His eyes finally lift to mine, sharp with recognition. Then, without missing a beat, he calls toward the back of the store. "Richard!"

"Shit," I mutter.

A door in the rear swings open so fast it smacks against the wall. "Well, well, well. Cassandra, my darling." Richard emerges, grinning like the devil he is. He points at me, twirling a ring-laden finger in the air, his nose wrinkling in mock dismay. "That's an interesting choice for a visit to your favorite auntie. Laundry day?"

"Auntie?" Bennet murmurs.

I shake my head. "Friend of the family."

Richard is short—no taller than Kevin—but what he lacks in stature, he makes up for in presence. His shock of white hair barely crests the shelving unit next to him, but his bright blue suit more than compensates, shimmering under the dim lighting. The black silk shirt beneath it is open just enough to reveal an opulent gold chain. With the dramatic blue eyeshadow dusted across his lids and the swipe of his glossy red lipstick, he's like a flamboyant, wizardy Papa Smurf. In one hand, he clutches a glossy cane topped with a gleaming gold handle, which he taps against the floor as he approaches.

His face is unlined, his nose a little too large for his features but somehow suiting him. I don't know how old he is. Mimi swears he hasn't changed a bit since she met him, over forty years ago.

"Hi, Richard." I pointedly ignore the jab about my outfit.

"Cassandra, my dear, it's been ages." His voice is high and lilting. He taps toward me, his heeled shoes clicking against the floor, and leans forward, kissing me on both cheeks. "You never come to see me anymore."

"I saw you last month."

Richard waves a dismissive hand. "That was ages ago and it was for work and not play. Come, come." He spins on a heel, heading back through the dark doorway he emerged from. "Bring your friend."

I jerk my head at Bennet to follow. "Brace yourself," I warn him as we step toward the gaping blackness where Richard disappeared.

"For what?"

"Literally anything."

Richard is powerful and strange, and every time I meet with him, I'm left with more questions than answers. He's a master illusionist—his magic can make you see whatever he wants you to see. But that's not all. He's been around a long time and picked up spells from all over, particularly from New Orleans's deep well of magic. Mom used to tell me stories about how he studied under voodoo queens, how he could change the way people perceived reality itself. Mimi met him years ago at a Mardi Gras ball, one of those exclusive affairs where people form "krewes" and carry on like royalty for a night. They got put on the same float and ended up sharing a flask of magical booze.

He has more power than anyone I know . . . except maybe Bennet, based on what he said of his abilities.

We step through the doorway, and the moment we do, the door slams shut behind us.

Bennet spins around. "Where's the door?"

I shrug. "Magic."

Any trace of Boutique du Vampyre is gone. The space is unrecognizable, transformed into a hobbit's dream. One side of the room is curved, warm wood, like the inside of a hollowed-out tree. A rocking chair with a blue flannel blanket flung over it sits beside a flickering fire, and shelves carved directly into the wood are lined with books. The opposite wall is entirely glass, revealing a stretch of bayou just beyond it—lush greenery, wet earth, a stagnant waterway snaking through towering trees draped in moss. The air is thick with the scents of wood and sawdust mixed with the dampness of Louisiana marshlands.

Bennet stares, wide-eyed. "What is this?" He turns in a slow circle, taking it all in. "It's incredible."

Richard flutters his fingers. "Oh, this?" He taps forward, cane clicking dully against the packed dirt floor. "Just a bit of glamour."

I clear my throat. "Listen, we need to know where the vamp will be tonight. It's important, and we're kind of in a hurry because I have work later, so—"

Richard hums, pacing toward Bennet with deliberate slowness. "Tell me, Cassandra, who is your friend?" He rests a hand on Bennet's bicep, giving it an appreciative squeeze.

"This is Bennet." I step between them before Richard can get any ideas. He loves to meddle and get involved in everything, but he's unreliable and expensive. He could probably help us find Helen, but I'm not sure we can pay the price. Just giving us the white vamp's location should be easy enough without payment. It's worth a shot, anyway. "Can you tell us where the vamp will be?"

Richard releases Bennet, stepping back like he wasn't interested anyway. He saunters toward a plush chaise lounge in the corner and flops onto it dramatically, his cane resting against the arm.

Richard examines his nails, then flicks an invisible speck of dust from his sleeve. "How is the poltergeist situation?"

I wave a hand. "It's fine, Richard. Now, the vamp?"

He clasps his hands together, expression positively beatific. "I am so pleased my hex bags were useful. You're welcome, by the way."

"I already thanked you for that." And paid you a small fortune.

Richard tsks, shaking his head. "Sarcasm doesn't become you, my dear. The magic I use is special and powerful, some may even say . . . evocative."

What is he talking about? "I know." I don't want to know. "I'm not asking you to use magic. I only want one tiny piece of information. Can you help or not?"

Richard exhales dramatically, like I've just asked him to donate a kidney without anesthesia. "You are so dreadfully impatient." He taps his cane against the floor. "Perhaps I should consult the spirits. Or divine the answer through—"

"No," I cut in. "No theatrics. No spirit consultations. Please tell me where to find him."

Richard pouts, then glances at Bennet. "Your friend here is terribly rude."

Bennet's mouth gapes open. "Uh."

Richard gives a delighted little clap. "Oh, I do love the quiet, bewildered ones."

"Richard."

"Fine." He waves a hand. "The vamp will be at Fritzel's tonight. Courtyard."

"And?" Is he messing with me?

Richard taps his cane on the floor. "And he won't be the one in leather pants and fake fangs. That's merely a diversion."

"When?"

"Around eight."

I lift my brows. "Are you sure?"

His head dips. "Yes, because that's when he gets his break."

"His break?"

"He's in the band." Richard chuckles. "He plays the saxophone. Such a sensuous instrument."

I resist the urge to strangle him. "Are we done?"

Richard snaps and the swamp vanishes, replaced by a solid red door. "Be gone, then. But do try to have fun, my dear."

I don't hesitate. "Great. Thanks, Richard."

My hand is on the doorknob when he calls out, "Cassandra."

I pause.

"Keep that man close. You're going to need him. And Bennet, darling?" Richard's smirk turns sharp. "You're welcome."

Bennet stiffens. "For what?"

Richard winks at him. "You'll see."

"Come on." I haul Bennet through the door with me.

We step into a park, under the shade of a sprawling oak tree, its thick roots bulging from the earth. The trunk is wide and solid, its bark unbroken, like we didn't just step out of it. Sunlight filters through the leaves, dappling the grass in gold and green. In the distance, children squeal with laughter, the rhythmic creak of swings blending with birdsong.

Bennet turns in a slow circle. "Where are we?"

"About a mile from where we were. Richard does this kind of thing." I chuckle, shaking my head. "When he was making us the hex bags, he insisted on staying at our place for a full week. He said he needed to 'sit in the space,' but really I think he just wanted to annoy us. He wouldn't leave me alone. Followed me everywhere, asking questions, and he kept stealing my hairbrush."

Bennet tilts his head. "He seems lonely."

I snort. "That's a nice way of saying obnoxious. He might consider not being an asshole if he wants friends who actually enjoy his company."

Bennet's brows knit. "He has a strange scent."

I glance at him. "Yeah?"

"Like oranges," he says slowly. "Dripping in sugar. Cloying and sweet, slightly off." His nose wrinkles. "But there's something else underneath the scent. Almost as if the scent is a mask, which is why it smells wrong."

"A mask for what?"

His eyes dart to the side. "I'm not sure. He kind of smells like you, but not."

Okay. That's weird. "Maybe that's left over from when he stayed with us? Although that was a month ago and I would hope he's showered a few times since then but who knows. What do I smell like?"

His posture stiffens, his mouth opening slightly before snapping shut.

A grin tugs at my lips. "Oh, come on. That bad?"

He clears his throat. "I—uh—"

My pocket chirps.

I dig out my phone and check the message. The job I was supposed to take later. I'll have to push it back. My stomach flips. They're asking if I can stop by tomorrow, but I don't know how I'll have my magic back before then. We don't even know if the vamp will be able to track Helen, let alone if she can fix this curse.

I blow out a slow breath and text back, pushing it to next week.

Bennet moves to a nearby bench, sitting with his back straight, scanning the park. He's close enough that our bond doesn't stretch to that weird, uncomfortable pull.

He takes in the park, and I scan our surroundings with him. A family plays in the grass, a little boy shrieking as his dad swings him into the air. A woman jogs past with a golden retriever trotting happily at her side. People living their lives, completely unaware of the magic in their midst.

Completely unaware of the djinn watching them from a park bench.

I bet they have hot water at home.

After a minute, I drop onto the bench next to him, leaving about a foot of space between us.

The breeze stirs his hair. "Tell me more about this vamp we are meeting. What does 'vamp' mean?"

"Vampires are creatures that can manipulate energy. They can feed on it, feel the source, track it. I'm hoping one of them will be able to sense Helen's magic. If she's powerful enough, they will be drawn to her."

He tilts his legs in my direction. "Would they harm her?"

"No. They might be able to draw on some of her energy, but it wouldn't hurt her. It would be like losing a little bit of blood. Your body replenishes it. They can't take enough to cause harm, or else it hurts them as well. A bit of magical energy blowback."

He nods. "What was the noise from your cell phone?"

"That was my next job. Had to push it back a week."

"Why?"

I rub a hand over my face. "Because my job involves magic."

"This makes you sad."

I huff a laugh, but it's hollow. "Yeah. In case you haven't noticed, my family needs someone to support them. And that someone is me."

Bennet hesitates, then asks, "What about Mimi?"

"She does as much as she can to help. But she's in her seventies. She has some health issues and she doesn't have the energy to work and cook and clean and run after two kids all day on her own. She helps me with them while I work, and does more than I could ever ask, but it's still a lot." Although she likes to say we all make her feel ten years younger, but I think she's just trying to lessen my guilt at relying on her so much.

His lips part, but then he presses them shut again. His eyes search mine. "You do all that, take care of everyone, hold everything together. You're—" His gaze dips to my mouth.

My heart stutters.

He moves closer. Or am I moving closer? His breath feathers against my lips. One more inch and—

I jerk back, heat flooding my cheeks. "Whoa. Okay. That, uh, that can't happen right now." I push off the bench. "Come on. Kevin'll be out of school soon, and I need to check on Jackie and some of my other clients. We'll head to Fritzel's after dinner."

Bennet lingers for a second longer, gaze sweeping the park, then stands and follows.

I spend a couple of hours in the kitchen alone, giving up my office to Kevin to get his schoolwork done on the computer. I take care of phone calls with clients, moving my schedule around and checking in on my regulars to find out what items they might be needing in the future—once I have the time and ability to search for them.

I'd give up my left arm to stop hustling for a day and just hang out in a museum. Or go back to school and finish my degree. Or just escape. When I was in college I had all these plans for a gap year, traveling through Europe or Asia or literally anywhere else.

Those dreams are long gone.

As I head upstairs, voices drift from my office. Bennet with the kids. I slow my steps, stopping right outside the door.

"... and those are reality shows," Kevin is saying, his voice serious. "They're not scripted, supposedly. Just people being dramatic on camera."

Bennet sounds skeptical. "So these individuals volunteer to be recorded while engaging in conflict and strange mating rituals?"

Jackie giggles. "Pretty much. It's like watching wild animals, but with more hair gel and bad decisions."

I peek through the crack between the door and the frame.

"Here, you have a lot to learn. Let's watch this." Kevin hands Bennet a tablet. The screen lights up his face. Probably one of those "top ten reality TV meltdown" compilations, Kevin loves those.

There's a pause and then Bennet asks, "Why are these people so scantily clad?"

My eyes widen. What the hell is he showing him?

"It's *Love Island*," Jackie says. "That's just what they do."

"Why?"

"It's like a game," Kevin says. "These people go to an island and they have to play games and couple up, and people who watch them get to vote on their favorite couple. The non-favorites get kicked off each episode. At the end, the best couple is given money and they get to choose to keep it all or share it with the other person."

"To see if they are legit," Jackie adds.

Bennet scratches his head. "Is this how courtship is handled in your world?"

"Only for people who want to be famous and get money."

They watch for a few more minutes. "Your world is . . ." Bennet starts, searching for words. "Excessively chaotic."

"Yeah," Kevin agrees. "It's great."

I press my lips together to keep from laughing.

Kevin steps closer and bangs his knee hard against the side

table. He yelps, sucking in a sharp breath through his teeth. "Ughhh, my knee."

Jackie sits up straighter. "Are you okay?"

"Fine. I already can't feel it. I'm basically a superhero."

Bennet drops the tablet, his eyes shooting up to Kevin, but my brother is already moving on, plopping on the couch next to Bennet and picking up the dropped tablet. "Anyway, wanna watch something else? Maybe *Vampire Diaries* since you're going to see a vamp later? It's not really accurate, but it's funny."

Oh, no.

I step in to the room. "Does everyone have their homework and chores done?"

Kevin hands the tablet to Bennet. "I did all my homework."

"My work is done too," Jackie says.

"And chores?" I lift my brows.

They exchange a glance. "No," Jackie says and Kevin says, "Not yet."

"Well get to it. They need to be done before dinner."

"Fine."

They trudge out.

Bennet sets the tablet on the table. "Your siblings are entertaining."

I gesture to the tablet. "Are you done learning about *Love Island*?"

Bennet's lips twitch. "Not even close, but I believe I have learned enough about television for one day."

"Want to learn about the magical washer and dryer?"

TEN

The courtyard at Fritzel's is quiet on a random Tuesday night in October. Just me and Bennet, a scattering of empty picnic tables bathed in the soft glow of overhead fairy lights—orange colored, for the season—and the fake vampire in the corner, posing for pictures with a handful of giggly tourists. Jazz notes float on the breeze, muffled by the brick walls that surround us.

Bennet shifts beside me, tapping his foot against the uneven cobblestone. "When I looked on the magic mirror Kevin gave me, it said vampires drink blood."

I glance at him. "I'm guessing you don't have vampires in Aetheria?"

"No." He tilts his head. "We are all djinn. Among us, there are the jann, which are my people, the marid, the shaytan, and the *ifrit*." He says "ifrit" like Jackie would say "cringe."

"What are ifrit?"

"They are technically djinn, but they are different from the jann and the rest. They have magic, they can shapeshift when they have enough power, but it is hard for them to maintain.

They are mostly made of smoke and fire. To take form, they must feed on us, drawing from our energy until they have the strength to take a form. Even then, it cannot last long."

I frown. "So, they steal your magic and use it to become something they're not?"

"Yes. They take from us in order to exist in the light."

I think on that for a second. "Sounds like fictional vampires."

Bennet's brow furrows. "*Fictional* vampires?"

I nod. "The *Vampire Diaries* isn't real. It's a show. Fiction. In reality vamps don't hurt people, at least, not any more than anyone else. There are at least a dozen vamps in the New Orleans area, though I've only met a couple." Haven't really had much use for them until now. "They are magic manipulators, of varying ability. Some can feel magic in others and feed off of it—like it gets them high, I guess, but it doesn't hurt the person they are taking from. There are made-up stories about vampires drinking blood, but it's not true. Simple human paranoia, making up monsters to explain what people don't understand."

Bennet hums, glancing toward the fake vamp, who is now ushering the tourists toward a staircase leading up to the bar. "Like him?"

"Right. No magic. Just a guy in a costume, playing a fictional vampire. There's a bar up there—it's actually kind of fun. You pay him, and they let you go up. The bar overlooks the street and it's decorated really cool, antique furniture, pictures that move, black lights, other visual effects. Stuff like that."

His eyes flick back to me. "Have you been there before?"

"Yeah," I admit. "A long time ago."

Years ago. Before Jackie got sick. Before everything changed. Back when my biggest worries were college, friends, and whether I had enough gas money to make it through the week. Those problems were crushing at the time, all-consuming. If only I had known what was coming.

Bennet studies me. "You sound sad."

I test the barrier around my mind. Still latched. Still intact. "Can you feel me?"

"No." His voice is quiet. "It's in your voice."

I turn to face him fully. The fairy lights above cast a soft glow over his face, highlighting the sharp angles—the aristocratic cheekbones, the straight, austere nose. He looks like a royal. *A royal pain in my ass.*

Except, not so much a pain in my ass. Not really.

My eyes slide over his chiseled jawline. What I need is a nice burlap sack to cover all of that up.

"It reminds me of a different time." I force my attention back to the present. "It's amazing how much perspective you gain when the real shit hits the fan."

He watches me for a beat. "It was before your parents left."

"Yeah." I glance at my watch. Eight o'clock. Any second now. Richard is never wrong.

"Have you met this vamp who will be here tonight?"

"I don't think so. He's kind of the big kahuna. Hard to find, hence the need to ask questions to get his location. He is the strongest vamp in the city. If anyone can find Helen, it'll be him." And hopefully he will help us. Otherwise . . . I am not sure what to try next.

The door to the bar slams shut as the fake vamp disappears with his latest group. The air shifts, the pressure dipping ever so slightly.

There.

"He's here." I incline my head toward the far corner.

Bennet blinks. "Where did he come from? He wasn't there a second ago."

"They move quickly. Come on."

The vamp is already settled at a table, poking at a container of food with a plastic fork. He looks like he could be any college Joe—clean-cut dark hair, a Tulane frat-boy kind of face, a green polo shirt. The kind of guy I used to date.

I hate this kind of guy.

As we approach, he sets his fork aside, gaze flicking between us. His brows draw together. "Well. This is interesting."

I sit across from him, already annoyed. Bennet settles beside me.

"What's interesting?" I ask flatly.

His lips curve. "The connection between you."

My brows lift. "You can see that?"

"Of course."

"Can you fix it?"

His mouth twitches. "No. And you wouldn't want me to."

I grit my teeth. He's absolutely the type of guy who has the audacity to tell me what I want. "Um, yes I would."

"You will change your mind." He leans back, studying us like a puzzle. "Not that it matters. I couldn't do it anyway. I can read energies, I can absorb energies, but I can't manipulate them in that way. The shape of it—this thing between you—is very unique." His eyes glint, a hungry shimmer beneath the surface. "Quite fascinating."

His expression makes my skin crawl, like he's looking at a particularly rare dish on the menu.

"That's not why we're here. I'm Cassie, this is Bennet."

His head dips in acknowledgment. "I am Edward."

"Of course you are," I mutter and then barrel ahead. "Listen, we are trying to find his sister. Can you help us track her?"

Edward's expression shifts, his interest sharpening on Bennet. "Yes. You have a lot of power but it's," his head tilts, "dim. I felt it when you crossed the barrier into our world. Your sister as well. Her power signature is similar to yours, but stronger.

"You can sense when something powerful crosses into our world?"

Edward picks up his fork, spearing a bite of chicken. "Sure. Happens all the time."

"It does?" That's news to me. People and creatures crossing dimensions like it's a damn revolving door? I have enough to worry about with what's going on in this world, let alone the others bleeding into it.

Bennet leans forward. "Can you tell me where she is, then?"

Edward sets his fork down, lacing his fingers together. "I'm not sure. You went into the French Quarter and then your power dimmed. And the other . . ." He lifts his brows meaningfully.

I sigh. Here it is. "How much?"

He smiles. "Just a little taste."

I extend my hand.

Bennet's arm shoots out, stopping me. "What are you doing?"

"Paying the man."

His gaze sharpens. "With what?"

"My energy."

Bennet's mouth pops open. "You can't do that."

"Of course I can. It's how things work. Don't worry, it doesn't hurt. I told you. It's like giving blood. I'll eat a good meal later."

His jaw tightens. "I can't let you do this."

I raise an eyebrow. "It's not your choice."

He doesn't flinch. "Let me pay him. It's my sister."

I hesitate, searching his face, then nod. "Fine." Let him deal with the subsequent headache.

Bennet reaches out.

Edward's eyes gleam, a flame flickering in the black depths of his pupils. He rests his fingers against the back of Bennet's hand.

A few seconds pass. Then, the glow in Edward's eyes flickers out. He frowns. "It's not working."

Bennet's brows furrow. "Why not?"

Edward blows out a breath. "It's this thing between you. It's blocking access."

I stretch out my hand again. "Try me."

He touches my palm. A second passes. Then another.

He shakes his head. "Nope."

I glance over at Bennet. "Maybe both at the same time?" The words register and my face fills with heat. "You know what I mean."

Edward grins. "Now we're talking."

He shoves his food container to the side, then reaches out, fingers hovering over both of ours before finally resting atop them. His touch is cool, featherlight.

Seconds pass.

Edward withdraws. "Still nothing."

Bennet shifts beside me. "Why?"

Edward studies us, his expression turning thoughtful, almost distant. "I've seen connections between people before, but this one is different." His eyes fall shut, brow furrowing. "There are two pathways, but they're woven together, like a braid. Instead of widening the link, it's jamming everything up. Blocking everything."

"What does that mean?" My voice is steady, but my pulse ticks faster. "How do we fix it? Can we unbraid it? Remove it entirely?"

Edward frowns for a few beats longer before opening his eyes. "You must make a choice to act in sync."

His words resonate inside me, like a string plucked deep in my chest.

A chill trickles down my spine. That is eerily close to the whole "move as one" thing.

I shove the thought aside.

Pay attention.

We need the intel. Neither of us can pay with our magic, but maybe . . . I tap Bennet's arm and lean in, clearing my throat.

His head dips toward me. He smells like soap and warmth and rich, hot summer nights laced with jasmine.

"We could try that whole shared intentions thing."

His eyes search mine. "Are you sure? You may have to lower your mental shields for us to connect on that level."

I spread my fingers on the table. "I can't say I like it, but do you have any other ideas? This guy only takes payment in magic, and our magic is stuck."

His jaw flexes. "I understand. But perhaps we can intend for the magic to come from me and not you."

The protectiveness radiating off him is not hot at all. Nope.

I shiver, but only because it's cold.

"Fine." Turning back to Edward, I clap my hands, rubbing them together. "Okay, Eddie boy. Let's try this again."

ELEVEN

I extend my hand to the vamp again, my mind racing. Intentions, shared intentions, what the fuck does it even mean?

Bennet puts his hand over mine, and then Edward reaches for us, fingers covering ours.

I drop my mental shields, despite the fear coursing through me of being that vulnerable. Like a turtle without a shell.

But then . . . nothing.

No spark, no jolt, no ancient well of power springing free. No choir of angels bursting out of the heavens. Just three idiots holding hands across a café table like we're in a throuple.

I glance sideways at Bennet. "Is this doing anything for you?"

His brow creases. "It should be." He shifts, angling his palm more fully over mine. "You must focus."

"I am focusing."

"Don't force it. Just focus on what we need our magic to do and let go."

"Let go of what, exactly?" The tenuous thread on my sanity? But I shut my eyes anyway. *Let go. Let go.*

Let go of fear. Of doubt. Of trying to control it.

A beat passes. Another.

Then there's a pinch and a tug, a release, like a clogged drain suddenly breaking free. Magic flows into me, molten and hot, causing a cascade of warmth.

It's hard to concentrate. And suddenly, Bennet is there, in my mind, like smoke rising through cracks, he's all around me. His emotions swirl with mine, heat meeting with heat, until I can't tell where his end and mine begin.

Wonder.

Surprise.

Confusion.

Fear.

Arousal.

A deep longing, raw and unshaped, slipping through my fingers before I can take hold of it.

My breath catches. *What is happening?*

Then, as suddenly as it came, it vanishes. The emotions bleed out, leaving me lightheaded. But clearheaded enough to slam my shields back into place.

But they're still in place. Locked down tight.

What the fuck?

Was he getting all that? Or is it just me? Or . . . both?

I steal a glance at him. The weight of his stare is more than I can handle. His cheeks are flushed. Okay, apparently he had the same experience.

I'm sure it will all be fine.

I turn to Edward.

His mouth is slack, gaze unfocused. "Wow," he breathes. Then his fingers tighten on my wrist. His eyes darken, hungry. "More."

I smack him over the head.

He blinks, the hunger in his gaze dulling to hazy and unfocused.

"Pull yourself together. You've got your payment. Now spill."

Edward slumps back into his seat, sighing, then picks up his fork and shovels food into his mouth with obscene satisfaction. "This tastes amazing."

"Edward." Goddammit. He's high as fuck.

Bennet moves faster than I can track, snatching Edward's plate away before he can stab another bite of chicken.

Edward frowns. "Hey."

"Answer the lady, please." Bennet's voice is smooth, but edged with steel.

Wow. I didn't know he had it in him.

Edward huffs, but finally mutters, "She went to the bayou."

Not exactly helpful. Louisiana has over twenty-five hundred square miles of swamp and wetlands.

"Where in the bayou?"

"To the witches who see beyond the veil."

Okaaay.

I try again. "How do we get to these witches?"

His eyelids droop. "There's a portal."

I groan. "I should have made him talk before we paid." I flick his ear. Useless. Like a well-fed cat who overdid it on the catnip. "Who do we go see, Eddie?"

He swipes lazily at my hand and misses by a mile. "Lafayette Cemetery One," he yawns. "Find the mausoleum marked with magic. Be there at dusk or dawn for it to work."

"And you're sure Helen is still there? With the swamp witches?"

He shrugs, eyes glassy. "She could be. I don't sense her anymore. She went there and then—" He snaps his fingers.

"Poof." Then he giggles and slumps forward. A snore rumbles out of him.

"Great." I shove back from the table. "We're not getting anything else out of him. Let's start walking back."

We exit the courtyard, walking through the bar onto the main road. The music follows us out, bluesy and rich, twining through the dimly lit street. The Tuesday night crowd on Bourbon is light, but present nonetheless. Tourists in windbreakers, twenty-somethings spilling from neon-lit bars, the occasional street performer crooning under a flickering lamppost.

I weave through a clump of drunk college kids, Bennet a silent presence at my back.

We reach a quieter street, and he turns to me. "How did you set your intention, exactly? What did you wish for?"

"I wanted us to be able to access our magic whenever we need to, to remove the block. It seems like it worked. Maybe now we can use our magic to find Helen ourselves." But I'm also a little freaked about how it basically erased any block between us as well. At least, while the vamp was drawing from us.

Maybe it was just a one-off. Freak occurrence.

"We could test it?" Bennet steps around a random pipe sticking up out of the sidewalk.

"Later. When we get home." I'm not quite ready for another emotional tornado. "Let's focus on Helen. So, either she's still in the bayou, or she asked the witches to block her or something so she couldn't be tracked."

Bennet's eyes are troubled. "She may have concealed her presence herself. Clearly she doesn't want to be dragged back to Aetheria. I have no doubt Uncle Hugh has sent someone after us since I haven't returned. He is probably worried sick."

"How would they find you? Can they track you the way you could track Helen?"

"No. Not many have that ability. And Helen and I—it's different. We have more magic than most. When we were kids, our connection was so strong we could find each other anywhere. Almost read each other's thoughts. We aren't as close as we once were." He steps off the curb to avoid a pothole, then falls back into stride beside me.

I shove my hands in my pockets. "Being able to read her thoughts would sure come in handy right about now. There is no way to bring that back to life?"

He shakes his head. "When I first tracked her even with my magic on this side of the veil, it was difficult. The channel between us is muddled with misuse, like a well-worn path that's been overrun with weeds and fallen logs. Things have not been the same between us since our parents died."

"Why did your relationship with Helen change?"

We stop to let a car pass.

He turns to me as we cross the street. "She had obligations to the throne. She was often sequestered away with Uncle Hugh, learning how to rule, while I had tutors. Sometimes I was sent away to foster with Uncle's councilors in their steadings, to learn about the more distant parts of the kingdom, so I might more capably assist my sister at court once she ascended. After our parents passed, we were thrust into our respective roles, no longer free to be children."

"How old were you?"

"I was nine. Helen was twelve."

My heart hurts for him, for both of them. To lose your parents so young—and then be separated from each other to attend to "duties." I can't imagine it. There's no way in hell I would have sent either Jackie or Kevin away after our parents went missing.

I would rather send myself away. After three years of playing mom, getting a night off from parenting duties? That might be actual heaven.

"What happened to your parents?"

His hand lifts to the ring hidden behind his shirt. "They were attacked by ifrit on the way home from a neighboring kingdom. My uncle was with them. He barely survived."

I wince. His story just keeps getting worse. "I'm sorry. The ring you wear, did it belong to one of them?"

His shoulders stiffen. "Yes. My mother."

Ah. I'm not sure how to react to that. I know firsthand what it's like to lose your parents. Words don't fix or help anything. Nothing I say is going to bring them back or fix the ache of loss.

Shit. Way to ruin a perfectly comfortable conversation with an insensitive question.

We walk in silence for a block.

Grief is personal. Death is awkward.

I open my mouth to backtrack, but he suddenly stops.

I halt beside him. "Look, I'm sorry—"

He lifts a hand, pointing past me.

I turn. "What is it?"

His head tilts slightly, eyes flicking behind us.

I listen. The night is quiet, save for the distant thrum of music and the occasional car rolling past the next intersection. The street we're on is empty, just pools of shadow and the occasional glow of light spilling from a high window.

Bennet murmurs, "Strange."

A flicker of unease curls in my gut.

The shadow against the nearest wall moves.

I freeze.

It peels away, detaching from the brick like liquid darkness, shifting, twisting, morphing.

A dim streetlight glints off something in its hand.

Is that a knife? It's shiny but glowing, prickling like light-ning. Shock locks my body in place. How the hell is a shadow holding a bolt of lightning? Let alone moving.

My limbs are ice.

Can't breathe.

The figure lunges, a flash of light arcing my way.

TWELVE

The world slows.

Bennet leaps in front of me, blocking the strike with a whip of his arm.

The shadow moves with an eerie fluidity, its edges rippling like liquid smoke. It attacks Bennet, each blow echoing down the quiet street.

My mind stutters over the impossibility. How is there a shadow throwing lightning at us and landing hits?

But Bennet is fast. His movements are sharp and efficient, almost unnatural in their precision, as he parries and evades each strike with effortless grace. He's some kind of freaking ninja or something. He can barely use a cell phone, has never driven a car, struggles with the dishwasher, but apparently, he can fight like he was born for it.

The shadow shudders, losing shape. Its edges dissolve, twisting and folding in on itself like a collapsing house of cards, and then it melts away entirely.

Silence crashes down in its absence.

I stand there, heartbeat hammering, breath trapped in my

throat. The night around us is too vast, and yet the darkness is pressing in too tightly.

"Come." His warm hand connects with my lower back, a comforting weight. "We must hurry, in case it returns."

My legs finally unlock. "We'll be safe at home. It's warded."

Then we're running, footsteps uneven against the cracked sidewalk. Bennet keeps pace beside me, smooth and steady, always half a step behind like he's shielding my back. My pulse thrums in my ears, drowning out the city's usual hum. I can't stop scanning the shadows, waiting for another one to rise, for another flash of lightning to lash out of the dark.

By the time we reach the alley leading home, my lungs are burning, my legs are lead, and I'm drenched in sweat. Bennet, on the other hand? Not even winded. Not a single strand of dark gold hair out of place.

So unfair.

I slam the door shut behind us, leaning against it, dragging in gulps of air.

Mimi rounds the corner from the kitchen, her sharp gaze locking on to us. "You're bleeding."

I glance down, pulse spiking, expecting I don't even know what, a bolt of lightning sticking out of my chest?

But no. It's not me.

A drop of crimson patters onto the floor. Then another.

Bennet's hand drips with blood.

Mimi spins on her heel. "I'll grab the first aid kit."

I curse under my breath. He got hurt protecting me, and I was too caught up in my own panic to notice. "Come on. Let's wash you up."

The kitchen light is too bright after the street's murky shadows. I guide him to the sink, turning the tap. Cold water. Great. Whatever, it'll have to do.

"Jacket off." I reach to help him shrug out of the leather

coat. It's heavier than I expected, still warm from his body. I fold it carefully, setting it aside, my gaze catching on the dark stains blooming at the cuffs.

I swallow hard. He didn't hesitate. Not for a second.

"Hand." I nudge him closer to the sink.

Bennet obeys, holding it under the stream. Water runs pink, swirling down the drain in delicate spirals. The cut on the base of his palm is deep, worryingly so. Might need stitches.

Mimi reappears, the bright red first aid kit clutched in her hands. "Here."

I take it, flipping the latch and rifling through the supplies. Maybe liquid bandages would be best. He'll rub regular Band-Aids off the second he touches anything.

Mimi clicks the stove on, setting the kettle to boil. "Are you going to tell me what the hell happened, or do I need to guess?"

I find an alcohol wipe and tear it open. "We were attacked."

Mimi blinks. "Attacked? By who?"

"Or by what." I press the wipe to his skin. "This might sting."

Bennet barely reacts, but his teeth are clenched.

Mimi frowns. "By what?"

I remove the wipe. The bleeding is already slowing. Another djinn ability? I open the liquid bandage bottle, dipping the brush inside. "A shadow. It came loose from the wall. And it had lightning."

Mimi's eyebrows shoot toward her hairline. "A shadow. With lightning."

"I know how it sounds." I slide the brush over his wound carefully.

"It was an ifrit." Bennet's voice is quiet but firm.

My fingers still. "*That* was an ifrit?"

The kettle whistles.

Mimi pulls it off the stove, shutting the burner off. "What the hell is an ifrit?"

His throat bobs as he swallows.

"You said they feed on magic. But that thing—" I gesture toward the door, toward the outside world. "That wasn't feeding. That was attacking."

Bennet shakes his head. "There is not enough magic here for them to fully manifest." His hand flexes under mine. "Even in Aetheria, they are mostly smoke and shadow. They feed on my people to take form, and even then they cannot sustain a physical shape for long. I don't know how it came here at all. I don't think it was trying to kill, only injure."

A chill prickles at my spine. "You think it was trying to take you back?"

"I don't understand why." His brows are drawn, gaze troubled. "Ifrits would benefit from my family's disappearance. Keeping Helen and me stuck here, away from Aetheria, should be in their best interest. Their land is all parched desert and scorched volcanic mountains. They have coveted the magic and lush life of my kingdom for centuries, trying to take over, attacking my people at every opportunity. It's why Helen's wedding was so important, uniting us against a common enemy, adding to our armies."

"Maybe they want you for ransom." I finish with the glue and put the top back on the bottle. "Or to torture? Are they the types to shake people down for . . . whatever?"

Bennet's expression is blank, but foreign emotions brush at the edge of my senses—an echo of confusion, faint but real. I reach for the shield, but when I check, it's perfectly intact. No stray emotions leaking through.

Strange. I'll have to ask him later if there is something he's not saying.

Mimi pours steaming liquid from the kettle into three cups

waiting with tea bags. "Well. That's just wonderful. Assassins made of shadow."

I blow on Bennet's hand and then motion him toward the table. "Don't touch anything until the glue dries."

Bennet slides into a chair, resting his arms on the table, keeping his injury up.

Mimi sits opposite, fingers laced around her mug.

I grab the remaining two cups from the counter, setting them down in front of us and taking the chair next to Bennet. "Where did you learn to fight like that?"

He reaches for the mug with his good hand. "I trained. Learned with the guards in the castle. After what happened to my parents, I wanted to be able to protect my sister."

A trickle of admiration seeps through me. He did it for his sister.

"Thank you." I reach over and rest my hand lightly on his wrist. "For protecting me."

His skin is warm beneath my fingers. A quiet moment lingers between us.

Then Mimi clears her throat, and I yank my hand back, heat creeping up my neck.

One corner of his mouth tilts up. "You're welcome."

I latch on to the next thought that pops into my head, before Mimi can make a comment about me needing to get laid again. "There's more. I don't know if it's relevant, but yesterday, when I was walking home with the lamp, I felt like something was following me." I hesitate. "I didn't see anything, though, so maybe it was nothing."

Mimi blows on her tea and takes a slow sip. "You mentioned that. It was after you bought the lamp."

"Yes."

What does it mean? Maybe nothing. Maybe something. I

rub my temple, the pressure doing little to ease the nagging itch in my chest.

I change the subject. "How was Jackie today?"

Mimi sighs. "It was a hard day."

"What happened?"

"She was okay in the morning, but as the day went on, she kind of faded." Her fingers clench into a fist against the table. "By bedtime, I had to practically carry her up the stairs."

A flicker of unease crawls through me. "Are you okay? You didn't hurt yourself getting her up the stairs, did you?"

She waves a hand. "I'm fine. My arthritis was acting up this morning, but moving around got the juices flowing. I'm barely feeling it now. Tell me what happened with the vamp, before the ifrit attack."

I go through everything—our encounter with Eddie, the deal we struck, unblocking our magic—minus the accompanying wild emotions—and what we learned about the swamp witches. As I talk, Mimi listens intently, her fingers curled around her tea mug, her expression unreadable. "The swamp witches. Yes. I've heard of them."

"You have?"

Mimi taps her fingers against her mug. "A friend of mine went to them once. Years ago. Her and her husband were having trouble conceiving, and she was desperate."

"And they helped?"

"She had a baby a year later." Mimi shrugs. "Who knows if it was them or pure luck? But she believed it."

"Do you remember how she got there? Where it was in the cemetery?"

Mimi frowns, rubbing her chin. "Not exactly. But I do remember her saying the spot is warded. The witches don't want just anyone finding them. Only people with magic can see through the spells keeping the place hidden."

"That makes sense," I murmur. "Do you remember anything else?"

Mimi nods. "She said the portal only activates at certain times, dusk and dawn, when the veil is thinnest."

"That's good to know." Relief washes through me. At least now we know Edward wasn't bamming us. "I want to be here in the morning before Kevin goes to school, and just in case Jackie has a bad night. So we'll have to get there tomorrow afternoon, early enough to find it in time for dusk."

Mimi's lips press into a thin line. "I wish I could do more."

"You do so much as it is. I couldn't function without you, and neither could the kids."

"Not enough. Not like I used to." She flexes her fingers, rubbing at her wrist. "Twenty years ago, I could have run around this city twice. Now? I can barely get up and down the stairs without feeling it the next day because of my damn arthritis."

Bennet's head tilts to one side. "What is this, arthritis?"

"It's an inflammation of the joints. Getting old is a pain in the ass."

"When did you start having this pain in your ass?"

I spit out my tea, sputtering into my hands and then getting up to grab a hand towel.

"Are you okay?" Bennet asks.

"Fine, fine." I wipe at my face.

Mimi chuckles. "The pain isn't in my ass. That's just an expression. It started . . . I don't know, maybe five or six years ago? It's nothing to worry about. The doctors have actually said it's a miracle it hasn't gotten worse. Most people with the same condition do much worse so many years after diagnosis."

I move back to the table and mop up my spit tea.

Bennet taps a finger on the handle of his cup. "And when did Jackie first start showing symptoms?"

Mimi's head kicks to one side, considering him. "Also five years ago. Why?"

I stare at Bennet. "Do you think there's a connection?"

Bennet's tone is careful. "Perhaps. If she's a healer."

"But Jackie doesn't have magic." Mimi's eyes are wide. "She's always been so upset about it, being the only one in the family with no abilities."

Bennet watches us both, steady and unflinching. "She might be using it without realizing it, for people other than Mimi as well."

"That's not possible." But even as the words fall out, pieces click in my mind. "Kevin."

Mimi's hand shoots out, covering mine, picking up my train of thought. "He hasn't been sick at all in years."

"His baseball injuries always heal quick too, but he's so young." I gasp. "She knew. About me and you." I look at Bennet. "She said we are connected, yesterday, is that how she knew?"

Bennet rubs his chin. "It's likely. She can sense injuries in people. Even subconsciously, she may have recognized the curse. In Aetheria, healers are rare. They need magical replenishment frequently, even if they aren't actively healing, and time to recover after using their magic. She needs to be trained to pull the power from external sources, to take from the land, from other living things, and not from herself." His gaze drifts around the room, settling on the cold metal, the artificial light. "Here, it's different. You have no pieces of the earth inside."

The walls close in around me, tighter and tighter. "Jackie doesn't even hurt bugs. She scoops them up and puts them outside, even when they're in her bed. She'd never take from anyone else to heal herself."

Mimi's voice is thick. "If that's true, how do we fix it?"

"She needs nature," Bennet says simply. "Living things.

Plants. Trees. The earth itself. Healing is based in water magic because all life is centered on water. She needs something to draw from that won't hurt her. It is easy once you know what to do, like with the shields over our minds."

"We don't have plants," Mimi says. "Because we have kids. And lives. And can barely keep up as it is."

"We have one plant." I wince. "It's on the porch, dying a slow death."

"Then you get more." Bennet's voice is firm. "Many. She won't need much from each. Just enough to balance herself. Enough to stop taking from her own body."

Mimi swallows hard. "Could this work?"

I want it to work. I need it to work. But I've had my hopes up so many times—Mimi and I both—and what if it doesn't? What if it's just one more dead end? I don't know if my heart can take another hit. But of course *my* heart isn't the one in danger here. I swallow a surge of dread and weariness. "We won't know until we try."

Mimi heads up to bed while Bennet and I put the empty mugs in the sink.

"We can go to the front room to try and track Helen together. The couch in there is more comfortable."

He follows me out of the kitchen and into the front room.

I drop onto the love seat, tucking one leg under me. "How do we start?"

He lowers himself next to me, resting his hand on his knee, palm up. "Your hand."

I place mine in his, palm to palm. Warmth passes between us like a slow tide, settling low in my stomach.

"Close your eyes. Drop your shields and focus on what we

want—to find Helen. I will conjure her in my thoughts and share her likeness with you."

I lower my mental walls and an image fills my mind. Helen. In Bennet's mind, she's laughing, standing on the edge of a cliff that's straight out of a *Pride and Prejudice* remake, all white rock and rolling green hills in the distance. She's petite, dark haired, dark eyed. She doesn't look anything like Bennet, who is all sharp cheekbones, green eyes, and dirty-blond hair.

I shut my eyes. At first, there's only silence. Stillness. My own thoughts, too loud.

Then a pulse, like a tugging, from somewhere deep in my chest. His hand tightens around mine, and it builds—warmth, pressure, and need. Not mine. His. Or is it mine? I can't tell.

My breath catches.

"Bennet—"

"I know." His voice is tight with strain. "It's not—just focus. Don't feed it."

But that's the thing. The harder I try to pull away from it, the more the bond winds around me like velvet and fire.

The tug intensifies, just for a moment—like something stretching out to meet us—and then snaps.

I gasp, eyes flying open. "Did it work?"

He looks just as startled as I am, his jaw clenched, chest rising and falling in slow, shallow breaths. "No," he says finally. "I mean, yes. I could access my magic, but she's not . . . *there.*"

"What does that mean?"

"I couldn't feel her. Which means she's either shielding herself, or someone else is doing it for her. Or . . . I don't know." He scrubs a frustrated hand through his hair. "Either way, we can't find her. Not like this."

My hand's still in his, and neither of us moves to let go.

"Well," I murmur. "That was weird."

He huffs a breath, not quite a laugh. "We may need more practice."

"Or better boundaries."

His eyes meet mine. Heat simmers there.

I slam my mental walls down and shoot to my feet. "Uhhh, do you think maybe we can try our magic on the water heater?"

The basement is cold and dark and creepy. I flick the light on before we head down ragged wooden steps. A single bulb at the bottom illuminates the concrete floors, piles of sagging boxes, and shelves of canned goods.

And the ancient water heater in the corner.

We stand in front of it.

I hold up my hand. "Once more with feeling?"

He wraps my fingers in his and takes a deep breath. "Are you ready?"

I nod. "Drop my shields, focus on the glory of hot water."

A corner of his mouth tilts up. "That should do it."

We turn back to the rusty old water heater and then I shut my eyes.

The pressure is back, coming quicker and easier than before, tugging and pulling, and then heat rushes through my core, spreading through my limbs like liquid fire.

What in the actual hell?

Arousal slams into me. Sudden and thick and drugging, spreading like molten honey down into my bones until all I know is *need*. I'm so full of erotic pleasure, it borders on the edge of pain. I suck in air, gasping for breath.

Holy shit. What is happening?

I need an orgasm like I need my next breath. It's primal. Desperate.

All my attention zeroes in on Bennet. Is he unaffected? I'm wound so tight, I might actually explode.

Dear goddess, I *ache* for him.

"Can you feel that?" He asks. "There's damage where there once was fire. Use your gift to locate where the damage is. I can help you."

Stop being horny and focus!

I draw on our power, letting it stretch between us and flow into the water heater. The shape of the pilot assembly forms in my mind—metal parts, too cold, too still. And a hairline crack in a bracket. The gas is flowing, but the flame flickers out almost immediately.

"It can't stay lit," I whisper. "There's a break in the piece that holds the flame. It won't anchor. How do we fix it?"

"I'll bond it with fire," he says. "You hold the fracture in your mind. Show me how it should be so I may shape it, still it. Give me something to channel."

I close my eyes. My magic wraps around the broken edge like invisible hands, holding it steady.

Then fire from Bennet seeps into the crack, melting the edges and welding them back together with molten precision.

We're almost done—

Another wave of arousal washes over me, black spots crowd my vision, and if it wasn't for my death grip on his hand, I would collapse in a puddle on the floor.

It has to be the magic. Do I stop him? Tackle him? Dry-hump a pipe?

He pulls the flame back, the work done.

"Bennet," I force his name through clenched teeth.

His entire body jerks. Shoulders heave. And then he turns.

Yeah, that's right, feel the heat, buddy.

"Cassie?" His voice is low and frayed.

We collide like magnets snapping together.

THIRTEEN

His hands slide under my thighs, lifting me effortlessly. My legs wrap around him, instinctive and urgent. His mouth finds mine, hungry, hot, claiming. I moan into him, tasting heat and chaos and passion that hints dangerously of destiny.

Fierce, my fingers grip his hair, thick and soft against my palms.

Then we're moving. My back presses against a wall, cold and rough, brick scraping my skin through the thin fabric of my shirt, but I barely register it. My world has narrowed to only the maddening friction between our bodies, the hard press of him through his jeans, the grinding rhythm that has me crying out for more.

Pleasure coils tighter and tighter until it's unbearable.

He tears his mouth from mine, blazing a path down my neck. His lips find the sensitive curve of skin between shoulder and throat and I shatter.

The orgasm crashes over me like a tidal wave. Stars. Shudders. Light. I fall apart in his arms, and he follows a heartbeat later, groaning against my neck, every inch of him shaking with release.

We stand there, chests heaving, sweat slowly cooling on our skin.

And then reality creeps in. I can't open my eyes and face him, not yet. I can't believe I did this. I got super horny and mauled Bennet. Well, mutual mauling, for sure, and we didn't even take our clothes off, but I basically forced him into it with the whole unlocking the shields so he could feel my arousal thing. Is that . . . morally gray?

Why was I so aroused? It was the magic. It had to be. We're definitely unblocked now. Too unblocked. Is this going to happen every time we use magic, this insane arousal? This can't be real.

"I'm sorry, Bennet, I don't know what came over me."

Horny magic. That's what came over me.

Bennet lifts his head, brushing hair from my face with a tenderness that melts me all over again. "Don't apologize. That was incredible."

I shift in his grip and he releases me, letting my legs fall to the ground.

I wobble a little before finding my footing. "Incredible, yes. But we have to be careful. We can't run around using magic all willy-nilly and then getting all, getting all," I wave a hand, "frisky." I lower my voice to a whisper. "Children live here."

He presses his lips together, the corners twitching.

Is he laughing at me?

I cross my arms, still catching my breath. "So. What was that?"

"I'm not entirely sure."

"I really hope this didn't happen with the twins you told me about when they accessed their magic together because that would be some *Game of Thrones* shit that I am not ready to hear about."

He chuckles. "I assure you, no thrones were involved in that story, but this did not happen to them, as far as I'm aware."

"Then what does it mean? Why would using magic make us—lose our minds like a couple of horny teenagers?"

He rubs his chin. "I'm not sure. It must have something to do with the bond, or with Helen's curse. I'm not sure."

"So it was just magic. A side effect. It doesn't have to mean anything."

He studies me. The laughter is gone. His mouth is a flat line. The silence stretches long enough that I fidget.

"It was just the magic," I repeat, more firmly this time, like I'm daring him to contradict me.

He gives a small nod. "As you wish."

That shouldn't sting. It really shouldn't. It *is* just the magic. Unexplainable, horny magic. Fuck my life.

He clears his throat. "I promise to be careful. In the meantime," he gestures to the water heater, "I think the shower's ready to go."

I stare at him, suppressing the urge to throw myself at him again, no magic needed.

I need to get a grip. A hot shower sounds divine, but honestly, what I really need is an ice bath and an exorcism.

The hot water works. Better than before, actually—like Bennet didn't just fix it, he upgraded it with ancient, mystical spa settings. I don't question it. I'm too busy sloughing off the residual embarrassment and magic-fueled horniness in scalding peace.

He insisted I go first, and I wasn't about to argue. The water pressure alone nearly makes me weep.

I wrap myself in my robe, mentally formulating the world's most awkward post-sex small talk.

What do I even say?

Hey, great magical orgasm, sorry I mind-blasted you with lust. Do you need a towel?

I half expect him to be waiting in my room, maybe in my bed, shirtless and smug. But instead, when I exit the bathroom, he walks by me, fully dressed and holding a pair of sweats. "I'll be quick."

"It's no problem."

He shuts the door without so much as another word or heated glance.

I get dressed and lotioned up, then grab the extra pillow and blanket I had planned on bringing him earlier—before the madness—and take it into the office.

The lamp in the corner is on, casting a soft glow over the space. Kevin's baseball gear is gone. My desk is no longer cluttered with papers and books; everything has been set in careful piles. The thin blanket Bennet used last night is folded on the couch.

He cleaned up.

After his attempt at washing dishes I expected him to be more, I don't know, like a spoiled trust fund baby expecting maids and room service. But instead he's been sort of . . . helpful. And amusing. Earlier, when he helped with chores, he tried to battle the vacuum before realizing it wasn't sentient, then used it on every rug in the house because it was "like cleaning with thunder."

I settle on the sofa, clutching the blanket and pillow against my chest. This whole evening has been surreal. Hell, the past few days have been surreal. I don't know what to think about any of it.

I must be staring into the distance for a while because when Bennet opens the door and steps inside, I startle so hard the blanket and pillow in my lap tumble to the floor at my feet.

"Are you okay?"

"Fine. I wanted to bring you more bedding." I reach down and grab the items from the ground.

"Thank you." He steps around my legs to the couch, plopping down next to me and taking the items from my arms, setting it all on top of the other blanket beside him.

I'm waiting for some kind of signal that he's weirded out or confused or—I don't know—*freaked out* by what just happened.

But there's none of that.

He glances over at me. "You're staring."

"No I'm not." I totally am. "Just surprised. I thought this might be awkward."

"Why would it be?" He raises a brow.

A startled laugh escapes me. "Because I acted like a sex-starved lunatic and mentally broadcast my horniness at you like a human speaker system?"

He considers this, then shrugs. "It was mutual."

The weirdest thing about all of this, sitting here with him, chatting about all this, is that it isn't weird. Somehow, this is *less* weird than every other interaction I've had with a man in the last decade.

It's not just the lack of weirdness. It's the way he fits into the space, into my space, like it's natural.

There's no tension. No guilt. Only the glow of the light, sharing silence that isn't heavy at all.

And he's not flustered or concerned at all. I'm not sure if

I'm more alarmed by the magic-induced orgasm, or by how completely normal this all feels.

"I wanted to thank you, too, for thinking of the healing thing with Jackie. I never would have even considered it."

One shoulder lifts in a shrug. "I might be wrong."

"But it makes sense. It explains why the doctors can't find anything, because she's not actually sick. She's draining herself." I swallow past the lump in my throat. "I can't tell you what it means to have a plan."

Maybe this isn't such a bad thing, getting tied to Bennet. It will be worth it if Jackie gets better.

I glance toward the door, debating whether I should go back to bed and stare at the ceiling for another two hours. Instead, words tumble out of my mouth before I can stop them. "Can I ask you some questions?"

His head cocks to one side. "What would you like to know?"

I hesitate before settling on, "What were you thinking earlier? About the ifrit attack? You acted like you weren't saying everything."

His expression darkens. "The only person who knew where I went was my uncle. He was supposed to explain our absence to the visiting courtiers while I retrieved Helen."

"Why didn't he come after Helen while you stayed behind?"

"He is not powerful enough to travel between dimensions, and he cannot track her the way I can." His jaw tightens. "The way I could. The way we *should* have been able to. It's like she's hidden herself from being found, blocked even from me. I suspected that might be the case when she trapped me in the lamp, but I had hoped . . ." He shrugs.

"We'll find her," I say automatically, even though I have no idea if the swamp witches will even deign to help.

But one way or another, we'll figure it out. We have to. And once we do, he can go back to his djinn life in Aetheria, and I can go back to my wonderful life of raising my siblings, working for pennies, struggling every day, and grieving the still unresolved loss of my parents. Best time ever.

"Your uncle." I shift my knees in his direction. "He raised you and Helen?"

His head bobs in a short nod. "Yes. My mother's brother. Before their passing, my uncle was meant to marry. His fiancée was heir to her own kingdom, and once they wed, he would have moved there to rule alongside her." He looks down at his hands. "They were returning from meeting her family when the ifrit attacked. Everyone else—our parents, the guards, even his fiancée—was killed."

I wince. "I'm sorry."

"He barely survived," Bennet murmurs. "And after that, he raised us. Taught us how to be ruling djinn. Especially Helen, since she is the heir. She always had more pressure, more eyes on her."

And being sequestered away from her only sibling, as a child, would definitely have decreased that pressure. Not. "That must have been hard, to be separated from your sister when you were so young and had just lost both your parents."

His lips turn down. "It was at first. But my uncle knew it was necessary, that she had to be better, sharper, more composed than anyone else. He made it clear she couldn't afford mistakes and I was a distraction."

I can't help a snort. It's clear he loves his uncle, but ouch. I would *never* send Kevin away from Jackie. No matter how sick Jackie got. They *need* each other.

Bennet nods, as if I've said some of that aloud. "Maybe it was too much. And maybe that is part of what prompted her to flee. He was always a bit harder on her than on me, since she was older and the heir. The expectations were higher."

His shoulders are hunched like the weight of memory sits heavier than he expected, and the shadows under his eyes seem darker in the soft lamplight.

"What about you? It must have been difficult for you to be apart from her as well, even without the same expectations being forced on you."

He blinks. "I suppose so. I never thought about it." He glances toward the hallway. "Your siblings, they are close. It's a good thing." He hesitates, his brow furrowing. "Helen and I were like that once."

"It hasn't always been easy. Jackie takes up a lot of our time and attention, but Kevin's never once acted like he resents it. He loves her. Looks out for her. They're good kids. They're kind." My throat tightens. "That's because our parents were too. They left us with something solid. I just picked up where they left off. Or tried to."

"They are lucky to have you." His eyes are too intense.

I squirm and wave a hand. "So, tell me more about Aetheria. The women in your kingdom, they can be rulers?"

"Yes. The eldest sibling inherits the throne, regardless of gender. Is that not how it is in your world?"

I wrinkle my nose. "Not entirely. Men are mostly in charge, although there have been some female rulers, queens and presidents and prime ministers, things like that. Men are physically stronger and so they've been basically running the show forever."

Bennet frowns, considering this. "In Aetheria, men are also physically stronger, but women usually hold more magic. And they bear children, which makes them even more vital. Our people struggle with conception. Matches are often made based on compatibility for producing offspring or solidifying political alliances."

I curl my legs under me. "That sounds wildly unromantic."

He shrugs. "It depends. My parents' marriage was arranged, but they loved each other deeply." His lips quirk slightly. "Eventually. At first it was a diplomatic nightmare."

I inch closer to him. "What happened?"

Bennet leans back against the couch, rubbing his jaw. "My father was arrogant and stuffy and my mother was a bit of a hellion."

I raise a brow. "Hellion?"

"Wild," he corrects. "She did what she wanted, when she wanted, and had absolutely no patience for politics or propriety. Helen is much the same. My father, on the other hand, was the definition of responsible. He thought rules were sacred, duty was everything, and that a queen should be graceful and composed at all times."

A draft hits the back of my neck and I shiver. I should have grabbed a sweater. "Sounds like a recipe for disaster."

He gathers my legs into his lap before covering them, tucking a blanket around me. "Oh, it was," he continues. It's almost like he isn't even aware of his own movements, pampering me without thought. "They were a disaster wrapped in calamity and then set on fire. Their first official event as a married couple, she got into an argument with a visiting ambassador over dinner, flipped the entire table, and challenged him to a duel."

I bark out a laugh. "What?"

"And she won."

"Oh my God. I love her."

He grins. "My father was mortified. He called her reckless, undignified, a menace to the throne. She called him a prissy little windbag with a stick up his arse."

I'm grinning with him now. "So how did they go from that to being in love?"

His thumb rubs my knee absently, heat from his palm sinking into me even through the blanket. "Their caravan was attacked by mercenaries on the way to visit Mother's parents. The guards were overwhelmed, and my father, in all his royal wisdom, started shouting about strategy. My mother, meanwhile, jumped off her horse and punched one of the robbers in the face."

My mouth pops open.

"And my father saw her fighting—truly fighting with skill —and he stopped barking orders, stopped trying to control the situation, and for the first time in his life, he followed someone else's lead. He fought with her, side by side, and together they took down half the bandits before the rest fled."

"And that's when they knew they were in love?"

"That's when my father realized," Bennet corrects. "My mother had figured it out weeks before but was waiting for him to catch up." A soft smiles lights his face. "According to her, the moment he jumped into battle, she thought, 'Oh, finally, he's stopped talking.'"

I chuckle. "I think I would have liked them."

Bennet's smile drops. "They bickered until the day they died. But they were inseparable. Fiercely loyal. A force to be reckoned with." He looks down, expression blank. "And they loved each other. Even if it took a war for them to admit it."

I lean further into the couch, resting my head against the back, suddenly exhausted, but I don't want to stop this conversation. Not only is it fascinating, his voice is so soothing. My thoughts and worries are a distant drum, barely audible. The rest of the world may as well no longer exist outside the glow of this small room.

"What about Helen's fiancé? Do they know each other? Any sparks either way?"

"They've met, but she never told me she was so opposed to the marriage she would rather flee to another realm. If she had, I—" He cuts himself off. "I don't know what I would have done."

"Why do you think she never said anything to you? About the marriage?"

For a long moment, he doesn't answer. Then, finally, he says, "It was my fault. After my parents died, I shut down. Helen tried to reach out, to talk to me about their death, but I didn't even want to think about it. I was angry at everyone. And then Uncle sent me on my first fostering before I could fix it."

"How did you get past the grief?" It's an honest question. My parents have been missing for three years, and still I find myself mired in dark thoughts, anger, denial, confusion. It's a long dark tunnel with no end in sight.

"Fighting. Sparring with the guards at the keep."

"Ah. You chose violence. The guards didn't have an issue throwing punches at their boss?"

Bennet huffs. "The head guardsman didn't give them a choice, though if Uncle Hugh had gotten wind of what we were up to, it would have ended in disaster for all of us."

I tilt my head. "Your uncle didn't want you to learn to fight? Even though your parents were clearly skilled at it?"

"Uncle Hugh has some old-fashioned ideals. Plus, losing his sister and brother-in-law in such a violent manner made him extra paranoid. He wanted me to be a good statesman, and to stay safe. But I needed an outlet. And I found one, or I should say it found me." His lips quirk.

I can't drag my eyes away from him. The tilt of his mouth

and the spark in his eye should be illegal. Definitely hazardous to my heart rate.

Ignore all that.

A silence settles between us and I slump deeper into the sofa, drowsiness sweeping over me.

He reaches over, brushing my hair behind my ear, his fingers trailing a warm path down my jawline. "Perhaps you should get some rest, princess."

I snort. "I am the farthest thing from a princess you can get."

He's right, though. I should go back to my room.

But it's so far, and I'm warm and comfortable right here, like floating in a syrupy haze. For the first time in ages it's like I could close my eyes and actually sleep and not lie awake with my thoughts or be jarred into heart-pounding alertness by all the fears and worries that won't leave me, even in slumber.

"What does Aetheria look like?" Truly, it's an excuse to get him to keep talking. He could read me the tax code and it would be riveting. It's gotta be the accent.

"Well, let's see." His thumb rubs against my leg again in a soothing motion and my lids drift shut. "Aetheria is divided into four kingdoms. I am from Zehraya, land of the jann. My home is full of endless emerald valleys and sprinkled with ancient stone cities. Thalassara is where the giants reside, the marid. Their kingdom is near the sea, rich with waterfalls and wildlife. Then there is Duskharan, land of the shaytan. Their kingdom has twisting labyrinthine forests and crimson rivers that glow in the dark. They are a very secretive people. Our spies struggle to obtain any information on their royals. Finally, the ifrit live in Ashkaran, a land of volcanic mountains and scorched canyons. The ifrit live in obsidian fortresses carved into cliffs, at least that is what they say . . ."

He continues speaking, but the words stop registering. Only the tenor of his voice, the soothing cadence, penetrates my consciousness.

For the first time in a long time, I fall asleep without worries crowding my mind.

FOURTEEN

I tuck a giant Swiss cheese plant onto the corner by the front windows, stepping back to check the positioning so the large glossy leaves aren't being pressed into the wall. The house already smells fresher, like damp earth and fresh air. It cost an arm and a leg but I ordered twenty plants and small potted trees from a nearby nursery. I had to get cheap plastic containers, but it doesn't matter. I only care if it works.

I pick up the rubber plant on the floor, admiring its ruby leaves, and head toward the stairs. A voice drifting through the air from the kitchen catches my attention.

"Close your eyes. Breathe in deep. Find the quiet place inside yourself."

I pause, fingers tightening around the plastic base.

Bennet and Jackie are in the kitchen.

His voice is low, smooth, steady in a way that makes my stomach flip, especially when I remember our conversation last night. At some point he must have carried me to my bed. I woke up a few hours later, but it was still the longest and best sleep I've had in years.

I step closer to the doorway, pressing my back to the wall, listening.

"Feel the breath in your chest. Let it settle. The quieter you become inside, the easier it is to connect to what's around you."

There's a beat of silence. Then Jackie sighs. "It's not working."

"You're thinking too much."

"How do you not think? When I try to tell my brain to be quiet it just gets louder."

Bennet lets out a soft chuckle. "Focus on your breathing. If thoughts come, that's okay. Let them come and go, like a boat floating in water. Or a butterfly. Don't push the thoughts away with force. Watch them, let them float around, and then return to your breath."

I set the plant down at my feet and lean back against the wall, letting my own eyes slip shut, mirroring them.

Bennet keeps talking, murmuring things to Jackie about letting go, surrendering to her breath, letting the burdens slip away. Maybe it's exhaustion. Maybe it's curiosity. Maybe it's the way his voice lulls me into the same calm spell from last night.

I inhale, slow and deep.

And then there's a shift inside me, like a puzzle piece locking into place. It's not magic, it's more like adjusting an internal radio to tune in to the world around me.

The walls around me no longer exist. I'm floating in a dark space, surrounded by glowing threads stretching through the space around me, fine as silk but impossibly strong, a web of fragile lines linking me to the world.

Everything is connected to me through delicate lines humming with energy: the plant at my feet, the wall at my back, even the lamp in the corner. Thicker strands branch in targeted directions, two leading upstairs—Mimi and Kevin are up there. Another flows from me into the kitchen, where Jackie is.

There's another one. The largest one. Thicker. Brighter.

It stretches from me to Bennet.

It's exactly like Edward said, a glowing, braided strand, pulsing like it's alive. Its golden light twines with threads that are darker, deeper. My breath catches as it stretches, and I reach for it.

The moment I do, emotion crashes into me like a wave.

This is more than simple magic.

His strength, warmth, and affection flow into me, drawn by a pull so strong it's like gravity, ancient and unshakable.

Like belonging.

It slams into me, filling every cell.

From the kitchen, Bennet's voice stumbles. "—and then you—ah—" He clears his throat sharply.

I jerk back, heart hammering.

Nope. That way lies danger.

Gulping down air, I jerk my thoughts and emotions together, reinforcing the barrier around my mind. I pick up the plant at my feet and stride past the kitchen without looking inside. If I catch even a glimpse of his face I might actually combust. Again.

I clear my throat, forcing my voice to sound casual as I pass the open doorway. "We're leaving for the cemetery in an hour. Gotta get there before sunset," I call out.

Then I pound up the stairs, running away from . . . whatever that was.

A black iron fence rises above us, its bars spiked like sentries standing guard over the dead. At the top of the arched entrance, white block letters spell out *LAFAYETTE CEMETERY No. 1.*

Beyond the gate, rows of stone mausoleums stretch into the distance, their surfaces streaked with age and weather. Some are grand, adorned with intricate carvings and wrought-iron gates, while others are simpler, their names and dates fading into the gray and white stone.

Twilight approaches, darkening the sky overhead.

I push open the heavy iron gate, and it groans in protest, echoing through the stillness.

The oak trees inside are draped in Spanish moss, their gnarled limbs twisting like old fingers reaching for something unseen. Despite the lack of wind, the moss sways slightly, shifting like ghostly curtains.

Bennet follows, his gaze sweeping over the rows of tombs. "What are these structures?"

I glance at him. "Crypts and mausoleums. We have to keep bodies aboveground because of the water table. New Orleans is basically built on a swamp. Dig too deep and you hit water, so if we buried people underground, well." I make a grossed-out face. "Things would get nasty."

His lips press into a thin line. "They'd resurface."

"Yep. Not exactly the kind of thing you want after a heavy rain." I shift the pack on my back. I brought a bunch of supplies, snacks, water, extra socks. Better to be prepared for anything.

He nods slowly, looking back at the tombs. "They are quite large."

"Entire families are buried together most of the time. They use the same tomb for generations. When someone dies, they put the body inside, and after a year and a day, they open it back up, push the remains to the back, and make space for the next person."

He winces. "Efficient."

"Yeah, well, space is limited. Gotta make do." There are a couple of mourners leaving flowers in front of a tomb about two hundred yards down the main walkway. I tilt my head toward the path on our right. "Let's go this way." Somewhere away from the main path and out of sight of normies.

Bennet looks around again, his gaze thoughtful. "We don't have cemeteries in Aetheria."

I frown. "What do you do with your dead?"

"When a djinn dies, their body turns immediately to dust. There's nothing left to bury."

"Like Buffy."

A divot appears between his brows. "What is a Buffy?"

"What isn't a Buffy?"

At his continued confused expression, I sigh, shaking my head. "Never mind." I guess Kevin hasn't shown him any vampire shows from the prior century yet.

"When we pass, we become one again with the earth and sky. It seems odd to surround one's body in such materials."

I shrug. "I guess. I've never really thought about it." But after experiencing that connection to the world around me earlier, it makes a lot more sense. I don't know how I was able to do that without using my magic. I want to ask, but I also don't want to delve too much into what happened during that encounter. But then the words just make a break for it. "Can I ask you about what happened?"

"What happened when?"

Heat fills my cheeks. "When you were helping Jackie in the kitchen and I was outside listening, I, uh, could feel you. And me. And us. Our bond. And Jackie and Kevin and Mimi too, and everything else. It was weird. I've never felt anything like it. How could I do that without accessing my magic?"

We turn down a narrower path, moving deeper into the cemetery, before he responds. "I don't think magic is necessary to be aware of the world around you, and your link to it."

"I guess that's true."

"Even those with little to no magic in my realm have this ability to sense our connection to the world. It is in all of us. Even mere mortals."

I glance around. No one is around now. I stop walking and face him. "And with Jackie, you think it worked?"

He shrugs. "It is too soon to tell. She's been using her own resources for a long time. Her magic needs to replenish itself and her body needs to heal. It's not going to be instant, even if I'm right. Since she is young, though, connecting to the world around was easier. She has not been around long enough to build up the defenses that lock us away from nature."

"That makes sense." It's hard to be patient, but I don't have a choice. Nothing to do but wait and see, and I have bigger fish to fry at the moment.

We have about twenty minutes until dusk, but who knows where the portal is, or how long it will take us to find it. Even though the cemetery only takes up one city block, there are more than eleven hundred family tombs and seven thousand graves.

We've already decided to use magic to locate the portal, and we'll just have to be prepared for any blowback.

I take a deep breath. "Are you ready?"

He nods.

He takes my hand and I reach inside, focusing on our intention. My magic is there and ready. No longer blocked. Relief blows through me. Along with something else.

Heat, starting at my core and spreading out through my

limbs. My skin tightens, sensitive to every brush of air and aware of Bennet's every move.

The lure of the portal is subtle at first, a whisper of energy moving through the humid night air. But then it clicks into place with a snap, then a pull, like a thread tugging deep inside me, guiding me forward.

Bennet is stiff beside me.

I open my eyes, breathing through the arousal filling my veins. "Are you okay?"

He's staring at me, pupils blown, breath coming out in quick pants through his tight jaw. "Fine." The word is clipped. "Can we get moving?"

I press my lips together. I shouldn't be deriving amusement from his . . . discomfort? But it's affecting me too. He doesn't look like he's in pain, but it's difficult not to find this whole situation a bit absurd.

We start walking, following the invisible call. The sensation is hard to describe—like a gentle pressure between my legs, surrounded by pounding lust. The deeper we go into the cemetery, the stronger it gets, a slow but undeniable pulse that leads us between towering white tombs and crumbling stone pathways.

Bennet paces beside me, hands clenched at his sides.

The wrought-iron fence surrounding the cemetery rattles in the wind, casting long, spindly shadows against the graves.

We round a corner, passing a particularly ornate mausoleum with ivy creeping up the sides and a weathered, cracked plaque at the entrance, when Bennet stops abruptly.

His hand snaps out, gripping my wrist. "Wait."

A shiver races down my spine. "What?" His skin against mine, even though it's just our hands, is more satisfying than scratching an itch, like a mixture of relief and pleasure.

His grip tightens. He muffles a groan, his thumb rubbing

against my palm. "You should step away from me because I am not sure I can let you go."

Hunger fills me. *Step away. Step away.* I can totally do that. I force my feet to move. His hand drops from mine. I swallow hard.

"Something is there," he grits out. "Ifrit."

My brain freezes at the word, not quite comprehending. What? Here? *Now?*

Murky shadows in the darkness twist and roil, shaping into solid form. Forms? I squint. Are there more than one?

"Run," Bennet murmurs.

He doesn't have to tell me twice.

I spin on my heel and bolt, surging in the direction of the tug of my magic, feet pounding against the damp cemetery ground. Bennet is right beside me as we dodge between the tombs, weaving through the maze of white stone.

I'm glad I wore leggings and my sneakers—the better to sprint with.

A blast of light, bright and jagged, scorches past us, barely missing my shoulder. I yelp, throwing myself behind a low grave marker as lightning explodes against a nearby statue, melting part of the marble into an oozing puddle.

"Keep moving!" Bennet grabs my hand, dragging me along.

I stumble and then run alongside him. The magic is getting stronger, pulsing through me along with the heady desire. The juxtaposition is alarming. Fear. Pleasure. I can barely focus on the task at hand. "We're almost there."

We must be close to the portal. My heart hammers as we push forward, darting between tilting grave markers and cracked tombs, the scents of ash and decay thick in the air.

Finally, we skid to a stop in front of a tall, imposing mausoleum near the back of the cemetery, its stone surface carved with strange, looping symbols.

Bennet's eyes flick to me and then he shuts them, breathing in slowly. "I'm finding it very hard not to touch you."

This is it. I cut my magic off, like snapping a door shut. "Is that better for you?" Because it isn't for me.

He swallows, hard. "No," he grinds out.

The ifrit are getting closer, wind pushing at my back. I press at the stone marker. There's no door. "How do we get in?"

Bennet reaches for the tomb, his palm next to mine. But nothing happens. His lips twist in frustration. "It needs something—it's locked—"

I brace myself for the ifrit's attack. We're out of time.

Then, suddenly, the symbols on the tomb shift, glowing brightly. They rearrange, forming two dancing flames.

I stare. "What does that mean?"

Bennet makes a strangled sound. "I may have an idea. But we need to act quickly. Do you trust me?"

"I don't really have a choice, we're about to be barbecued."

The shadows behind us have grown into a dark moving cloud, gathering speed and size as it approaches, lightning flashing within.

"Cassie," Bennet snaps, grabbing my shoulders and taking my attention from the rapidly approaching fog of doom.

Then he kisses me.

FIFTEEN

The world tilts. Or maybe it's me that's falling.

Bennet's mouth on mine is a demand filled with desperation. His lips part, tongue stroking against mine. His arms wrap around me. My fingers weave into his hair. Heat floods through my body, insistent and full of the magic surging between us, like a circuit finally being completed.

Beneath us, the ground rumbles.

The darkness descends.

Bennet yanks me toward the tomb, his mouth still fused to mine, and then *snap*.

The world falls silent.

Our kiss breaks apart. For a moment, I can't breathe. My ears are ringing.

Not just because we almost died, but because my lips still tingle with the ghost of his lips pressed against mine.

We're lying on the ground and I'm sprawled on top of him, my thighs bracketing his hips, our faces aligned, breath mingling. My fingers clench on his chest. He's all hard muscles and barely restrained lust and he's rigid, *oh my*, everywhere.

Is the magic is still affecting him? There's one way to find out.

It's a terrible idea and yet I'm helpless to stop. I unlock my mental shields and lift the cage around my mind a mere crack and—*stars above.*

Hunger slices through me, white-hot and brutal. It's unbearable, primal and pure. A startled cry escapes me.

How can he stand it? How did he feel all this in the cemetery and still retain enough of his faculties to get us through the portal?

But then all thoughts and questions are erased by Bennet himself, stretching up to nip at my lips, and the excruciating longing turns into an exhilarating frenzy.

I shrug out of my backpack and toss it somewhere behind me. I slide my hands down his chest and yank his shirt up, then chuck it to the side.

I lean forward, running my mouth over the exposed flesh. He tastes amazing, like spice and heat, all sinewy strength and smooth skin over solid muscle.

His hands skate under my shirt, rough palms against bare flesh, branding heat across my spine. He drags his mouth from mine to trail open kisses down my throat, teeth grazing just enough to make me arch into him.

"Cassie," he rasps.

There's a question buried in the way he says my name. A plea. A warning. Maybe all three.

"I know." I don't. Not really. But I don't want to stop.

We rip my shirt off, the bra flying with it, and then we come back together, and the press of his bare skin against mine is *everything.*

He flips us with terrifying ease, pressing me into the cool earth beneath us. His body covers mine, all strength and tension barely leashed. His hips grind down, the friction between us electric, maddening. I moan, wrapping my legs around him to bring him closer, chasing the pressure, the high, the storm that's building between us.

His lips brush my jaw, my cheek, the corner of my mouth like he's trying to memorize every piece of me.

"This isn't just magic," he says hoarsely.

I freeze beneath him, breath stuttering.

But before I can answer, he kisses me again—soft this time. Reverent. Like I'm something fragile he doesn't want to break.

It undoes me more than all the fire and fury that came before.

He props himself up, rolling to one side, creating enough space to brush the skin of my lower stomach with the tips of his fingers. "Is this okay?"

Does he need to ask? He could offer to pinch me and I would be begging for the touch.

I shift, spreading my legs. "Please."

His eyes are dark and hot, spearing me in place with their intensity. His hand slips easily under the waistband of my leggings and below my panties. When his fingers encounter the slickness between my legs, gliding over heated flesh with ease, we both groan at the contact.

The world around us ceases to exist. My entire being focuses solely on the pressure of his hand at my core, the murmur of his voice in my ear, and the incessant need pounding in my blood.

His free hand fumbles at his pants, freeing his massive erection, and I reach out, grasping his hard length in my palm.

He moans, his fingers between my legs faltering for a second before resuming their ministrations, his palm pressing against the most sensitive part of me while his fingers slip into my wet heat.

Then he leans over me and draws one tight nipple into the

heat of his mouth and I buck and cry out as the orgasm overtakes my body, making me arch and contract, the world tilting once again, except this time we aren't falling through a portal.

Bennet shudders next to me as his own release finds him.

We lay there until the last tremor fades and we're lying tangled and spent, hearts pounding in sync.

He shifts just enough to drape an arm across my waist and lets out a slow, contented sigh. "Well," he mutters, "that's one way to travel."

I release a shaky laugh and meet his amused gaze. "Maybe the best way . . . minus the lightning and terror part."

Slowly, I sit up, rubbing my now chilled arms. The ground is damp beneath me. The air is thick with the scents of moss and earth. Overhead, the moon hangs low and swollen, casting silver light over the inky water and glinting off surrounding trees.

Did we move forward in time as well? In the cemetery it was still dusk. Here, the sky is pitch-black, dotted with stars visible through the leaves and branches overhead.

Torches glowing with eerie blue flames float in the air, trailing into the distance, lighting a path through the thick trees around us. The sounds of croaking frogs and rustling leaves float on the breeze.

Bennet pushes himself up next to me. "I suppose we found where the witches live."

So we're not going to talk about the romp on the swamp floor. Got it. Straight back to business. It shouldn't bother me. I'm the one who insisted it was just the magic. But didn't he say it was more than that?

I swipe my hair out of my face, like I can swipe the memories of the past fifteen minutes away with it. "Maybe we'll find Helen here too."

He swings to his feet, buttoning up his pants and reaching for our clothes, handing me my shirt and bra. "Maybe."

Thank the gods I brought wet wipes. I offer him one before cleaning myself up and tugging my clothes back on.

He shrugs his own shirt over his head, covering up the masculine perfection that I'm pretending not to look at.

He offers me a hand and I take it, clambering to my feet.

"I suppose that's the way we go." I point out the lighted path.

We pick up our bags and get moving. The blue lanterns bob in the thick night air, leading us forward like ghost lights over the bayou. Each one drifts just far enough ahead to keep us going in the right direction, vanishing the moment we draw close.

Bennet walks beside me, footsteps soundless.

The path narrows, trees pressing in around us, their gnarled roots rising from the dark water like skeletal hands. Spanish moss drapes from their limbs, shifting in the breeze.

He glances behind us. "The portal, when we crossed over, it felt familiar to me. It was like passing through Aetheria. It may be a fold."

I purse my lips. "What is that?"

"A place where the space between worlds folds in on itself, where the veil is thin. When you step through a portal like that, you're passing through Aetheria and then ending up in the same plane, just farther away."

That makes a weird kind of sense, even if it makes my brain throb. "So, what, these places are all around us? Random portals in the universe?"

"Not random. Certain places are naturally thin. Old places. Powerful places. Places that have seen both great and tragic events." His eyes flick to the glowing lanterns. "And I suspect the witches know exactly how to use them."

A bird cries somewhere in the distance, long and haunting. The usual hum of the swamp—frogs croaking, cicadas buzzing—dulls as we walk, like the world itself is holding its breath.

I step around a log jutting into the path. "Those ifrit—they were ifrit, right? There was more than one. They seemed more powerful than the last time."

"Yes. They consolidated their powers to enable the manipulation of the elements. I have heard of such a thing but never seen it."

A chill creeps over my skin. "Creepy."

"Very."

The attacks are escalating.

My family.

I should call and check on them. The wards should keep them safe, but if they leave for any reason . . .

Sliding my phone out of the pocket of my jacket, I lift it to my face. The screen is black. I push the button to try and turn it on. It was fully charged when we left, it shouldn't be dead already. Nothing happens. Maybe the portal zapped it. Perfect.

"Great." I shove it back into my pocket.

Bennet raises a brow.

"My phone doesn't work." I glance back the way we came. "I can't check on my family."

"I am sure they will be okay. The ifrit have no reason to attack them."

"You aren't even sure why they're attacking us."

Before he can respond, the last of the lanterns floats ahead, circling a massive cypress tree at the heart of the swamp. The trunk is as wide as a house, its roots arching like ribs into the murky water. At the base, beneath a tangle of moss and creeping vines, a hollow gapes open. The lantern illuminates a dark, yawning mouth leading down before it circles back around the tree and flickers out of existence.

This is all totally normal. Sure. Not scary at all.

I stop. "Please tell me we're not going in there."

Bennet glances at me. "Would you prefer to wait out here alone in the dark?"

I glare. "Fine. But if this turns into some horror movie crap, I'm leaving you to be mauled by the zombies."

"I've seen this zombie on the magic mirror. I am sure I could take them on. They move slowly and have little skill."

I chuckle. "Okay, Daryl Dixon."

His brow creases in confusion.

"Never mind. You first." I gesture to the giant hole at the bottom of the tree.

He ducks, stepping into the hollow.

I take a breath and follow close behind.

The ground slopes beneath us, like a steep ramp, shifting from dirt to cool, smooth stone before leveling out.

A few steps in and the moonlight behind us fades. It's pitch-black. The darkness presses against me. It's like being in a tomb.

Where is Bennet? I grope forward, my fingers hitting his back, and relief floods through me.

He slows. "Are you all right?"

"Peachy."

"Here." His hand fumbles for mine and I grip it, thankful for the contact.

The air thickens, colder, heavier, charged with energy that crawls along my skin.

Ahead, a blue glow flickers in the darkness.

The tunnel widens into a huge cavern, damp and echoing. Twin lanterns float overhead, casting long, flickering shadows over the figures dominating the center of the space.

Three figures, to be exact, hooded and shrouded in darkness, sitting on carved stone seats facing us. Their features are hidden in the depths of their deep black cloaks, the bottoms brushing against the ground in a rumpled heap.

"You seek something."

The voice is unlike anything I've ever heard. The pitch is somehow high and low all at once. Not masculine or feminine but both and nothing all together. It's not one voice but many, layered one over the other, thick with age and time and wisdom, so ancient it makes my teeth ache.

Bennet steps forward. "I'm looking for my sister, Helen. We traced her magic here. Can you help us find her?"

Silence stretches. Then the one in the center lifts a hand, pale and thin, and points at Bennet. "All knowledge has a cost."

Of course.

Bennet tenses. "What's the price?"

The witches don't answer immediately. Instead, the one on the right tilts its head, then the voices speak again. "You walk between worlds, tethered to another."

A chill rolls down my spine.

The one on the left turns, the blackness under the hood of the cloak facing us. "Yes. An unusual bond. One that weakens and strengthens in equal measure."

Enough with the cryptic bullshit already. "What do you want?"

The figures still. Then, in unison, "An offering. Something cherished."

My stomach dips. "What does that mean?"

"A piece of your past. A tether to what once was. Freely given, never returned."

Bennet's hand lifts to the chain around his neck.

"No," I whisper, realizing a beat after he does.

"You want this?" He pulls the chain over his head, revealing the delicate gold ring that hangs from it. Simple, worn smooth with time.

The center figure inclines its head. "It belonged to your mother. It carries memory. Love. Loss. That is the price."

I glance at Bennet, hoping he'll refuse. But he's already holding the ring in his palm, the chain dangling through his fingers. He hesitates. Just for a second. Then he steps forward and extends the ring toward them. "Take it."

The tallest figure reaches out, long fingers brushing his as it accepts the ring. For a moment, Bennet's eyes flutter shut.

The figures sit back. "The debt is paid."

The center one lifts both hands wide in the air.

A large, glowing map forms above the witches, lines of streets and wisps of buildings and the blue glow of water. It's New Orleans, taking a shimmering form. Then a single dot pulses in gold near the Garden District.

"There." Bennet steps forward, studying it.

You've got to be kidding me. "That's literally right by where we just were."

The figure closes its hands. The map vanishes.

"Why is she there?"

"That was not your question. Would you like to pay more for it?"

Bennet exhales. "No. We'll find her ourselves and ask."

The figures lower their heads. "Then go. But the veil has closed. You must stay the night."

I glance around at the cold, damp cave and the unsettling blue firelight. "Here?" I'd rather pluck my eyelashes out while walking on Legos than have a sleepover in a damp cave with the three creepiest witches to ever exist.

The one on the left tilts its head. "Follow the golden lanterns."

The blue flames blink out, plunging the cavern into total blackness.

I suck in a sharp breath, grasping for Bennet's arm. He's already reaching for me, our hands colliding, fingers linking effortlessly.

We shuffle back the way we came, moving slowly in the darkness.

Then, from behind us, the voice whispers, the sound echoing in my ears like the words are being delivered straight into my head.

"The ones you lost have crossed the veil, but not to Hades. Not to death. To the plane of light and magic."

My breath catches. *The ones you lost?* Helen and Delores? They haven't crossed a veil, they're in the Garden District. What are they talking about?

A single golden lantern flickers to life ahead, illuminating the way out. I glance behind us, but the cavern is empty.

They're gone.

Bennet nudges me forward. "Come on."

We follow the golden glow back to the surface.

CHAPTER

SIXTEEN

Following the lanterns, we circle behind the giant tree where a stout wooden cabin sits, surrounded by trees.

I stop in my tracks. "That wasn't there before, right?"

Bennet steps up beside me, his expression unreadable. "No."

It's small, barely more than a shack, its wooden boards warped with age and moss creeping up the sides. The porch is so frail it might collapse under the weight of a strong breeze, and the whole thing leans slightly to the left, as if tired of standing upright. A single window glows with warm, golden light, almost inviting.

We approach slowly, our steps creaking as we navigate the steps and porch.

The door swings open on its own, a slow, creaking motion that sets every nerve in my body on edge.

I glance at Bennet. "That's not ominous at all."

But he's already stepping inside.

The interior is simple. One single room. A fireplace crackles, casting flickering radiance over the space. A narrow

136

wooden table runs along one wall, holding a tray of bread, cheese, and a carafe of water with copper cups. There's no couch. No chairs.

The center of the space is dominated by the bed.

It's raised on a platform, draped in a thin, white net, the material shifting gently in the breeze from the open door. The mattress is decent enough, plush with thick blankets folded at the end.

One bed.

Bennet crosses his arms. "I can take the floor?"

"This floor?" I stomp on the hard wood. "I mean, we're adults. Adults who have now brought each other to orgasm twice. We can—" I wave a hand at the bed like that somehow makes it less of an issue. "We can stay on our own sides. Avoid magic. That kind of thing."

Do not think about the mind-boggling, earth-shattering orgasms.

Do not think about the way his mouth moved against mine alternately hungry and tender, like he was starving for the connection.

Do not think about all the fun things we could get up to in a bed that's way more comfortable than a dusty basement or the dirty ground.

Nope. Not thinking about it.

This is all temporary anyway.

I clear my throat. "I'm going to use the facilities."

The bathroom is about the size of an airplane lavatory, just big enough to turn in without hitting the walls. The mirror above the sink is old and warped, stretching my reflection in odd places. I splash cold water on my face, gripping the edges of the sink to steady myself.

It's only one night.

It's fine. I can do this.

When I step back into the main room, Bennet is already on the bed, partially obscured by the netting. He glances up as I enter but says nothing, reaching for a piece of bread from the tray.

I tilt my head, eyeing the net. Lovebug season is over. "I wonder why—?"

A skittering echoes across the floor and I give a strangled cry. It's definitely not a scream, but it is also definitely not dignified. In one completely instinctual motion, I launch myself onto the bed, shoving my way inside the net.

Bennet snaps upright, body tense. "What happened?"

"Bug," I gasp, heart hammering.

His brows dip. "A bug?"

I nod. "It was huge." So I didn't actually get a look at it, but he doesn't need to know that. The skittering sounded big enough.

He blinks. "Where?"

I point to the floor. A tiny, barely visible insect sits there, unmoving.

Bennet stares at it. Then at me. Then back at it.

"That?" he asks flatly.

I nod, still breathless. "Did you see the gleam in its eyes?"

He tilts his head. "It has eyes?"

"I'm sure it does. And I'm sure they have a wicked gleam in them."

He leans forward slightly, moving the net to study it. "It's half the size of your pinky nail. I can't even tell if it has a face."

When all else fails, double down. "Well, it does. And it's full of malice. It could be poisonous."

There's a pause. A slight twitch at the corner of his mouth. "I'm sure you're correct."

I glare at him. "This is not funny."

His amusement presses against my senses like a warm pulse.

And then, despite myself and my cursed pride, I laugh. It bubbles out unexpectedly, half exhausted, half hysterical, and then he's laughing too. A quiet, breathy chuckle.

"I hate you."

He smirks. "No, you don't."

I kick my shoes off and dump them over the side of the bed, wiping off a few bits of dirt I brought with me when I leaped inside the net.

He puts the tray between us, breaking off a piece of bread and handing it to me. We sit side by side, sharing food under the glow of the fire.

"I'm sorry about your mother's ring." I pick up one of the copper cups he's already filled with water.

He's looking down at the hunk of bread in his hands. "It's okay. It's just an object. Helen is more important."

"Still. It sucks." I would be absolutely devastated to lose something of value that belonged to either of my parents.

"Yes. It does."

"Maybe we can find a way to get it back, once all this is over."

His eyes lift to mine. "That would be nice."

He turns back to his food and we eat for a few minutes in silence.

"What do you think they meant when they said, 'the ones you seek have crossed the veil'?" He wipes a crumb from his mouth with the back of his hand.

"You heard that?"

He nods. "Though it felt like they were speaking to you. I don't think it was about Helen and Delores. They are still in the mortal world." He rubs the back of his head. "Do you think they were speaking of your parents?"

A bite of cheese lodges in my throat and I cough. "My parents? You think that's what they were talking about?" How could they still be alive? Crossed the veil but not to Hades . . . cryptic much? I force words out over a suddenly bitter tongue. "I don't know. Maybe."

I've spent years clinging to the idea that my parents will walk through the door, or I will be handed a neat explanation and a happy ending.

I've longed for the day when Jackie will suddenly wake up better. When life will make sense again.

But hope, when it's unanswered, starts to hollow you out.

Miracles don't happen. Not to me.

His gaze sharpens. There's a beat of silence before he asks, "Will you tell me what happened to them?"

"They went missing." My voice is flat. I stare down at the food tray. "I don't know where they are, if they're alive or dead or what. We'll probably never know. We tried everything. We went to the cops. I used my magic, but that went nowhere. I asked Richard for help, but even he couldn't do anything. Kevin asked his ghost friends. We thought maybe they . . ." I trail off, unable to finish the sentence.

They have not met Hades. The witches' words echo in my mind.

"We put flyers up all over town," I continue. "Even got the news to report on it. No one had seen them. They disappeared into thin air."

"I'm sorry," he says, his voice softer now. "The authorities were unable to find any hints at all?"

"The cops were useless," I mutter. "They didn't say it outright, but they thought my parents bailed on us. Thousands of people go missing every year. Some end up dead, some are never found. Some don't want to be found."

Silence stretches between us. The bread in my hands has

turned to dust in my mouth, dry and tasteless. I set it down and take a sip of water, but it does little to ease the tightness in my throat.

After a moment, Bennet asks, "Did they have magic? Your parents?"

I take a sip. "Mom was a spellbreaker. Magic didn't affect her. She could block anything tossed her way, and she could break any ward or negate any spell even directed at people around her. I think that's why Richard liked her, or was fascinated by her. He couldn't affect her like everyone else."

Bennet listens intently. "And your father?"

"His power was similar to mine."

"A seeker then?"

"Yes. He was more in tune with people though, and their vibrations. I can kind of sense people but it's more natural for me to feel objects. Kevin wandered off once when we were at a carnival. He got into a game booth and was hiding behind one of the giant stuffed prizes. I have no idea how he even managed to get in there, but Dad found him no problem. He could find us anywhere."

Bennet studies me for a long moment, then gestures toward my half-eaten bread. "Are you finished?"

I nod, and he slips out from under the netting, crossing the small space to set the tray back on the table. I lean back against the pillows, letting my eyes drift shut.

There's the quiet clink of him adjusting the tray, the soft shuffle of his footsteps as he stirs the fire. Then, a moment later, the mattress dips again.

I open my eyes. He's sitting on the bed, watching me, his dark gaze steady in the dim glow of the firelight.

"They disappeared before Jackie's illness began?" he asks.

"No." I frown slightly, thinking back. "Just after. Maybe a year or so after it started."

"Hmmm." His brow furrows. "And then you stepped in to care for your siblings."

"Yeah."

There's no pity in his expression. He nods, like he's fitting the pieces together.

"What were you doing before they disappeared?" he asks.

"Nothing much." I let out a small, humorless laugh. "I had just graduated from college. I was about to start my master's degree in art history."

His brow furrows. "Art history?"

"Yeah." I smile a little at his confusion. "It's the study of art through different cultures and time periods. Understanding techniques, symbolism, how movements evolved. Basically, a deep dive into the stories people have told through art."

He nods slowly, considering it. "That sounds significant."

I snort. "Not really. It's not like there's a huge job market for it."

"Still. You had to put it on hold for your family."

I shrug, trying to play it off. "Eh. It's not like I was walking into a high-paying job or anything. My options were basically become a professor or work in a museum gift shop. Although it has helped me get jobs finding antiques for people, along with my magic."

His expression turns thoughtful. "Do you miss it? School?"

I hesitate, then admit, "Yeah. Sometimes. I loved what I was studying because looking at art from the past is like a way to see the world through another's eyes long after they're gone. It's a moment in time, preserved. A glimpse into how someone thought, how they felt, what they feared or hoped for, centuries ago. It's not just history, it's like a memory made visible."

The fire crackles. I stare at the flicker of flames through the net, unable to meet the weight of Bennet's stare. "You are not what I expected."

I look over at him. "What do you mean?"

His fingers spread over the blanket between us. "Uncle always says mortals tend to be selfish creatures, obsessed with wealth and their own comfort."

"Well. He's not wrong." I sink down further into the bed. "A lot of people are like that."

His lips purse. "Hmmm."

I take a deep breath and for a second allow myself to enjoy Bennet's solid presence beside me, the warmth of the little room, the comfort of the space between conversation and silence.

I turn toward him. "Did you go to school? In Aetheria?"

His head dips. "I had tutors."

"What did you study?"

"Magic, languages, politics, mathematics, courtship," he waves a hand, "things useful to a second son."

My brows shoot up into my hairline. "Courtship? They have tutors for that?"

He leans back against the pillow, shifting until he's reclined on one elbow on his side, facing me. "I am expected to make a good match, after Helen gets married, of course."

Jealousy slides through my veins, hot, burning, and intense. My jaw clenches. This is ridiculous. Bennet isn't mine. I cannot possibly be murderous toward some vague woman I've never met and may not even exist.

I take a breath before speaking, so my voice won't emerge as a screech. "Are you . . . engaged?"

"No. I've met a few potential candidates at balls and feasts with other kingdoms, but," he rubs his chin, "it's never sat well with me."

I'll ignore the relief that rolls through me at learning he's not engaged. "What do you mean?"

He shrugs. "I don't like feeling out of control of my own destiny. I would rather pick a partner I love, rather than be matched for political advantage."

"That's understandable."

"Yes, for you and your world. In my world, that is not the way of things."

"There was never some fair maiden that caught your eye?"

I want to roll my eyes at myself. *Fair maiden?*

But Bennet doesn't notice my internal berating.

He rubs an invisible spot on the pillowcase. "No. They were nice enough, but there was no spark."

Our gazes clash and hold. The irrational jealousy over the nameless, faceless maidens morphs into another kind of heat entirely. There is no lack of sparks here.

The fire has mellowed into burning embers, darkening the room.

In the thickening gloom my eyes track over his figure, his broad shoulders filling the space on his side of the bed, and the tapering of his waist. He's less than a foot away. So close.

No.

No no no.

He's going back to his djinn life and his fair maidens. I'm going back to my simple mortal life. This wouldn't be anything more than a night of pleasure.

Arousal blooms, spreading through my limbs. Would that be so bad? Only one night?

Yes. It would be bad. We still have to work together and find Helen and anything more will just complicate matters further. This can't be anything more than just magic sex between us. I can't risk him catching feelings. Or me.

It's simple attraction and shared emotions. Nothing more,

nothing less. He's not even human. Once we break this curse, he's going back to Aetheria, a whole different dimension.

I mean, there's wanting what you can't have and then there's *this*.

"Um. We should get some rest." Lord only knows what's going to happen tomorrow. I force a yawn and shift, slipping under the covers.

"Right. Yes. Of course." Bennet settles in next to me, staying on top of the covers.

It's for the best.

I'm staring up at the netting when he murmurs, "You're sure you're safe?"

I frown, turning my head to face him. "What?"

He props himself up on one elbow, his expression completely serious. "I wouldn't want you to wake up with one of your wicked-eyed friends crawling across your pillow."

I groan, smacking his arm. "Oh my God, don't say that. Now I'm going to be paranoid all night."

He stifles his laugh. "I could always stand watch."

"You're not funny." I tug the blanket higher like that'll protect me from potential creepy-crawlies.

The rumble of his laughter brushes against my senses like a soft feather.

And damn it, I laugh too.

SEVENTEEN

Banging drags me out of a deep sleep. I haven't slept a full night like that in *years*. With the exception of the night before last. I'm going to pretend like Bennet didn't have anything to do with either of those amazing slumbers even though he is the only common denominator.

I shift to stretch, but I'm held back. I'm wrapped up in cozy heat. I settle back down. Stretching can happen later.

Warmth tickles my nose along with spice and sugar.

I open my eyes and am confronted with the strong column of Bennet's throat.

I'm half on top of him, my face wedged into his neck. His arm is wrapped around me, holding me in place, our legs entwined.

The room is gray with hints of dawn creeping through the windows.

Dawn. The portal. We have to get out of here before the portal shuts.

Wait. What woke me? Was there knocking?

I stir, attempting to untangle my limbs from Bennet's.

Before I progress more than an inch, he rolls in my direction, holding me tighter, flipping our positions so now his head is in the crook of my neck. He breathes in deeply, contented noises rumbling in his chest. The bristles of his jaw brush against the delicate skin of my neck and collar. He's rubbing his face on me like a cat.

A wave of jumbled emotions crashes over me: satisfaction, possessiveness, and arousal. Are his shields down? Are mine? I search inside for the bond between us, lifting my shields a crack. Words filter through the emotions, rising into my awareness like buoys in the water. *Mine. Comfy. Mmmm.* He breathes deeply. *Delicious.*

I guess he thinks I smell okay. Good to know. But how is it that I can hear his thoughts? Is the bond getting stronger, even though we've clamped down our mental defenses? Are his clamped down at all?

Whenever I lift my shields in his presence, the bond is there, his emotions are there, flaring brighter than the sun . . . Has he even bothered to lock his mind away from mine?

The knocking returns, a staccato of thumps.

Bennet snuffles and wakes. I rebuild my defenses, locking out his thoughts as he rises to consciousness and blinks his eyes open.

He gazes at me sleepily, a smile lifting his lips. "Good morning."

An awake and alert Bennet is handsome. A sleepy, rumpled Bennet with messy hair is devastating.

I don't have time to contemplate any of it. Whoever is at the door is about to break it down.

Bennet's eyes snap to awareness. "Stay here." In one smooth movement, he rolls away from me and slips under the net, stalking on quiet feet to the door.

I sit up.

Dammit, his protectiveness is way too hot.

The hammering at the door abruptly ceases.

He lifts the curtain to peer through the narrow front window, then frowns and swings the door wide open, sticking his head out. "No one is here." He turns to face me.

I make an attempt to contain my sleep-mussed hair, sliding my palms over the tangle around my head. "I think that was our wake-up call. We have to get back to the portal by dawn, before it shuts and we're stuck here another night."

Although part of me wishes we could stay here, sequestered together, away from the real world and real responsibilities.

What would it be like spend the night with Bennet and not have to rush out of bed the next day?

He squints outside into the slowly brightening gloom. "Looks like we'd better hurry."

Quickly, we take turns using the restroom and getting our shoes on.

We exit the cabin, jog down the rickety porch steps, and head back in the direction we came from the night before, circling around the giant cypress. The bark is whole, unblemished, no cavernous hole at the bottom.

Okey dokey then.

We keep moving down the path.

Mist curls over the swamp's surface, thick and ghostly in the early morning light. The lanterns that led us through the night are gone, leaving only the gnarled trees and dark water stretching endlessly in every direction. My shoes sink into the damp earth. We approach the area where we entered the swamp through the portal. At least I think we're close? It's all the same.

I glance behind us. The cabin is out of sight. Were we supposed to go in a different direction?

The splash of water against wood catches my attention.

A shadow emerges from the mist to our left.

A voice calls out, smooth, smug, and entirely too familiar. "Well, well. Look what the gators dragged in."

I suppress a groan. "Richard?"

The figure comes into focus, standing at the bow of a rickety flatboat like some kind of swamp-bound river god. One hand on his hip, the other lazily resting on a pole, Richard is dressed like he's ready for a high-society brunch, despite the mud-slicked hellscape around us. His suit is lime green, bright enough to be blinding, with lace along the sleeves rolled up just so, rings glinting on his fingers, and a golden scarf tied dramatically around his throat.

Richard's gaze flicks between us, then he grins. "I'm so glad you survived. I was worried there for a minute, with the lightning cloud and whatnot. That creature was absolutely teeming with magic. A bit dark for my tastes, but I could have made an exception."

I prop a hand on my waist. "How did you know we would be here? Why are you here?"

"I'm your ride, of course. I knew as soon as I saw you and your handsome man here that I would be needed. This one's on the house, sweetie."

He knew we would be here? "Why didn't you tell us about the swamp witches?" We could have bypassed the whole vamp experience.

Richard presses a hand to his chest. "I didn't know you were looking for the swamp witches. You said you were looking for the vamp."

"But you knew where that would lead, and that we would be here today."

"Well, yeah. I had an inkling you would be my favorite damsel in distress." His attention drifts over to Bennet. "And I see you're still distressing yourself with tall, gold, and broody."

Bennet stiffens beside me. "Did you know where my sister was?"

"Yes."

I lift my hands. "Richard! This whole time?"

His eyes widen, the picture of innocence. "You never asked me about his sister."

I pinch the bridge of my nose.

"Well, are you two needing a ride back to town or are you going to stand there being cranky and performing histrionics? Come, come. Hop aboard before something with too many teeth decides you're breakfast." He waves a hand at us.

I want to punch him, but I step onto the boat, gripping the wooden railing as it rocks under my weight. Bennet hesitates for a second before stepping in behind me. Tension radiates off of him, but Richard just smirks and pushes a button on the pole in his hand. The boat rumbles beneath us and then pushes through the mist, away from the shore.

The silence of the swamp presses in around us, broken only by the soft splash of the oar cutting through the water and the low hum of the magical motor. Mist clings to the surface, curling and shifting like it's alive.

Richard shoots me a look. "You know, Cassie, darling, you've gotten yourself tangled up in something real deep this time."

I snort. "Yeah, no kidding."

Richard tilts his head, his expression unusually thoughtful. "Magic's been shifting. I've felt it—whispers in the wind, dreams pulling at the edges of reality. You're not walking blind into this, are you?"

"We're looking for Helen. The swamp witches told us where to find her."

Richard hums. "And they charged you for it, didn't they?" His gaze flicks to Bennet, sharp and measuring. "I'm guessing the price wasn't cheap."

Bennet's jaw tightens, but he doesn't answer.

The swamp thins as we drift on, the boat moving faster and faster, the dark waters expanding around us.

"Mind the bump."

The boat lurches, like we've run over a giant log or wave. I stumble into Bennet, his arms wrapping around me while he braces against the rail.

The swamp and mist have disappeared. We're on the Mississippi, near Woldenberg Park, right in the thick of the city. The sun beats down overhead. Did we lose time again? It is no longer morning, but midday at least.

"Will you take us toward the Garden District?" It's just up and around the bend.

"As you wish, darling."

A few minutes later, we've exited the boat and Richard glides away, yelling out, "Call me!" on the breeze with a dramatic wave. His boat vanishes back into whatever strange existence he operates in.

Bennet and I step onto the sidewalk. The Garden District stretches around us, a picture-perfect slice of old New Orleans wealth. Grand mansions sit behind wrought-iron fences, their facades covered in ivy and creeping jasmine. The sidewalks are cracked but clean, shaded by the sprawling arms of ancient oak trees. Their roots bulge up through the concrete in places, making the path uneven.

I pull out my phone and release a breath. It's no longer dead. My stomach unclenches a little as I dial home. It rings twice before Mimi picks up.

"Cassie! Are you okay?" Her voice is bright, but there's a thread of worry beneath it.

"I'm fine." I step around a pile of magnolia leaves. "We, uh—things got a little weird last night. But everything's fine now."

"Define weird."

"We were chased by more ifrit. Have you all been safe there?"

"We've been fine."

"Maybe don't leave the house unless strictly necessary, just in case. How are the kids? How is Jackie?"

"It's too soon to tell. She seems better to me, but it could be wishful thinking."

Please let it be more than wishful thinking.

"Other than that," Mimi continues, "Kevin made waffles. Jackie burned a waffle. Then she cried about the waffle, so we gave it a funeral in the trash can."

I let out a breath of a laugh. "Sounds about right."

Mimi hesitates. "Did you find Helen?"

I glance at Bennet. "Maybe. We're about to check out a lead in the Garden District. I'll call you later, okay?"

"Okay. Be safe."

I hang up right as we reach the address the swamp witches showed us.

The house is exactly what you'd expect in this neighborhood, stately and pristine with history baked into its bones and leaking into the surrounding area. It's a three-story Greek Revival, complete with towering white columns and an iron-railed balcony on the second floor. The paint is a soft white with dark green shutters, and the wraparound porch is lined with neatly trimmed ferns.

Bennet steps up to the heavy oak door and knocks. The sound is deep and solid, echoing through whatever space lies beyond.

The door creaks open almost immediately.

A man stands in the doorway, holding a giant, colorfully wrapped present complete with a bright red bow. He barely glances at us before his gaze darts over his shoulder, distracted by the sound of a child screeching somewhere deep inside the house. "Oh good, will you take this to the back?"

Bennet and I exchange a glance.

The man frowns, shifting the oversized package in his arms. He's middle aged, fit, with salt-and-pepper hair and a neatly trimmed beard. His shirt is slightly wrinkled like he's been running around all day. "You are here for the party, right?"

We both gape for a second. Then I snap to attention.

"Yes," I blurt out. "The party."

He nods in satisfaction and gestures behind us. "Follow the signs. Everyone's in the backyard. Here." He shoves the present at Bennet, who catches it instinctively, his arms tightening around the box.

I glance behind us and spot a single glossy pennant flag fluttering in the breeze, set between the porch railing and a tree: *Birthday Party This Way!* A collection of balloons tied to the fence confirms it, but they would have been hidden by a tree near the front of the yard when we approached.

I turn back to the man, forcing a sheepish smile. "Must've missed the signs."

But he's already shutting the door.

Bennet and I stare at each other, then shrug almost simultaneously.

"Well. I guess we're crashing a party."

He adjusts the weight of the gift. "At least we brought a present."

We step off the porch and follow the signs, slipping around the side of the house and into the backyard.

It's a scene straight out of a lifestyle magazine. The yard is sprawling and meticulously manicured, with towering oaks draped in Spanish moss casting cool shade over an opulent patio. A turquoise-blue pool glistens in the center, kids splashing wildly while adults lounge in chairs sipping drinks. A long table set with trays of food—sandwiches, fruit, pasta salads, an entire roasted pig—stretches along the patio. Another table, covered in a bright pink tablecloth, is piled high with presents. Bennet deposits the one in his arms there, his movements stiff, like he's walking in a dream.

I scan the crowd, searching for someone who resembles the image he shared with me the other night when we tried to track her.

"Helen." His voice is low, hoarse with disbelief.

I follow his gaze to the woman sitting at a table near the pool. She laughs, her expression open and warm, a baby nestled in her lap. The woman beside her leans in, their conversation intimate, easy.

Bennet's frame grows impossibly tighter, the tension rolling off him. His sister left without a word. She ran from everything. Trapped him in the cursed lamp. And now, she's just here? Laughing, smiling, carefree?

I reach for his hand without thinking. His fingers clasp around mine.

Across the yard, Helen's laughing eyes land on us.

The smile dies, her face draining of color. Her arms tighten around the baby for a split second before she carefully hands the child off and stands.

She crosses the space between us. When she reaches us, she doesn't greet Bennet. Doesn't hug him. Doesn't try to explain.

She glances behind her at the party, and then returns her gaze to Bennet. "Not here," she says instead. "Come."

She leads us away from the party, deeper into the property,

weaving past the trees until we reach a secluded sitting area, partially hidden from the backyard by heavy, draping branches. A stone bench sits beneath a weeping willow, and the air is thick with the scent of honeysuckle.

She crosses her arms over her chest. "What are you doing here?"

Bennet's mouth pops open. "What am I—? What are *you* doing here? You cursed me. You trapped me in a damn lamp."

Her brows knit together. "What? I did not. I merely sent you back to Aetheria."

His hand grips mine tighter. "Then why am I still here?"

Helen's eyes close, her jaw tightening. "He lied," she whispers. "Of course, he did." Her hands curl into fists at her sides. "Delores tried to warn me—"

"Helen," Bennet cuts in. "What are you talking about? Who lied?"

She lifts her chin. "Uncle Hugh. Who else?"

Bennet flinches. "What—?"

"Despite what he may have told you, I didn't come here on a lark. Or to escape my marriage. Well, not *only* to escape my marriage." She swallows hard. "I came here to find my father."

His head jerks back in shock. "What do you mean, your father? Helen, our parents are dead."

"No." She shakes her head. "You're wrong. Our mother is dead. But we had different fathers, Bennet. My father was human."

EIGHTEEN

Ten minutes later, we're seated in an opulent sitting room with high ceilings and intricate crown molding. Velvet drapes frame tall windows, their heavy fabric muffling the sounds of the party outside. The furniture is rich and antique, deep mahogany pieces with plush cushions, a marble-topped coffee table sitting between us, and an ornate fireplace with a grate clean enough to eat off of.

I sit beside Bennet on a cushy white sofa. His posture is so rigid I half expect him to vibrate out of the seat. Across from us, Helen perches stiffly in an armchair, her hands gripping the arms. Delores is beside her on another chair, quiet but watchful, her dark eyes flicking between us like she's assessing potential threats.

Shortly after Helen dropped her lineage bombshell, Delores found us in the backyard and insisted everyone come inside to chat in private. Delores is petite with a button nose and blonde hair pulled back from her face in a low bun.

"Why do you think you have a mortal father?"

Helen's fingers tighten further on the arm rests. "I don't think. I know. Uncle confirmed it to me, months ago."

A muscle jumps in Bennet's jaw. "What did he say?"

"That our parents were struggling to conceive, and that it is a known recourse, for djinn to seek assistance in the mortal realm. It is not widely discussed, but whispered of in dark corners. No one else knows why I'm here. Only Uncle, and us." Helen glances at Delores, a flicker of acknowledgment passing between them.

The lightbulb clicks. "The swamp witches," I blurt. Mimi mentioned they'd helped her friends have a baby.

Bennet stiffens. "You're saying they, what, made you?"

Helen shakes her head. "No, they helped find a donor, so to speak. Our parents made a deal. A mortal man, one who carried magic in his blood, was found. Magic in the blood means they are part djinn."

Does that mean I'm part djinn? I don't have time to ponder the thought.

"The witches guaranteed success," Helen continues. "In exchange, he was given riches enough to support him and his descendants. His mother's health was ailing and he wanted her to live in comfort for her final days. The mortal realm, at least this part of it, does not take care of their most ill, apparently. They would have been on the streets to pay for her treatments and medicine."

"Do I have a mortal father as well, then?"

"No. You were a surprise. A happy surprise. Our parents didn't think they could conceive without assistance. And then you came along." She offers a small, sad smile. "How were you able to find me? I blocked myself from being tracked."

"Cassie helped me."

I fidget in my seat. "We were able to trace your power

signature to the witches, and that's where it disappeared. We went to them for more information on where to find you."

Helen nods. "Yes. The witches warned me there were other forces seeking me." Her lips press together. "They warned me to keep my presence hidden with magic. I didn't think Bennet was the 'other forces' on the hunt. I thought he would be back in Aetheria by now."

His brows dip. "Who did you think was tracking you then?"

She shrugs. "I didn't know. The witches wouldn't say."

"You didn't think it might be your uncle?" I asked.

"Of course not. Uncle and I started making plans shortly after he confirmed the story of my heritage to come here, to search. Uncle *helped* me."

Bennet's brow furrows. "But he told me to bring you home. Why did he help you leave, only to send me right after you?"

She bites her lip. "I don't know. He knows I don't want to marry Lord Wallace. I want to be with Delores."

Delores reaches over, covering one of Helen's clenched hands with her own.

Oohh. That makes a lot more sense. "Is that not allowed?" I ask. "I mean, in Aetheria? Are queer people looked down on? We have a lot of homophobia here too, it's a real problem."

"Not exactly. There's no real stigma against who you love. It's not like here, not the same kind of judgment." Helen shrugs. "But I'm a royal. The heir. I'm expected to marry someone with standing, to form alliances, to produce heirs. It's not about who I love. It's about duty."

Delores's thumb strokes over Helen's knuckles. "But you're not just an heir. You're a person. And you shouldn't have to choose between duty and your heart."

Helen releases her death grip on the chair, turning her hand over to weave Delores's fingers with her own. "I don't know why Uncle told you to come fetch me. He gave me the lamp to return to Aetheria with once he was able to scuttle the marriage. I was going to use it myself to come home because we weren't sure how strong my magic would be here and if I would be able to generate a portal back. That's the only reason I used it on you, to send you home."

Bennet shakes his head. "Except the lamp didn't send me to Aetheria. It took my powers and trapped me. If it wasn't for Cassie, I don't know how long I might have been stuck in there."

Helen's face drains of color. "I—I didn't know, I swear. Honestly, I had no idea that would happen. I wouldn't have used it if I had."

Bennet doesn't say anything, but the silence stretches through the room as the weight of everything that's happened sinks into place. Their uncle orchestrated so much of this. It's like he's been moving pieces on a board, playing a game none of them knew they were a part of. Did he mean for Helen to get trapped in the lamp when she attempted to return? Did he send Bennet right after her, to be stuck here on a fool's errand or knowing Helen might use the lamp on him? Were the ifrit meant to find him—just in case? Why? So he can take over in their place?

"This isn't a normal spell. It's a curse," Bennet finally says. "We are tied together."

Helen straightens, like she's ready to latch on to something she can fix. "Maybe I can help with the curse. With my magic."

Bennet nods slowly. "Yes. We can have you test it, but later. First, tell me why you came in search of your mortal father."

"I wanted to know where I came from. I've always wondered, since the moment I realized the truth, and I intended to come here as soon as my duties allowed. Then Uncle convinced me this was the perfect time. I could leave and find my father, and in the meantime he could sort out the impending wedding, take care of everything at home." Helen searches his face. "I would never hurt you. I wasn't intending to leave forever, I was going to return. You understand why I could not marry Lord Wallace."

He blows out a breath. "I am beginning to."

Helen straightens, her mouth twisting. "You honestly didn't know? About Delores and me?"

Bennet rubs the back of his neck. "How would I?"

She rolls her eyes. "I don't know, maybe the fact that we've been in each other's pockets for months, or that one time you walked in on us leaving the bathing room together and holding hands?"

"Women are always doing those things."

She gives him a pointed look. "Kissing in dark corners?"

Bennet rubs a hand down his face. "Okay, okay, I should have known."

Helen and Delores exchange a glance and burst into laughter.

A reluctant smile tugs at Bennet's mouth and then he laughs too. With the humor, the tension in the room finally breaks, dissolving like steam.

After a moment, Bennet leans forward in his seat, elbows on his knees. "Will you tell me about him? Your father?"

Delores squeezes Helen's hand and then stands. "Cassie, would you like something to eat or drink?"

Reading between the lines, I stand. "Absolutely. I would love to see more of the house, it's beautiful."

"Yes. Come right this way."

I follow her to the door. She eases it closed behind us and gives me a knowing smile. "The tension in there was thick enough to swim in."

I let out a laugh. "That's one way to put it."

She slips her hand in my arm with a sunny smile. "Come.

There is a lack of magic in your realm but the kitchens are marvelous. You must tell me what is going on with you and Bennet."

I swallow. "Um . . . what do you mean, what is going on?"

"You smell like him."

Of course I do. We spent most of the night wrapped around each other and then he rubbed his face against me like a contented house cat marking his territory.

"It's nothing."

"Right. The bond and the flirting and the intense looks. Nothing at all. Bennet has been so sheltered and closed off his whole life, I've often wondered who would be the one to break through his walls."

I wave a hand, heat creeping up my neck. "Oh, it's nothing. It's just the curse, you know? We've been basically tied together since I freed him from the lamp. Not that there's been any actual tying up—we're not like that. There's nothing happening here, is what I'm saying. Nothing at all."

No wild orgasms in the swamp. Nope.

"Right. I understand. Nothing going on." She nods solemnly—then bites her lip, failing to hide her smile.

We step into the kitchen, and my mouth falls open at the sheer extravagance of it. White marble counters stretch for miles, their surfaces gleaming under the recessed lighting. A massive island sits at the center, its top covered with an array of food, trays of fresh fruit, imported cheeses, and delicate pastries that are too pretty to eat. There's a double-door fridge that could probably hold an entire grocery store inside, and state-of-the-art appliances line the walls, their polished steel surfaces reflecting the golden glow of the lights overhead.

"Tell me how it all happened, the lamp and Bennet and finding us?"

I settle onto a stool at the island and give her the short

version of everything that's happened over the past few days, finding the lamp, releasing Bennet, the search for Helen and being chased by ifrit.

"Ifrit? Here?" She taps her finger on her chin. "It's all so bizarre, isn't it?"

"No ifrit followed you and Helen?"

"No. But Helen did mask our presence. How did they find you, I wonder?"

"I have no idea."

She quickly describes their adventure so far, which is much less dramatic than Bennet's and mine. They've basically been hanging out here since they found Helen's father, meeting Helen's extended family and helping prepare for the birthday party—it's for the daughter of one of Helen's half-siblings who just turned one.

"That must have been strange for her, discovering she had other siblings."

"Four of them." Delores pours water into a beveled glass and slides it to me. "Three sisters and a brother. Two of the sisters live here in town, one is overseas, and the brother is off at school."

We snack from the platters of food as she tells me about their arrival. They weren't sure what Helen's father would think, if he'd reject her or want nothing to do with her. But to their surprise, he was welcoming.

"He doesn't know about Aetheria or djinn or any of it." Delores lowers her voice. "He thought he was just helping out by donating some of his essence to wealthy people willing to pay. He had agreed to not seek her out."

I pop a grape in my mouth. "What did she tell him?"

She leans against the counter. "The truth, mostly. That her parents passed and she tracked him down through the agency that arranged it. His wife died a few years ago. He was happy she came to find him. He had always wondered if anything had come from his donation."

Right then, a man walks into the kitchen, the same one from earlier who handed off the gift.

Delores beams. "Mr. Landry. This is Bennet's lady friend, Cassie. Cassie, this is Mr. Landry, Helen's father."

Lady friend?

"It's nice to meet you." I wave.

Helen's father chuckles. "It's nice to meet you too. I'm so glad Helen's brother was able to make it. Thanks for coming out today. Help yourselves to anything you like." He gestures to the food. "We always over cook. I came in to grab more drinks for the kids."

We make idle chitchat for a minute and then he disappears with a handful of juice packs.

"What do you think of their uncle Hugh?" I ask, when we're alone again.

She makes a moue. "I'm not sure. He's always seemed like he has their best interest at heart, but now I wonder. It doesn't make sense though. Why would he do all this work to get Bennet and Helen out of his way? For power? How would their disappearance do anything but cause a crisis?"

I drum my fingers on the countertop. "Chaos is a ladder."

"I suppose that's true. But what does he want that he can't already achieve with his proximity to the throne?"

I shrug, then double over, clutching my middle.

"Cassie! Are you okay?" Delores is at my side instantly, a gentle hand on my back.

Black spots swarm my vision. Damn. This is not the charged arousal I'm used to. This is actual physical agony, like when we were too far apart. "Bennet," I manage to choke out.

Panic claws at my throat. What if he's hurt? What if one of the ifrit came into the house and took him, and he can't fight back because of this—this bond that keeps twisting tighter?

The pain recedes suddenly, like a balloon deflating.

And then Bennet appears in the doorway, his grip white-knuckled on the frame. "There you are." Relief bleeds into his voice.

"You felt that?" I ask, still breathless.

"Yes." His chest rises and falls heavily. "Our bond is strengthening. Helen wants to see if she can break the curse."

"Now?"

"Yes. The sooner the better. Then you can go home to your family, and we can make plans to return to Aetheria." His voice is measured and calm, his expression carefully blank.

Something inside me screams in protest. But no. That's not right.

This is what we wanted, right? To break the curse. To go our separate ways.

But as I follow him back to the sitting room, a hollow ache blooms where the scorching pain once resided.

NINETEEN

I can't shake the strange achiness in my chest.

It doesn't settle, even as I lower myself onto the same couch as before. Bennet sits beside me, close but not touching, his hands in his lap.

Helen stands in front of us, her expression focused. Power hums in the space around her, the air growing thick and charged.

She lifts her hands, her fingers moving through the air like she's weaving something invisible. "I'll need you both to stay still."

Bennet doesn't move. Neither do I, though my heart thuds a little harder.

The air shimmers around us, gold and violet threads of magic spinning into existence, wrapping around Bennet and me in a delicate web. It reminds me of the connections I saw when Bennet was doing breathwork with Jackie, the forces that link the world and everything in it.

The gossamer strands make contact, tingling where they touch my skin. It's not painful or anything, it's like the moment before a static shock, energy coiled and waiting to snap.

Helen's brow furrows in concentration. She speaks words I don't understand, her voice low and firm. The threads tighten, pulse, then—

Nothing.

A flicker of unease crosses her face, but she smooths it away. She tries again, her magic pressing against the bond between Bennet and me, probing, searching for a weak point to unravel.

I shut my eyes and breathe, searching for that silent place inside. The awareness rushes over me, faster than before, and the bond throbs to life in my mind's eye.

Is it getting larger?

The gold cord is brighter and thicker than before. Helen's magic weaves around it, probing and poking.

It doesn't budge.

Helen exhales sharply.

I open my eyes.

A bead of sweat rolls down her temple.

Bennet shifts beside me, his thigh brushing against mine. "Something wrong?"

Helen's fingers twitch, the magic around us flickering unsteadily. "The curse—" She shakes her head as if to clear it. "I thought I could sever it, or unweave it, but . . ." She presses her lips together. "It's not working. It's not a normal bond."

My stomach flips. "What does that mean, not normal?"

"I don't know. Let me try once more." She waves her hands wider, the threads of her magic brightening as her face darkens with strain. The power crackles and flexes—but still, the bond holds. A shudder ripples through her magic before it snaps apart entirely, sending a burst of light through the room.

I flinch. Bennet tenses beside me. Helen stumbles back, blinking rapidly.

Silence hums loud in my ears.

Helen rubs her temples. "That shouldn't have happened."

Bennet leans forward. "Meaning?"

Helen looks at me, then at him, her brows furrowed. "The curse is stronger than I expected. It's deeply woven into your magic, Bennet, and into Cassie's now too. I was trying to break it apart like unraveling a knot, but it's not a knot—it's fused, welded together."

I bite my lip. "The vamp said it was like a braid."

She shakes her head slowly. "It does appear that it was a braid at one time. But now there are no separate parts. Only one."

I stare at her. "What does that mean?"

She hesitates. "It means I don't think I can break it."

Bennet sits back, his jaw tight. "There has to be another way."

Is he upset? Does it bother him so much, being tethered to me?

"There might be," Helen says slowly. "But not with the kind of magic I have."

The weight of her words settles over me. This whole time, we've been working toward this moment, breaking the bond so we can go our separate ways. I can get back to my life and he can get back to his.

But we're still bound, the bond apparently even more unbreakable than before. I don't know whether the fluttering in my chest is panic or relief.

I clear my throat. "What do we do now?"

Bennet's gaze is distant, lost in thought. Then, slowly, he reaches across the space between us, placing his hand over mine. His warmth seeps into my skin, calming me. "I'm sorry."

His hand squeezes mine. "We'll think of something. In the meantime, we need to mask our presence from the ifrit that have been stalking us, and figure out what Uncle is really up to."

I nod, trying to tamp down the uneasiness curling in my gut. "How?"

Helen tucks a loose strand of hair behind her ear. "I can take care of the masking, and then use deeper magic to see into Aetheria and spy on him, but it's difficult. I'll need time to rest and prepare, and we don't know if we'll learn anything relevant."

Only in the movies would a villain just so happen to be doing something incriminating at the exact moment they were being spied on.

Bennet taps a finger on his chin. "We may be able to see what's happening with Lord Wallace or the other visiting families too. Is he still there waiting for your marriage, or did Uncle truly 'take care of' the upcoming nuptials? Perhaps we can eavesdrop on the staff as well. They're always gossiping."

Helen's mouth twists in contemplation. "Maybe. We'll have limited time. It's a lot of magic and I'm the only one who can do it."

"If we do it when the veil is thinnest, that may help." Bennet leans forward, elbows braced on his knees.

Helen glances toward the sky beyond the window. It's barely three, so we have a few hours, at least. "It's worth the attempt."

Bennet straightens. "Dusk tonight?"

She gives a short nod. "Dusk. When the night meal is served at court. If anyone of note is in residence, Uncle must attend, so we can listen in on their conversations and find out what he is telling them. We'll need to gather some supplies."

"What kind of things help with spying across the veil?" I ask.

"There are multiple herbs and stones that aid vision, but I'm not sure what's easily accessible in this realm." She counts off on her fingers. "Mugwort, star anise, and blue lotus, maybe. And for crystals, labradorite, clear quartz, amethyst, and obsidian work well."

I perk up. "We have some of those at the house." Relief washes over me at the thought of going home, even if just for a short while. It'll be good to check on how Jackie is doing.

Bennet nods. "Write down a list, and we'll help gather what we can."

Helen smiles, the tension in her shoulders easing a fraction. "Thank you. Now, let's mask you two before we're attacked."

Familiar scents wrap around me the moment I step into our house, garlic and basil and lemon and a touch of Mimi's perfume. She's making spaghetti and garlic bread. It's only Thursday. So much has happened since Monday, when I brought home the lamp. Has it only been four days? The smell is comforting, a tether to normalcy, even when everything else is spiraling out of control.

Mimi walks out into the front room, sharp eyes scanning me from head to toe. "Took you long enough. You look like you've been through hell."

"It wasn't exactly a spa retreat." I drop my bag onto the nearest chair. "Where's Jackie?"

"Upstairs, resting." Mimi pats my shoulder. "She's better than she was, but let's not get ahead of ourselves."

We head into the kitchen, where Bennet and I fill her in on

everything—the ifrit, the swamp witches, Helen's father, and the scrying spell we're planning for tonight. Mimi listens, nodding along, only interrupting to ask occasional questions.

When I finish, she pinches the bridge of her nose.

Kevin thunders down the stairs. "You're back from the swamp. Did you bring me anything? A cursed amulet? A cool dagger? Crocodile skin boots?"

Bennet laughs and rubs Kevin's head. "None of the above. We need some herbs and stones. Will you help me search in the office?"

"I know all the best places to look for rocks."

"Not rocks. Stones, like crystals," Bennet says as they head out of the kitchen.

"What's the difference?"

Their voices retreat up into the house.

Mimi turns to me, lowering her voice. "Did you jump his bones yet?"

"Mimi!" Heat fills my face.

She smacks the table. "You did, didn't you? I hope you did, otherwise you're turning bright red over nothing."

"It's nothing. It meant nothing. I mean, nothing happened. It's just this curse."

"Uh-huh, that's what I said about your uncle too, God rest his soul. Man was an animal in the bedroom though."

I slap my hands over my ears. "I do not want to hear this."

She tsks. "Bennet not much of an animal then?"

My mouth pops open. I force it shut and grind out the words, "I do not know if he's an animal or not because we didn't sleep together."

Her eyebrows lift. "You didn't sleep while you were in the swamp?"

"We slept together but not *together,* together."

She nods. "So you thought about it."

"Yes," I answer without thinking. Wait. "No!"

She laughs.

I groan. "I am not having this conversation with you. I need to go check in on Jackie."

Mimi's laughter follows me up the stairs.

Jackie is in her room, curled up in the chair in the corner with a book.

Her complexion isn't as ghostly pale as before, but lavender shadows pop out like bruises underneath her eyes.

"Hey, you." I cross over and perch on the arm of the chair, placing a gentle hand on her shoulder. "How are you feeling?"

She sets the book face down in her lap. "Better, I think? I was worried about you and Bennet, that something bad might happen to you."

Great. My sleepless anxiety is rubbing off on her. "We're fine."

"That's what Mimi said. Kevin said if something happened to you, he would know."

"He's probably right. I would haunt all of you for eternity."

She smiles.

"Have you been doing the exercises Bennet taught you?"

She nods. "Yes, and I did my schoolwork and I've been eating all my food and drinking lots of water."

I lift my hands in surrender. "Okay, okay."

"You found his sister?"

"Yes."

Her face brightens. "So you can stay home now? It's over?"

"No. Bennet and I are still connected." I give her a much abbreviated, much sanitized version of events.

When I finish, she watches me with dark eyes, so similar to my own. "Is he your boyfriend now?"

My hands flap and I stand. "Are you and Mimi in on this together?"

She lets out a peal of laughter.

I try to hold on to some righteous anger, but she hasn't laughed like this since Mom and Dad disappeared.

My heart clenches in my chest. I bend over and kiss the top of her head. "Keep reading your book, munchkin. I'm going to check on Bennet, make sure Kevin isn't traumatizing him with more reality shows."

I make my way up the stairs, stopping by my room to grab fresh clothes.

Up in the office, Bennet is over by the bookshelves. He opens a small wooden box, sniffs the contents, then sets it back down.

Kevin is in the corner where an old chest sits open, rifling through shoe boxes of stones and leather pouches filled with dried herbs.

"Any luck?"

"We found labradorite and black obsidian," Bennet says.

Kevin squints at the list in his hand. "Still looking for quartz and amethyst."

"We can get the star anise in the kitchen. I know we have an amethyst on one of these shelves." I move over next to Bennet, reaching up to a higher shelf, fingers seeking a jewelry box. It's around here somewhere. "It's an old brooch, Mom kept it around here somewhere."

An object shifts, sliding against the wood above my head, not visible from below. A whisper of movement that makes the hairs on my arms stand up. A corner appears over my head, a box sliding along the very top of the bookcase.

"What the—?"

Then it falls, aiming straight toward my head. I duck.

Bennet, quick as lightning, reaches out and snatches it out of the air before it can knock me in the head.

"Kevin. Did you ask the ghost to help us?" I ask.

He shrugs, standing up and wiping his hands on his jeans. "Maybe."

"Could you maybe have asked for him not to brain me with the object?"

"He can't help where it was."

Bennet opens the jewelry box. It's a butterfly-shaped brooch, the wings lined with amethyst. He holds it up. "That should be everything. Or close enough."

I glance around the office one last time. There's something about being here, going through these things—my parents' things—that makes me painfully aware of their absence.

Bennet must sense it, because he rests a hand on my back, and the tension ebbs.

I inhale deeply and nod. "All right. Let's go see what Helen can do."

TWENTY

The sky is painted in deep shades of violet and umber three hours later as we step into the garden, the last golden slivers of sunlight sinking below the horizon. A crisp autumn breeze stirs the air, carrying the scents of damp earth and charred firewood.

Helen kneels on the cool grass and spreads out her tools on a flat stone nestled between the roots of an oak. She moves with quiet precision, drawing symbols into the dirt with the tip of her finger. A small brass dish rests at the center of her setup, filled with the herbs we helped gather.

She places three crystals around it while Bennet and I settle in the grass in front of her. Delores is at her side.

The air hums with energy as she strikes a match, dropping it into the brass dish. The herbs catch instantly, the smoke rising in slow, curling tendrils, the scent thick and intoxicating.

She presses her hands to the earth. "We'll start in the great hall. Try not to speak. I'll have to concentrate to scry where we wish."

A glow pulses beneath her fingertips, like embers smoldering under the soil. The smoke thickens, coiling toward the stone as if drawn by some invisible tether.

At first, the surface remains dark. Then it ripples and a picture forms, like a projection.

A grand hall comes into view, opulent and glowing. Chandeliers glint overhead, casting warm golden light over long tables dressed for a feast. Laughter echoes from the image. Servers glide past noble guests carrying silver trays.

It's some kind of party, I guess, a scene straight out of *Game of Thrones*, or *Robin Hood: Men in Tights*.

At the far end of the hall, a raised dais dominates the room with four people seated around the head table. One of the occupants—middle aged, dark hair threaded with silver—lifts a goblet in toast. "Thank you all for being here to celebrate the marriage of my beloved niece to Lord Wallace."

Helen's breath catches.

Bennet stiffens beside me.

Two figures step up beside their uncle. A man with Bennet's sharp jaw and calm poise. A woman with Helen's same long dark hair and graceful smile. The crowd erupts in cheers.

Then another man steps into view with broad shoulders, his bearing regal and confident. He takes the false Helen's hand, presses a kiss to her knuckles.

What is going on?

I glance up from the vision to the real Helen. Her face is flushed, her jaw clenched, her eyes flashing with anger.

The image ripples. The view shifts, weaving over the crowd, moving to the fringes of the room and coming to a halt over a servant, red-faced and hauling trays of empty dishes.

The servant hurries out of the great hall and through a maze of narrow passageways and into a giant, bustling kitchen.

Dozens of servants weave around one another in a choreographed frenzy, carrying baskets of herbs, trays of raw meat, and gleaming platters.

Steam hisses from an enormous oven. Is it magic? The burners flare hotter at a snap from a cook and a pot of soup stirs itself lazily near the back, the ladle rotating in slow, deliberate circles under a soft magical glow.

In the opposite corner, scullery maids scrub dishes with rags that dance and wring themselves out.

A harried steward passes into view, holding a list longer than his arm, muttering too low to make out. He's reed thin, balding, and dressed fully in black.

Bennet's head snaps up to stare at Helen.

Without removing her gaze from the vision, she nods.

Bennet looks back down at the image.

The steward grabs a rolling cart ladened with food trays from one of the maids and exits the chaos of the kitchen through another side hall.

We follow, the vision hovering over the bald spot on his head as he moves down the hall, unloading trays as he goes by sliding them into slots in the wall, ringing a bell, and waiting as they lift somewhere out of sight.

Medieval room service?

Finally, there is just one tray left on the bottom of the cart with a small cup of water, a hunk of cheese and bread.

He picks the tray up, leaves the cart behind and carries it through a door, then along more winding corridors, and finally down a narrow flight of stone stairs. Damp stone walls flicker into view.

A heavy iron door creaks open. Inside, chained to the far wall, is a man in a rumpled white tunic. His dark hair is disheveled. His face bruised, but he looks vaguely familiar.

Bennet sucks in breath through his teeth.

The prisoner's voice is hoarse but furious. "Tell your master I'll see him burn for this."

The steward shoves the tray through a slot in the bars and leaves without a word.

The vision pulses again, and we're back in the great hall.

Lord Wallace leans toward the fake Helen, smiling as they prepare for the toast.

Recognition slaps me in the face. The man in the dungeon is Lord Wallace. Who is this guy then? What the hell?

The projection shatters.

A violent burst of wind slams through the garden, sending the crystals skittering across the stone. The smoking herbs snuff out in an instant.

The garden is dead silent. Smoke curls from the remains of the rock.

Helen's fingers dig into Delores's arm as she straightens, her face pale. "Sorry about the dramatics, my magic dried up."

Bennet curses, pushing himself up. "Tell me that wasn't what it looked like."

"It was exactly what it looked like."

"So what does that mean? You two have twins you didn't tell me about?" I guess I make terrible jokes when I'm confused and terrified.

"That was him," she whispers. "That was the real Lord Wallace. In chains."

Bennet braces his hands on his knees. "They imprisoned him. But why? What is the point? And how does Uncle have the power to create three lookalikes that could maintain our likeness so well and for so long?"

Helen lifts a hand. "Assuming that was our uncle at all. What if he was a doppelganger as well? We didn't have time to search the whole castle. Maybe he's in the dungeon too, or gone."

A heavy silence falls. It's like the vision has dropped a boulder on top of all of us.

I stand, wiping my hands on my jeans. "How will we find out?"

Helen looks at Delores, then Bennet, then me. "We have to go to Aetheria. As soon as possible."

Bennet's eyes fall shut a moment. Then he turns to me. "I am sorry I brought you into this."

I put my hand on his arm. "It's okay." He didn't ask for this bond either. "We all have family drama," I tease, but the joke falls flat.

His jaw tightens. "Cassie, your family—"

"They'll be fine." I wave a hand in the air. "I'll call Mimi, make sure the wards are secure and they don't leave unless necessary. They can survive without me while we deal with this. Besides, with us no longer in the mortal world, the threat of ifrits here should be nil."

Delores folds her arms over her chest. "And I'll stay here. I can help your family, watch the house. Keep the kids safe. As Helen's mate, I can be a link back to this world."

Mate? What does that mean?

Helen stares at her. "I want you with me but I don't want you in danger."

Delores steps over to her, takes her hand. "I know. That's why this is the best choice. You can focus on what needs to be done, and I'll be here waiting when you come back to me. We will be able to feel each other, even through the veil."

Helen hesitates, pain flashing across her face, then nods. "Then we leave at first light. When the veil is thinnest."

"And once we're through?" I ask.

Bennet crosses his arms. "We figure out what is truly happening in our kingdom."

"And," Helen adds, "we can find a way to fix your curse so you may return to your family."

Right. That's what all this is about. Splitting the bond. I know this.

Then why does my chest ache like something precious is slipping through my fingers?

I stare at the ceiling.

The guest bedroom is luxurious. Too luxurious. Silk sheets, an absurd number of pillows, and a mattress so soft I sink into it like a cloud. It should be comfortable, but it isn't. I can't sleep.

Maybe it's knowing we're leaving in the morning, stepping straight into danger. Maybe it's the fact that my life has changed so completely in such a short time, and I haven't had a second to catch up. Maybe it's just this stupid, fancy bed.

Anxiety twists low in my gut. We're not planning to walk into a fight. We're just supposed to gather intel, figure out what their uncle is up to, and get out before anyone realizes who we are. But if he's orchestrating a coup, or using dark magic, or been replaced by a pod person, then what happens if we're caught? I huff out a breath and turn onto my side, punching a pillow in frustration. A glance at the clock tells me it's close to midnight. Fantastic.

Shoving off the covers, I slip out of bed. The house is quiet, the kind of quiet that is almost unnatural after a day filled with so many people. I don't even know where I'm going at first until I find myself standing in front of Bennet's door.

This is stupid. I'm stupid. I should go back to bed.

But then my fingers are curling around the doorknob, and before I can talk myself out of it, I push the door open.

The room is dimly lit by the glow of the moon shining in through the window. Bennet is lying on his back, one arm resting over his forehead, his jaw tense even in sleep. His brows pull together, lips parting slightly like he's on the edge of speaking.

I shift, about to turn and leave—

"Cassie?"

I freeze. "Sorry. I didn't mean to wake you."

He pushes himself up onto one elbow, blinking at me. "You didn't. I can't sleep either. What's wrong?"

I shake my head. "Nothing. I just couldn't fall sleep."

He studies me for a moment before scooting back, making space. "Come here then."

I should say no. I should go back to my dumb luxurious bed. Except last night was the best rest I've had in forever, and the man in front of me is most likely the reason I could close my eyes and relax without worry.

I step forward and slide under the covers beside him.

The warmth of his body seeps into mine immediately, cutting through the chill of my skin. I settle on my side, my back to him at first, but it doesn't last long. A moment later, I turn to face him.

He's watching me, his face a smudge in the dim light. "Are you worried about tomorrow?"

"Aren't you?"

He runs a hand through his hair. "Of course." He's quiet for a long moment before his voice drops lower. "I keep wondering why? Why would he do this? If he's behind all this, which seems the most likely explanation. Either that or a doppelganger took his place months ago, which I can't quite believe."

I don't have an answer.

He shakes his head. "My whole life, he was there. I thought he loved me. Protected me. Now I don't know what to think.

He must have been the one to send the ifrit after me. I can't think of any other explanation. I don't understand why."

I hesitate before reaching out, resting my hand over his. "It's not your fault."

"Isn't it? He could have been plotting against us this whole time and I was too blind to see it."

"When your parents died, you were only a child. You had no reason to not trust him. He was the one adult in your life you thought you could rely on. The fact that he broke that trust is on him alone."

His hand turns over, fingers lacing with mine. "Your siblings are lucky they have you."

I swallow a lump in my throat. "I worry I will fail them somehow. That I am failing them. How can I be good enough? I'm not a parent."

"It's obvious how much you care about them. Your love is a blinding light. Anyone can see it. They can too, and that's all that matters. Everything else can be sorted."

I blink. "You make it sound so simple."

"I don't mean to trivialize the loss of your parents."

"No. You're not. I know what you mean. Whatever happened to them, I might never know. I think that's worse than knowing something terrible did happen. The not knowing. I wouldn't be living in this roller coaster of hope and despair and fear and loss and rage."

His hand squeezes mine.

We fall into an easy silence.

But despite the comfort of his presence, my thoughts spiral back to the swamp witches, their strange warning. *The ones you seek are not gone.* What did they mean? Did they know something about my parents? About me?

"What Helen said, about your parents needing a mortal with djinn blood to help," I wave my free hand, "and mortals with magic, they must be part djinn, does that mean I have djinn blood?"

He considers me. "I suppose it must."

So we could make babies together. Got it.

Don't think about having babies while you're inches from Bennet in a bed.

This still can't happen.

We still come from different worlds. I absolutely could never leave my siblings, and obviously, he has some things to work through in Aetheria. We'll figure out what the hell is happening in Aetheria, and then I will go back to my life.

I don't have the rest of my days with Bennet, but I have today. I have right now.

My heart picks up at the thought.

He clears his throat. "Kevin asked me if I was your boyfriend."

"He did?"

"Yes. He mentioned you had a boyfriend before, but he said he was really cringe and had zero aura."

I chuckle. "Yeah, that sounds about right."

"What happened?"

"Nothing." I squeeze his fingers. "I left school, moved back home, when our parents disappeared. He tried to be there for me, but he couldn't handle it. He made excuses over and over, gradually disappearing until he just wasn't there. I haven't even attempted to date anyone since."

"Truly?" His voice is incredulous.

I scoot closer to him. "Truly."

"I've never courted anyone, ever." His thumb rubs the back of my hand.

"Even those ladies at the balls?" I tease.

He shifts a little in my direction. "We only danced and had mindless, generic conversation. Hardly dating as you do it in the mortal realm, half naked and broadcasting to the world on a magic mirror."

I laugh. "Not all dating is like on *Love Island.* You never lie with any of them like this? In the dark, in the same bed, only inches apart?"

His breath stutters. "No." The word is low, rough. Honest.

"Did you kiss any of them?" I whisper.

He swallows. "Um. I may have engaged in a little kissing with one or two of them."

"Really?"

"It meant nothing."

I move so close our lips almost touch, heat building between us. "No portal opened? That's fortunate."

He chuckles, breath fanning over my mouth. "Is it? I quite enjoyed what happened after the portal opened."

"Me too." I lean back, wishing his expression was clearer in the dim light. "Whenever I've lifted my mental shields—like in the basement, in the swamp—all your emotions are just there. Waiting. Do you . . . have your mind locked up?"

He doesn't move. Doesn't speak.

"No," he says finally, and the word is barely audible.

"Why not?"

"Because I want you to be able to feel me," he says, voice hoarse. "Always."

My heart stutters. The air between us crackles, charged and heavy.

"You do?" Why is that such a turn-on?

I trace a finger up his bare arm, trailing along the muscle. Goose bumps rise under my touch. His skin is warm, alive, trembling. He's holding himself back, restraint hardening the line of his body, in the way his breath hitches with every inch my fingers explore.

"I mean, if you want. If you need anything, since you have

your shields engaged, it doesn't matter if—ah, Cassie—" My name comes out on a groan, like he's breaking apart.

This might be the worst idea ever. But here in the quiet, with no magic humming under our skin, no glowing lights or visions or supernatural heat, a whispered truth echoes between us, too heavy to contemplate.

I should be scared. But I'm not.

Maybe it won't be the same without the magic. Maybe it'll be slower, less intense. But maybe it'll be better. More real. Like touching something solid after drifting in a dream.

And if we go into Aetheria tomorrow—if anything happens to him, or to me—if this all falls apart, I want this. I want a memory to take with me when he's long gone.

Because I can't imagine ever being this close to someone again. Not like this.

I take a breath and then a leap. "I want to be with you, now, without magic compelling us. Is that okay?" The words start strong, but grow weak by the end, rising in pitch with uncertainty.

In one smooth motion, he rolls me beneath him, his body caging me in, and then his mouth is on mine, hot, seeking, and perfect.

Everything disappears.

There's no danger, no fear, no looming dawn. There's only this, the heat of his mouth, the weight of his body, the way his hands slide through my hair like he's anchoring himself to me.

I arch into him, desperate to be closer. His kiss deepens, turning hungrier, messier, like he's trying to memorize the shape of me with his mouth.

I thread my fingers through his hair, pulling him tighter. He groans into my mouth, one hand fisting in the sheets as the other traces down my ribs, my waist, my hip, setting my nerves on fire.

His control is unraveling and it's amazing.

The kiss goes on and on until all that exists is his mouth, our breath mingling, his tongue brushing against mine, until we're nipping at each other with barely leashed hunger.

I gasp, and he drinks the sound in like he needs it to survive.

No magic, and still I'm unraveled.

My fingers skate over his shoulders, down his back, and he shudders. His lips trail down my neck, teeth grazing, tongue soothing. Every nerve in my body sparks. I arch into him, desperate for more, and he gives it—grinding against me slowly, deliberately, until I'm gasping into his mouth. Even with clothes between us, I'm about to lose it.

I need more.

"I want to feel you," I whisper. "All of you."

We shift, moving to our knees, clothes vanish in pieces, tossed aside in the dark, and when there's nothing left between us, his eyes strike me again, taking me in. Not just my body, but me. Like every fear, every scar, every wall I've ever built is on display and he accepts it all. Wants it all.

His chest is magnificent and I take the time to graze my fingertips over the moonlit flesh before following with my tongue, moving farther and farther south, gripping the length of him in my palm.

Air hisses between his teeth.

The muscles in his stomach twitch and leap under my hands, his breath coming out in gasps.

Drifting lower, unable to stop myself, I suck the tip of him into my mouth.

He growls. "I want to be in you when I release." He yanks me up and then we're kissing again, drinking each other in.

His hands roam over me, not urgent, but exploring, reverent. His fingertips trace the curve of my waist, the dip of my spine, the inside of my thighs. Everywhere but where I want them.

His mouth moves down my throat, teeth grazing my skin in a way that makes my toes curl.

"I've never—tell me what you like. I want to—I want to make it good for you."

The words hit me harder than any touch.

I guide his hand between my thighs. "Start here."

He follows my direction, tentative at first, then bolder as I arch into him, showing him exactly how to touch me. His mouth finds my breast, tongue flicking over a nipple, and I gasp, threading my fingers into his hair. I fall back onto the soft sheets, tugging him with me.

His forehead rests against mine.

I reach between us, guiding him to me.

"Wait," he pants, lifting his head to meet my eyes. "What about—do we need something?"

"I'm clean. And I'm on the pill."

"Pill?"

"It prevents pregnancy."

"Ah. Lovely mortal world inventions." He kisses my neck. "I have never been with another." The words are a puff of air against my neck, making me shiver.

"Good." Possessiveness burns through me. *Mine.*

He chuckles, as if I spoke aloud.

A smile tugs at my lips and then falls when he sinks into me, inch by aching inch. I cling to him, breathless and burning.

When he's fully inside, buried to the hilt, we both go still.

His breath is ragged. "You feel like—" He breaks off. "Like mine."

Wait. Did he hear—?

And then all thoughts flee as he moves.

Slow at first, deliberate. Like he wants to memorize every

second. I match his rhythm, our hips finding each other in perfect synchronicity. Each thrust sends pleasure coiling tighter inside me, dragging small, broken sounds from both of us.

It builds gradually, unbearably, our bodies slick with heat and sweat, fingers digging in like we're trying to fuse together. His mouth is everywhere, my neck, my collarbone, my lips.

I look up at him, and his face is my undoing. It's shining. Not with lust, but devotion. Awe.

I whisper his name as my climax hits, fierce and consuming. My whole body tightens around him, and I fall apart with a cry that echoes through the dark. He follows with a raw, desperate groan, thrusting deep and shuddering as he loses himself inside me.

He doesn't let go. Not after. He buries his face in my neck, arms wrapped around me like he never wants to let go.

We don't move for a long time.

His weight is half on me, his breath warm against my throat, our legs tangled beneath the blankets. I trail my fingers over the back of his neck, letting them dip into the soft hair at his nape. His pulse flutters under my touch.

Finally, he lifts his head. "Are you all right?"

I nod. "More than all right."

The corner of his mouth twitches like he's fighting a smile. "You're all flushed."

"Which is your fault."

He chuckles, and it rumbles through both of us. His hand comes up, gentle fingers brushing hair back from my cheek. His touch is reverent, careful again. Like he's not sure what the rules are now.

I'm not sure either.

I want to ask what this means. I want to ask if it changes anything. If we'll pretend tomorrow that it was just the magic again. That it didn't matter. But I can't make myself break the moment. Not yet.

So I say nothing.

Instead, I shift closer, press a soft kiss to the underside of his jaw.

"I'm glad it was with you," he whispers. "My first."

We lie there in silence for a while, skin cooling, hearts slowing.

Eventually, he shifts so we're on our sides, facing each other. One of his hands finds mine under the blanket, fingers curling together. He brings them to his lips and kisses the back of mine, then holds it there, against his chest.

"You're thinking," he says, voice low.

"I always think."

"Loudly."

I huff a laugh, then fall quiet again. "What if something bad happens tomorrow?"

His thumb brushes over my knuckles. "Then we'll face it. Together."

My throat tightens. I don't say *what if we don't come back*. I don't say *what if we do come back and then I never see you again*. I nod and press my forehead to his.

We fall asleep like that—tangled together, warm and quiet in the dark.

Tomorrow, we'll step into danger and I'll deal with the fact that we did what we did with no magical excuses.

TWENTY-ONE

When I wake up, Bennet's side of the bed is empty and the sun is just beginning to rise, casting pale light through the window.

I stretch, muscles deliciously sore, and the memories come flooding back—his mouth against mine, the brush of his breath, the heat of his palms on my bare skin.

Yummy.

But also complicated.

I draw the blanket tighter around me, staring at the ceiling as the weight of it settles in. What happened between us last night . . . it was real. And I don't know what to do with that.

I can't pretend it meant nothing, no matter how badly I want to keep things simple. But I'm also not ready to deal with what it might mean. Not when the world is on fire, and everything we're walking into could tear us apart.

We come from different worlds. He's light and power and magic, and I'm just trying to hold the pieces of my life together with duct tape and late-night panic attacks.

And maybe that wouldn't matter if I weren't already cracked open by too much heartache.

I've given up most of my hopes and dreams. College. Travel. Friendships. Sleep. I traded the future I once imagined for an endless parade of school plays, little league practice, and doctor's visits.

My choices haven't been my own since the day my parents disappeared. Until Kevin and Jackie are grown, I don't get to be selfish. I don't get to want things just for myself.

Bennet is amazing. But he's also a prince. A man raised on duty and sacrifice. He didn't hesitate to chase after his sister the second he thought his realm was in trouble. He belongs to his people and his very different world.

I can't live in Aetheria. I can't disappear and leave my siblings behind. No matter how much I want to fall into his arms and never come back up for air, I won't be the reason they lose another parent.

Now, with Bennet, I'm terrified.

Terrified that even if he wants to stay now, something will change or take him from me later. That love, no matter how fierce, isn't enough to make people stay.

Maybe when all this is over, we'll go back to our worlds like nothing happened. Maybe we're just a moment. A beautiful, bright thing that burned fast and hot in the dark.

If that's all this is, I'll take this time and lock it away, and when the fear creeps in, when everything else gets too big, I'll remember the stolen moments we had.

I'll take what we have, and leave the rest.

I shake myself. No time to think sexy—or emotionally destabilizing—thoughts. Time to get moving. Today I take a portal into another world.

Wild times. I'm terrified and yet thrilled. I've always

wanted to see more of the world, and now I get to see an entirely new one.

I pad to the bathroom. Voices travel up the stairs along with the intoxicating scent of brewing coffee. After taking care of bodily functions, I head down the stairs.

Bennet is alone in the kitchen when I enter the room, the others probably packing.

He's leaning against the counter, completely edible in jeans and a tee, his feet bare, his hair still damp from a shower. There's a mug in his hands, and when our eyes meet, his expression softens.

My heart flips.

"Morning."

His voice does weird things to my body, my flesh trembling with memories of hands on me, his gasps in my ear, his mouth devouring mine.

"Morning," I manage.

He crosses the room in a few strides and hands me the second mug. Our fingers brush and then linger. "I didn't mean to wake you."

"You didn't." I wrap my hands around the warmth of the mug, unsure what to say. Last night still clings to my skin, like the imprint of his hands is tattooed onto me.

There's a long beat of silence, but it's not uncomfortable. It's full of all the things we aren't quite ready to say.

"I don't regret it." His eyes are steady on mine.

My heart does a backflip in my chest. I take a sip of coffee. "Me either."

He nods once, then reaches up and tucks a piece of hair behind my ear. "Whatever happens on the other side of that portal, we go together. That's what matters."

I nod and sip more coffee, afraid to open my mouth and let out all the jumbled emotions boiling inside me. I let his hand linger on my cheek for a second longer. And I let myself believe, for now, that this thing between us doesn't have to have a label or a future to be real. It can be what it is.

We finish our coffee and then head upstairs. Packing is quick since we can only bring what we can carry. The portal may or may not open up close to the castle, since the magic here is weak. Even with the tools we gathered, Helen isn't sure exactly where we will end up. It's like throwing an arrow at a map with your eyes closed. Pin the tail on the donkey. Coming here, it was much easier for her to find her destination since the magic in Aetheria is so strong, it was like having a telescope. Now she is going back blind.

Before we leave, I call home. It's still early, but Mimi picks up on the second ring.

"Cassie? Everything okay? How did it go last night?"

I rub a hand over my face and tell her everything that happened. The doppelgangers, the dungeon, all of it—minus the R-rated content.

A sharp breath on the other end. "So what happens now?"

I lean against the dresser, gripping the phone tighter. "We are going to Aetheria."

Mimi is silent for a long minute. "I don't like it."

"I can't be apart from Bennet. It's not like he can go and leave me here. Delores will come stay with you and the kids. Her and Helen are linked. She'll be able to keep you updated as to what's happening."

"Cassie . . ."

I bite my lip. "You're the one who's always telling me I need to live a little."

She chuckles. "I meant travel to New York or date or something, not cross into another realm and get between some maniac and the throne." She releases a gusty sigh. "All right. I'll hold things down here. And Cassie, be careful. I mean it."

Warmth spreads through my chest. "I will."

"Good. Then go kick some djinn ass."

I laugh. "I'll definitely offer moral support while Bennet and Helen do the ass kicking. Love you, Mimi."

"Love you too, kiddo."

By the time we step out into the crisp early morning air, the city is still quiet, just a few early risers moving about. I tug my black cotton jacket tighter around me, the layered weight of my clothes a small comfort—sturdy pants, boots I can run in, and enough layers to handle whatever Aetheria throws at us. We move quickly, keeping our heads down as we make our way through the streets.

The portal location is in an alley tucked behind an old wrought-iron gate. To anyone else, it's merely an abandoned courtyard, overgrown with ivy and half hidden behind the remains of a crumbling archway. But the air hums with magical energy.

This is where Helen and Bennet both came through from Aetheria.

Helen and Delores linger near the entrance.

Bennet and I walk into the center of the courtyard to give them the illusion of privacy, but in the quiet morning air, their conversation is audible.

Delores speaks first. "I don't like this."

"I know."

"Don't you dare die, or I'm coming after you."

Helen laughs, though there's a watery edge to it. "Understood."

When they finally break apart, Delores's gaze flicks to Bennet and me. "Take care of her."

Bennet nods. "We will."

Helen joins us in the center of the courtyard. She kneels, drawing a small vial from her pouch and pouring a shimmering blue powder onto the ground. Then she whispers under her breath, tracing a sigil into the dirt with the tip of her finger.

The air shivers.

A thin sliver of golden light appears in the empty space before us, stretching and widening until it forms a glowing archway. Through it, towering trees with glossy emerald leaves appear through the mist, their trunks wide and spiraled with vines that glisten in the dim light. The scents of blooming flowers and damp earth brushes over me.

Holy shit, magic land.

Helen straightens, shoulders squaring. "It's time."

Bennet steps forward first, glancing back at me. "Ready?"

I take a breath. "As I'll ever be."

And together, we step through the tear in the world, leaving the mortal realm behind.

The second we land on Aetherian soil, the portal snaps shut, the strength of it making me stumble forward.

Bennet reaches for me, grabbing my arm. "Okay?"

I nod. We're surrounded by dense jungle, abundant leaves above blocking the light, dark soil below our feet. The air is thick with moisture and touched with magic, like it's holding an electric charge.

"Where are we? Are we close to the castle?" My pulse is unsteady from the journey through the portal.

Helen shakes out her hands, her face pale, the usual glow of her magic dimmed from the strain of the spell. "We're in the land of the marids. Thalassara."

I blink, my mind rummaging through the information

Bennet told me the other night about Aetheria as I was falling asleep. "Giants? We're in the giant part of djinn land?"

"You can tell by the humidity and the trees. They are bound by water magic. They once ruled vast territories, before the current kingdoms formed." Bennet squeezes my shoulder. "It will be fine. We'll stay quiet and out of sight. The odds of us running into a giant are slim. They sleep during the day."

"And if one of them decides to wake up?"

Helen winces. "It won't be good. They don't like visitors. They think the other kingdoms betrayed them and stole their lands. They see all outsiders as invaders, no matter who they are."

"So they might want to crush us for *historical* reasons?"

"Essentially. We'll be quiet." He glances around at the dense canopy overhead filtering sunlight into shifting emerald patterns on the forest floor. "We need to figure out which way to go. Thalassara is south of our kingdom and it's a two- to three-day hike from their border to our kingdom." He tilts his head back, scanning the thick trees. "I need to see where the sun is to ensure we head in the correct direction."

Without another word, he strides toward the nearest trunk, fingers searching for a handhold as he pulls himself up. He moves swiftly, disappearing overhead.

I turn to Helen. She's catching her breath, her hands on her hips.

"Are you okay?"

A smile touches her lips. "I'll be fine. A little tired, but now that we're back in Aetheria, my magic will replenish itself quickly."

We wait for a minute in silence, catching our breath, and then I ask, "Is it hard to be so far away from Delores?"

Helen's smile turns wistful. "Yes."

I hesitate again before pushing forward. "She said

yesterday she is your mate. Is that how you refer to partners in Aetheria?"

"It's more than a mere partner, it's the other half of one's soul. Mates are rare and sacred. Not every djinn finds theirs."

I absorb that, rolling the idea around in my mind. "So it's like fate or destiny?"

She tilts her head. "Something like that. At first, it's like a pull, a knowing. It's subtle. I didn't even realize who Delores was to me at first, just this strange sense of connection and attraction. But the bond doesn't fully settle until both people accept it."

"Once you knew what you had, you accepted it?"

She nods. "Immediately. I was all in. But Delores took a little longer."

"Why?"

Her brows lift.

I guess I'm being a tad invasive. "If you don't mind me asking," I add.

Helen leans against the rough bark of a tree. "She comes from a humble family. My uncle brought her to our kingdom as a hired companion. And since I was technically her employer, there was this power imbalance she didn't want to cross." She grimaces. "Understandably. And I didn't either. I didn't want to pressure her, or for her to feel beholden, you know? But she makes me happy. And I make her happy. Once I convinced her of that, and she finally accepted the bond, it was like everything made sense. There is no imbalance anymore because we are together in all."

Together in all. I can't imagine what that's like but the thought of that, with Bennet, sends nerves and hope twisting through me. What if Bennet is my mate? But how could I be sure, what with our cursed bond and all that? What if I'm mistaking it for more than it is?

And even if we are mates, what could I do about it? Leave my family behind, leave Mimi on her own with the kids?

Sorry got a hot djinn to mate, byeeeeeee.

The alternative would be to ask him to leave his world behind.

We can't belong to each other. It's impossible.

Even if it was possible, like when the kids are grown, who's to say he would wait that long? I've got the better part of a decade before Kevin is a legal adult, assuming the kids are even ready to be on their own by then.

And yet I can't stop myself from asking, "What does it mean, accepting the bond? How do you even do it?"

Helen's eyes focus somewhere beyond me. "It's hard to describe. It's like opening yourself up completely. Seeing the other person for exactly who they are, and letting them see you. No shields. No fears. No judgment or shame. Only trust and a true understanding. That's when it gets really good." She closes her eyes. "Even now, in another realm, I can feel her. Like a buzz in my chest, letting me know she's okay. When we're together, it's like the rest of the world fades, and nothing else matters."

I don't know what to say to that. It sounds beautiful. But impossible.

Bennet drops down from an overhead branch, landing smoothly a few feet away from us. He points. "This way."

We move through the trees, Bennet in the lead, Helen behind me. Somewhere in the distance, water rushes, maybe a river or waterfall hidden among the dense foliage.

"Do you know about how far we might be?" Helen calls out.

Bennet tosses a glance over his shoulder. "It's hard to say. I believe we are in the middle of the Veilwood somewhere. We can't be too far south because I could not see the Abyssal."

I duck under a branch. "What is the Abyssal?"

"The sea south of Aetheria." Bennet holds back a prickly bush growing into the path for us to pass by.

Helen winds her hair up on top of her head, knotting it. "It definitely feels like Thalassara. This whole kingdom is like walking through water."

Bennet takes position behind me. "There is a town, right outside the forest on the north edge of the border to Zehraya. Depending on how deep we are in the forest, perhaps we can make it there by nightfall. If not, we will find a place to camp."

We lapse into silence, trudging along the path. I want to ask more questions about Aetheria, but I need to save my breath so I can keep up. I should have done more cardio with all my nonexistent free time.

The surroundings are wild and colorful. I focus on putting one foot in front of the other, and absorbing the sights of a whole new freaking world that we're walking through. It's unreal.

Shrubs dotting the path drip pink and purple flowers, kind of like orchids but bigger and bolder. Like orchids on steroids. Some of the trees are tall and twisted with clusters of orange-red flowers, so vivid their branches are on fire.

Strange, luminescent creatures flit between the branches, leaving soft trails of light in their wake, like lightning bugs, but different colors.

Bennet shifts his course. "We should head toward the river and follow the water north. There is a river that goes through the town. This might be it, or it might be a tributary."

We walk. Forever. It's beautiful. But also wet. And exhausting. The underbrush is thick in places, thorny vines and springy moss tangling around our boots.

My calves are screaming by the time we stop for a quick break on a fallen log. Helen passes out our prepacked sandwiches and we eat in silence, grateful for the calories and the stillness.

Then we keep moving.

The trees press in closer, the shadows get darker. And despite the warmth of the sun above us, a chill seeps into the air. My skin prickles.

A bone-rattling thud shakes the ground beneath my feet. Then another.

My stomach drops. "Uh, what was that?"

Bennet's entire body goes rigid, his hand darting out to grip my wrist. "Run."

I don't hesitate. Helen bolts beside me, the three of us crashing through the undergrowth. The rhythmic pounding grows louder, the trees shuddering in time with it. Something huge is moving fast.

A deep bass roar rumbles through the trees. I risk a glance over my shoulder and my blood runs cold.

Giants.

TWENTY-TWO

Kevin had a picture book he loved when he was younger, *Jack and the Beanstalk*. I read it to him every night for months, the pages worn and creased by the time he outgrew it. I had it memorized. I could recite it in my sleep. The giants in the story were bumbling, slow-witted creatures who said *fe-fi-fo-fum* and ate Englishmen.

These marid are not bumbling. They are massive, easily twenty feet tall, their deep blue skin almost blending into the shadows, their eyes glowing like embers in the dim light and glinting with intelligence.

One carries a weapon—a spear as long as a tree trunk— while the other simply clenches its enormous fists.

I stumble over a root, barely managing to keep my footing as Helen grabs my arm, yanking me forward.

One of the giants roars again, a sound that shakes the foliage around us. I don't need a translation to understand the rage in it.

He's hungry and we're dinner.

Ahead, the trees break into a clearing. But as we sprint

toward it—*oh, shit*. There's no ground beyond it. The forest ends at the edge of a steep, rocky drop, a sheer cliff plunging down into a rushing river far below.

I skid to a stop, my breath coming in sharp gasps. "Umm, okay, now what?" Bennet can't use his magic, it's too risky. I can't run if I'm fighting the inevitable wave of magic-induced horniness.

Hysterical laughter bubbles up in my throat. *Keep it together, Cassie.*

Helen turns, eyes flashing. "I have an idea. Buy me a few seconds."

Bennet and I spin to face the oncoming giants. The nearest one raises its spear, aiming right for us. My chest clenches. There's nowhere to run.

A thick mist erupts from the ground, swirling up like a living thing. Helen's magic. The fog coils around the giants, obscuring their vision. They bellow in frustration, their steps faltering.

"Move!" Bennet shouts, pointing downstream, but before we can take off, one of the giants roars and swings a massive arm blindly through the mist. A gust of wind rushes past me as the sheer force of its movement cuts through the air. I barely dodge in time, stumbling backward as my heart slams against my ribs.

A second giant, slightly farther away, growls. The thud of heavy feet shaking the ground approaches. Too close. Too fast. A shadow looms in the mist, a dark mass of muscle and rage.

Then, Bennet moves. Faster than I would have thought possible, he lunges forward. With a flick of his wrist, a knife gleams in his grip. He ducks low, slipping past the giant's flailing arm, and slashes at the tendons behind its ankle. The giant roars in pain, stumbling, its balance momentarily thrown.

Where did he get the knife? Wait. Is that a steak knife? What the hell kind of damage can that do? Did he steal it from Helen's dad's? Could he not have gone for the butcher knife?

"Cassie, go with Helen!" He twists just as the first giant attempts to swipe at him. Bennet vaults onto its arm, using the momentum to propel himself higher. He kicks off its elbow and lands on its back, gripping the thick leather straps that cross its chest.

I stumble after Helen, who's moving downstream, adrenaline pushing me into motion. My feet slam against the forest floor, branches tearing at my arms as we run, but I keep glancing over my shoulder, unable to tear my eyes away from Bennet.

The giant twists, trying to shake him off, but Bennet moves like he was born for this. He climbs up its broad back, positioning himself near its thick neck. Then, with a sharp jerk, he wrenches something free from his belt. Another steak knife.

I would laugh if we weren't about to die.

With a fierce shout, he drives it deep into the giant's shoulder. The creature screams, the sound reverberating through the trees, and its knees buckle for just a second.

That's all Bennet needs. He kicks off, flipping backward and landing in a crouch before sprinting toward us. Behind him, the mist thins, roiling with more giants headed our way.

"This way!" Helen leads us toward the cliff's edge.

I panic. "Helen, what—?"

Bennet secures the knife in his waistband and reaches for me. "Trust me."

Before I can argue, he grabs my waist and jumps.

For a moment, there's nothing but open air and the rush of wind in my ears. The swell of water below rises like a soft, waiting cushion. Instead of hitting the river with bone-breaking force, we sink into it gently, as if dropped into a deep, cool embrace.

I break the surface with a gasp, my heart hammering in my chest.

Helen floats beside me. "Told you I had an idea." She grins, baring her teeth at me.

"You're a psycho."

She laughs.

Bennet pops up next to me, shaking the water from his hair. "Are you okay?" He paddles over, his hands roaming my body like he's searching for wounds.

"I'm good," I tell him. But he doesn't stop checking me over.

"Are you okay?" I push my dripping hair from my face.

He nods and then grabs me, his mouth crushing mine. We slip down into the water for a second and then surge back up.

He tosses me a lopsided grin that does funny things to my heart, and then we paddle together toward the opposite shore.

The giants are somewhere on the cliff above us, their massive forms blurred by the mist, their angry voices rumbling through the trees. But they don't jump. Small favors.

Helen exits the river onto a sandy bank where sun cuts through the trees. "It's going to take forever to dry off in this humidity." She shrugs out of her sopping jacket, wringing the fabric and squeezing water into the sand.

Bennet wades toward her and I follow him onto the bank.

"Let's get as dry as we can and then keep moving," he says.

We spend a few hurried minutes attempting to compress the water from our outer layers of clothes and dump the liquid from our packs. Thankfully the food is all still edible since most of it is in baggies and airtight containers.

Now is not the time to be checking out the muscles flexing

in Bennet's back as he tugs his wet shirt over his head and the sun glances off the dips and curves of his body.

Dammit, he's way too hot for me.

Helen smirks at me. "Catching flies, Cassie?"

I snap my mouth shut and get to work squeezing water out of my outer layers.

Once we are somewhat dry, Bennet squints up at the sky and then points. "This way."

Then there's more endless walking.

I lose track of time. Once the adrenaline from the giants and our cliff diving wears off, I'm trudging forward on legs that have turned to lead, and muscles that are little more than mush.

"Let's stop here for the night." Bennet gestures to a small clearing tucked behind a thicket of brush.

Helen recites a quick incantation, fingers sketching protective runes into the dirt around our camp. The spell settles over us like a weighted blanket.

She sinks to the ground beside a semicircle of stones and conjures a fire with a flick of her fingers. The flames bloom to life, crackling and golden.

Convenient. No need to worry about wet matches.

Bennet pulls out two sleeping bags from his pack, rolling them out near the fire and zipping them together before tossing another to Helen. "You set up a ward?"

She nods. "We should all be able to get rest. If any giants come within fifty feet, we'll hear them, and even if we don't, the protection spell will keep us hidden."

I drop my pack and collapse beside it, letting the warmth of the fire melt some of the tension in my shoulders.

We eat some fruit and bread we packed, passing around a canteen of water. No one talks much. The silence isn't uncomfortable. It's heavy, but shared, the same weight of exhaustion pushing down on us all. Tomorrow, we go deeper. Tomorrow, things get even harder. But tonight, we're safe. Or as safe as we can be.

After we eat, I crawl onto the sleeping bag, thankful Bennet assumed we would sleep together. I don't want to be apart from him. I make room for him.

He lies down beside me, his body radiating heat. There's a careful pause before he settles his arm around my waist, pulling me back against his chest. "I'll wake you if anything happens. And I'll protect you from any creatures with wicked gleams in their eyes, even if they are smaller than the merest pebble."

I chuckle. "My hero."

"Yes." His thumb brushes slow circles at my hip, relaxing me.

Across the fire, Helen curls up on her side, one hand resting over her chest. The flames cast dancing shadows over her face.

She must really miss Delores.

And then sleep takes me, slow and deep, wrapped in warmth and exhaustion and the quiet understanding that this might be the last peaceful night we get together.

TWENTY-THREE

I wake to dwindling smoke and the distant hush of birdsong.

The fire's burned down to glowing embers, casting soft light through the thinning mist. My back is warm, pressed against Bennet's chest.

His arm is draped over my waist, fingers splayed across my ribs like he's afraid I'll slip away.

I don't move.

Not yet.

Because I know the second I do, the illusion will shatter. We'll be back in Aetheria, fugitives sneaking through foreign woods, hunted by giants and goddess knows what else.

But here, in this flickering space between dreams and daylight, I can pretend.

Pretend I'm not scared out of my mind. Pretend I'm not starting to want things I have no right to want.

His breath stirs the hair at the nape of my neck. Slow. Steady.

Helen stands. "Morning."

I move away from Bennet and stretch, rolling my shoulders

and trying to shake off the fog in my head. Bennet stirs behind me but doesn't wake.

"We should move soon." She disappears behind some trees, presumably to take care of morning business.

I turn back to Bennet. I don't want to wake him. He's so peaceful in sleep. But Helen's right. It's best not to linger.

As if he can hear my thoughts, his eyes blink open. "Hey." His smile is sleepy.

My heart jerks in my chest at the warmth in his face. I lean over and brush my lips against the expression, wanting to hold on to it.

I draw back but his hands come up, locking me in place, deepening the kiss.

"Okay, lovebirds. Let's get going."

We break apart.

After a quick breakfast of granola bars and dried fruit, we continue our trek.

The morning sun filters through the dense canopy, casting fractured beams across the forest floor. The air is thick with the scent of damp earth and moss, every breath heavy and green. Our footsteps crunch on the loamy path, and distant animal calls echo through the trees.

My muscles ache from the relentless hiking and a night on the unforgiving ground, but I push on, falling into step behind Bennet and Helen.

I should be focusing on the path ahead, the mission, the dangers, but instead I keep replaying his voice from the other night, low and breathless in my ear.

And goddess help me, I want it again.

I'd convinced myself this thing between us couldn't be real. That it had to be the magic, proximity, shared trauma, anything but actual affection. But I'm not sure I can pretend anymore.

Maybe he's worth it. Worth the fear, the risk, the uncertainty.

Worth giving up everything I know.

And then reality slaps me in the face. I have the kids. And Mimi. Like I can just pack up my life and move to a magical kingdom in another dimension.

Sure, Jan.

We walk on, and on, and then something shifts. The air thickens, presses in. A prickling sensation crawls up the back of my neck. My shoulders tighten. It's like walking through invisible static, every nerve on high alert.

I stop in my tracks. Please, no more giants.

Pressure builds between my shoulder blades.

I drop the shield around my mind like a curtain falling, reaching instinctively. *Bennet?*

He halts and then whips around, leaping toward me.

A blast of heat sears past my shoulder and I instinctively flinch away.

He yanks me down, Helen diving to the ground right next to us as a lightning bolt explodes against the nearest tree, sending burning bark and embers scattering over our heads, stinging my exposed skin.

Okay. Not giants.

They emerge from the shadows, living smoke and flames, their skin flickering between red and black and molten gold. There are five of them, circling us like predators.

Definitely freakier than the shadows they manifested back home. And more solid.

I scramble up, heart hammering.

Bennet steps between me and the advancing ifrit. Helen's hands glow with gathering power.

One of the ifrit lunges.

Bennet meets it head-on. He ducks the first swing of burning flames.

Helen chucks magic at the creature, slicing across its arm, dark liquid sizzling as it drips to the ground. The ifrit hisses, and another rushes in from the side.

Helen throws up a shimmering barrier just in time. The ifrit's lightning collides with the shield, sending cracks skittering across its surface before the magic disperses. She lets out a strangled breath, sweat beading at her temple.

Bennet distracts them, dodging and parrying like a whirlwind, his limbs a blur. Helen uses his distraction to throw more magic at them, but they recover like it's nothing, like Bennet and Helen are angry kittens and they are, well, beings of fire and smoke.

And I just stand there.

Shit, shit, shit. How do you fight a thundercloud with fists that have never thrown a punch?

They're made of fire and smoke and rage. And I'm just a rando human with a magic I can't use. I'm going to get them killed because I have no idea what I'm doing and never trained as a ninja. I should have taken that self-defense class.

They move closer and closer.

No exits. No options.

I press against Helen, both of us backing up as Bennet stumbles to regain his footing. We're out of time.

The ifrit raise their hands in unison, fire blooming in their palms, ready to burn us alive.

And then—

An arrow slices through the air.

It buries itself deep in the ground inches from the lead ifrit's foot, quivering with the force of its impact. Purple magic smokes from the arrow, and when it comes into contact with the ifrit, they hiss as one.

Another smoking arrow flies. Then another.

The ifrit freeze. Their heads snap toward the trees.

Figures drop from the branches with impossible grace, their faces obscured by scarves and hoods. They move fast, loosing arrows and blades in fluid motions.

One of the ifrit snarls, twisting to launch a lightning bolt, but a shimmering wall of magic absorbs the attack, swallowing the flames before they reach us.

The ifrit hesitate.

More figures step into view, surrounding them.

With a final, frustrated snarl, they vanish in a burst of flame.

The moment stretches, thick with tension.

My breath rasps in my throat as I take in our rescuers—cloaked, weapons drawn, their faces hidden. One of them steps forward, her movements familiar in a way that knocks the breath from my lungs.

She lifts a hand, yanking down her scarf.

And the world tilts.

"Mom?"

TWENTY-FOUR

"Cassie."

Everything narrows to the woman standing a few feet away.

Alive. Here.

What the fuck?

I can't move. Can't breathe.

And then another figure steps up next to her, pulling his hood down.

Dad.

My brain is shrouded in fog. The adrenaline from the fight and now the shock of my parents, here, in Aetheria, not dead, but alive and here? In Aetheria? Am I dreaming?

How did they find us? The answer slaps me in the face. Dad. I look at him. "You felt me come through the portal."

His gaze locks on to mine. "I knew you would figure out where we were."

I don't know what to say. I didn't figure anything out. This is all happenstance, isn't it?

The weight of years of questions, of pain, of missing them slams into me at once.

Mom steps forward and I'm in her arms.

Her scent wraps around me. Like the warm hugs after nightmares, the way she'd tuck me under her chin and hum softly until I drifted off again. Like the afternoons she spent brushing my hair, untangling knots with infinite patience while telling me stories about the magic in my blood. Like home.

My chest tightens. It's too much. It's not enough.

I grip her tighter, my fingers fisting into the fabric of her tunic as if she might disappear again if I let go.

And then—*Dad.*

More gray than black has taken over his dark hair, and half his face is covered in a thick beard. I barely recognized him. But his arms wrap around us both, solid and strong, just as they always were. His hand cups the back of my head.

Time blurs. Seconds, minutes—hours. None of it matters.

Finally, I pull myself together enough to let go, my face damp with tears.

Mom cups my cheeks, her thumbs swiping over my wet cheeks. Her own gaze is shining. "We have much to talk about."

I look around at the people with them.

"These are our friends," Dad says. "People like us, trapped here or needing a safe place to stay. Some human, some djinn."

"This is Bennet and Helen." I gesture behind me. "And these are my parents, Dan and Blair." I'm too dazed to elaborate further.

Mom squeezes my shoulder and then gestures toward the trees. "Come. We have a safe place. We can talk more once we get there."

We follow them deeper into the forest.

Bennet takes my hand and squeezes. Numb with shock, I grip him back like he's the only thing tethering me to the earth.

These are our friends. People like us, trapped here. The words snag in my mind, catching like thorns.

How did they get trapped here? Why haven't they tried to get back to our world, or have they? Did they come here on purpose? Why? Did they know about Aetheria and djinn—that we are potentially related to djinn, even? Why didn't they ever tell me?

After endless minutes of walking through the trees, we stop. Mom chants, and then the forest in front of us wavers, like an image flickering in and out of focus.

Once the whole group moves forward ten feet, she chants again and the forest trembles behind us.

Mom. She's created a null space, devoid of magic, to mask the area.

We keep going and within minutes, an entire treetop village appears before us, tucked within the forest overhead.

The canopies are laced with suspended walkways weaving through the branches. Houses nestle in the crooks of enormous trees, their walls built from carefully joined wood, their roofs lined with woven leaves and moss.

Water trickles through a cleverly designed system, flowing from the canopy into carved basins, filtering down through the layers of the village. Bridges arc between treehouses, some swinging in the wind, others solid enough for multiple people to walk across.

It's incredible. A world suspended above the ground.

We climb up into the nearest treetop via a solid ladder with rope supports and then Mom leads us to one of the treehouses, its entrance framed by draping vines and the soft glow of enchanted lanterns.

She pushes open the wooden door. Inside is a cozy interior

with polished floors and woven rugs. There's even a small bathroom tucked into one corner, and the scent of fresh herbs lingers in the air.

"Get settled, take a breath. Then come to the main cabin. It's where we keep the kitchens and shared spaces. You can't miss it, it's right in the center. We'll eat. And talk." Then she leaves.

In a daze, I turn to Bennet. He opens his arms and I step into him.

Helen slips past us into one of the bedrooms.

He wraps me up in the warmth of his embrace and I take a full breath for the first time in hours.

I don't know how long we stand there, wrapped in each other while I draw on the strength of his arms around me.

Eventually, we break apart.

"Are you okay?" His eyes search mine.

I take a deep breath. "I will be."

The shock has started to ebb and curiosity has surged in its place.

He takes my pack from my back. "Come. Let's clean up and then go get some answers."

Thirty minutes later, Helen, Bennet, and I enter the main cabin. Wooden beams stretch overhead, crisscrossed with vines weaving through the structure. Lanterns hang at varying heights, unlit since sunlight steams in through open, glassless windows.

Long wooden tables line the space, worn smooth from years of use, their surfaces cluttered with bowls and platters of food. People sit together, talking in quiet, easy conversation, sharing meals like one large family.

Mom leads us toward a round table in the corner, slightly apart from the others for a semblance of privacy. Dad gestures for us to sit as he grabs a clay pitcher of water, pouring it into carved wooden cups.

The scent of cooked meat, roasted vegetables, and fresh bread fills the air, making my stomach throb with hunger.

"Eat something first. Then we talk."

I don't argue. I grab a plate, loading it with whatever is closest—a spiced grain dish, slices of some kind of roasted root vegetable, chunks of seared meat. Bennet and Helen do the same, and for a few minutes, conversation fades in favor of eating.

Finally, when our plates are nearly empty and my stomach is no longer an aching pit, Mom clears her throat. "Tell us everything. The kids. Are they okay? Kevin? Jackie? Mimi?"

I should have thought to tell them right away. They must be so worried, as worried as we've been about them. "They're all okay. Mimi is with the kids now. They miss you, but they are both doing well. Kevin is playing little league. Jackie is . . . she's still sick. But I think she's getting better."

Mom's eyes widen. "She's better?"

Dad looks over at her, then back at me. "We came to Aetheria hoping to find a cure."

My hand clenches around my fork. "You knew. You knew she had magic and it was making her sick."

Mom presses her lips into a line. "We didn't know for sure, but we suspected. Her sickness wasn't normal, not in the way the doctors thought. We could sense the magic in her, but something was wrong with it. We needed answers."

Dad covers her hand with his. "Richard helped us come here. He believed Jackie's condition was connected to our bloodline."

Because we must have djinn blood to have magic.

Mom leans into Dad, their shoulders touching. "He helped us find a tether to Aetheria. He warned us it wasn't stable, said we'd have only one shot to return."

Richard knew? This whole time? That ass-face. Why didn't he ever say anything? Ugh, I could kill him. If he tells me something blasé like *you never asked*, I absolutely *will* kill him.

"Then it didn't work," Dad continues. "We didn't mean to vanish without a word. The window to act came fast and we barely made it with mere seconds to spare. There was no time to explain. We thought it would be fine. It was just a scouting trip. In and out. But we ended up stranded. The tether snapped before we could return. We tried everything. We searched for ways back, but nothing worked."

Mom picks up the story. "We didn't know what to do. But then Rebecca found us." She tilts her head at a tall woman with short blonde hair sitting at a table nearby. "She takes in strays. Most of the people here are refugees from the borderlands, cast out of their kingdoms or caught in the middle of conflicts. We help each other survive. But we've been so worried about Jackie too, about her condition progressing, about all of you not knowing where we were."

I tap my finger on the edge of my plate. I don't know how to deal with all this information. I can't believe they didn't tell me. No time for a quick text to let me know they're fleeing to another realm? They were crunched for time and stressed, but the past three years of my life were spent wondering what if, and what if that could have been avoided? "Bennet figured out what may be wrong with Jackie. Bennet taught her how to redirect the energy, how to draw power from outside instead of within. We think it's working, but it's only been a couple of days."

Mom presses her hand against her mouth.

"All these years I have been worrying." My voice is thick. "Wondering if you were dead, or if you'd just left."

"We never stopped trying, sweetheart." She blinks back tears. "We couldn't get back."

Emotion swirls through me, thick and tangled. Relief. Grief. The sharp ache of time lost. "It's okay. We found each other. And we're not leaving without you. Helen can open a portal to help all of us get back. Kevin, Jackie, Mimi, they're going to be so happy."

"But first," Helen says carefully, "we've got some problems to solve."

Mom and Dad straighten.

"What kind of problems?" Dad asks.

I take a deep breath and launch into the story—how I bought the lamp from Ernie with Bennet inside, how the curse bound us together, the failed attempts to break it, and how we found Helen in the mortal world.

Helen picks up from there, detailing her uncle's attempts to trap them, their roles in Aetheria's court, and what we saw scrying: the doppelgängers, the real Lord Wallace imprisoned, and a wedding being orchestrated with someone pretending to be Helen.

"So we had to come," I finish. "We need to find out what their uncle's endgame is. Why fake a marriage between two imposters? What's he planning?"

Dad twists around, scanning the room. "We need Darius."

Bennet leans forward in his seat. "Who is Darius?"

A chair at a nearby table scrapes back.

One of the men—broad-shouldered, with sand-colored hair and intense golden eyes—rises to his feet.

Mom motions him over. "Can you tell our guests about Dominic? It's important."

He stands at the head of our table. "Dominic is my brother.

I was recently in your uncle's court, visiting as a delegate of my kingdom. A few months ago, I discovered Lord Hugh was working with ifrit. When I threatened to expose him, he had me marked for death. I escaped. My brother didn't. He is still there. We have been making plans to rescue him."

Helen pales. "You're saying Uncle Hugh is colluding with ifrit?"

Darius nods. "I overheard his plans. He is offering them power and freedom and what they've always wanted, land of their own in Aetheria. I don't know what his final move is, but ifrit are involved, that much is certain."

A cold knot tightens in my chest.

Bennet frowns. "Could it be ifrit posing as us? They can change form, but I've never known them to have enough magic to mimic one of us so perfectly for a considerable length of time. It would require tremendous power. Is it even possible?"

Darius shifts closer. "He has the Ring of Solomon."

Helen's mouth goes slack. "What? How? It's *real*?"

"We aren't sure how he obtained it." Darius rubs his chin. "Only that he's using it with the ifrit, to control them, give them power and enhance his own magic."

Mimi did say myths often come from twisted kernels of truth. But this sounds like a heck of a lot more than a kernel, if Hugh is using it to control a whole *people*.

Mom leans forward in her seat. "We've suspected the ring has been in play for months now. Conflict has been brewing with the ifrit for years, but recently it's been escalating, and their powers increasing. We've been searching for ways to weaken its influence and rescuing as many people as we can caught in the ifrit attacks."

Helen's voice hardens. "So Uncle has the ring. But what does he gain by marrying two ifrit posing as me and Lord Wallace?"

No one has an answer. Silence fills the space.

Helen's foot taps against the wood floor. "Maybe, if an ifrit is put in my place, in my name, they could change the laws of the land."

"That could be it," Bennet says grimly. "He's not just replacing us. He's selling Aetheria to the ifrit. But we still don't know *why* Uncle would do such a thing. Why steal the kingdom only to give it away?"

Helen rises to her feet. "It doesn't matter. We have to expose the fakes. We need a plan. We need to retrieve the Ring of Solomon and expose Uncle before the wedding."

Dad nods slowly. "We've been working on a way to sneak into the castle and save Dominic. It's heavily guarded."

Bennet clears his throat. "I can help with that."

TWENTY-FIVE

An hour later, we huddle around a makeshift map, a sketch Helen and Bennet drew from memory. Tunnels, passageways, and guard patrol routes snake across the parchment in charcoal lines. Darius stands beside my dad, his arms crossed over his chest as they quietly argue about the timing of the distraction.

They've been working on setting up a portal just beyond the border of their camp that will open in the forest near the castle. It's been in the works for weeks now. Darius created the gateway, but he isn't as strong as Helen and he had to store up the magic on the site a bit at a time. It's been ready for a few days, but they haven't finished their plans for infiltrating the dungeon because they didn't know all the routes and passages.

"We'll draw the guards from the wall out front," Dad says. "Start the fires here and here." He jabs at two spots along the outer wall. "Gives you a ten-minute window before reinforcements circle back."

Helen nods. "That should get us inside the west wing."

"We'll need to be fast." Bennet crosses his arms over his chest. "Once we're in, if we run into any guards, I can help. I know their routines."

"We'll get in, find Dominic, and locate the Ring," Helen says. "We have to go tonight. When it's full dark. We can't wait. We're running out of time."

"Agreed." Dad scratches his beard. "Everyone, go get some rest. We leave an hour past sunset."

Mom wraps an arm around my shoulder while the others file out. "I don't like you going in there."

"I have to. Bennet and I can't be too far apart." Unless we want to contort in agony.

She squeezes me once and then releases me, Dad swooping in to give me a hug too. We all make our goodbyes before heading back toward the treehouse.

Bennet falls into place beside me. He doesn't say anything, just catches my hand and laces our fingers together. Helen follows us, then disappears into her room, shutting the woven door without a word.

The bedroom where we placed our bags earlier is barely big enough for the bed. The frame is carved from smooth, pale branches, knotted with bark in places. Woven ivy and old cloth banners are draped above like a canopy. The mattress is some kind of soft, worn linen.

Bennet shrugs off his cloak, setting it on the foot of the bed, then looks at me with that careful intensity he saves just for me. "You should rest."

I nod. Without words, we both undress, shrugging out of everything but our underthings.

It's not long before we're lying like spoons, his arms around me, warmth seeping into my skin like it belongs there.

For a while, we're quiet. Listening to each other breathe.

His hand tightens around my waist. "I think I know why Helen was unable to break our bond, and why it keeps growing stronger."

I turn my head, our noses almost brushing. "The curse?"

"Not just the curse." He pauses. "I think it's more than that. It's us. You and me."

My heart thumps a little harder. "What do you mean?"

He's quiet for a moment. Choosing his words. "Djinn have a concept. Fated mates."

My heart picks up speed. "Helen told me. She and Delores are mates."

"Right. Someone your power recognizes before your mind does. Someone you're drawn to so fiercely, you can't stay away. I think the curse mixed with our bond, and that could be why we have the added side effect of . . . extreme excitement when we use our magic. That isn't normal with mates."

I turn my head to stare at the wall, the knotted wood patterns. "And you think that's what we are?"

"I know it is." The words are raw. Honest.

"How do you know?" I've wished it was true and hoped it was not in equal measure. I want Bennet to be mine, but I'm terrified at the same time. Fated mates sounds entirely too big, daunting, unreal. "What if it's just the curse?"

"It must be more than that. I've suspected from the start. Since you threatened me with the bat and I first caught a whiff of your scent." His nose brushes against the back of my neck. "You smell like you belong to me. That is no curse."

Mine.

The same word that wouldn't leave me alone when I found the lamp.

It's impossible to believe. It's impossible to refute.

"It would explain why we are so drawn to each other when

our shields are down and use our magic together," Bennet continues.

"Drawn to each other is one way to put it. We're like sex maniacs."

His arms tighten around me. "Then there was the portal in the cemetery."

"What about it?"

"The twin flames etched into the stone. The two flames represent a single soul split into two physical bodies."

And when we kissed, the portal opened. "Why didn't you say anything before?"

He chuckles. "Because I knew you'd panic."

Fair enough. Even now, my heart is about to pound out of my chest and my palms are sweating. I would bolt for the door if there was somewhere to actually run to other than a wild forest full of giants, ifrit, and evil uncles.

His fingers brush against the curve of my waist. "The curse bonded our magic together, but it didn't make this. It got tangled with it. Twisted the threads. That's why it acts up every time we use power together. That's why Helen couldn't undo it. She's trying to separate something that isn't just a spell."

I squeeze my eyes closed. "And how do we fix it?"

His lips brush against my nape, a whisper of a kiss. "You have to accept the mate bond. That might untangle what the curse fed off of. Your magic would settle. Mine too."

I can't breathe for a second, the truth pressing against my ribs, heavy and undeniable.

The curse can be broken, but only if I bind myself to him in a different way. Bound as chosen, fated mates instead of cursed with proximity.

Accepting the bond would give us the freedom to be apart, to live without agony, but it would also mean being tethered for life. Like marriage, only there's no possibility of divorce. No walking away. No loopholes. No escape hatch.

It's everything I want. And it still terrifies me.

"I care about you, Bennet. It's not that I don't—"

"I know," he says, quietly. "I'm not asking for anything from you. Just please consider it."

I close my eyes and focus on the warmth of him around me. I can't ignore the pulse in my chest that always beats faster when he's near. All the times he's protected me. Made me laugh. Let me fall apart.

"I'm scared," I admit.

"I know." He reaches down and tangles our fingers again. "But I'm not. I've already accepted you. That's why I never bothered putting up shields. I wanted you to feel everything. To know I wasn't hiding from this. From us."

Tears sting behind my eyes. I roll over to face him, resting my forehead against his. "You're an idiot."

"Your idiot."

I let out a shaky laugh.

And then we're kissing. It's slow, and sweet, and gentle.

The hum of magic between us is like the air right before lightning strikes. But it's not our magic, it's us. This thing between us flaring to life. Powerful. Undeniable.

His fingers slide up my spine as if memorizing me, every motion careful and full of wonder. We take off the rest of our clothes slowly, like this isn't a stolen night. Like maybe, for a little while, we're not two cursed souls about to fight for a kingdom, we're only Cassie and Bennet.

We make love quietly, wrapped in the hush of leaves and the soft rustle of ivy. His breath is warm against my neck, his heartbeat thudding in sync with mine. There's no rush. Just us —his hands, my lips, the electricity between our skin.

Release finds us both rolling first through me and then him

like a wave of thunder, brutal, intense, and crushing in intensity.

When it's over, we don't speak. We hold each other. My head rests against his chest. His hand settles over my back.

A calm certainty spreads through me. Like maybe, just maybe, it will all be okay.

TWENTY-SIX

The castle rises ahead, shrouded in clouds, dark towers looming under the moonlight. Magical lanterns glint through the fog, illuminating windows and parapets.

It's giving Dracula vibes.

I still don't know what to think about Bennet's mate revelation earlier. And I don't have time to sit and process it. I have to focus, stay close to Bennet and Helen, and try not to get in the way. Or killed.

We crouch low behind the ridge.

Damp moss soaks through my pants, breath fogging in the chill.

The plan is for Darius to free his brother and Lord Wallace, while Bennet, Helen and I go in search of the Ring of Solomon, since they are the most familiar with the layout of the castle and their uncle's rooms.

The rest of our group is spread out around outside the castle, about to set off a distraction.

There are no guards outside the door we plan to infiltrate,

which leads into the cellar. The guards are positioned between the cellar and the kitchen.

But we won't need to go through the kitchens, because there is a secret passageway within the cellar. It's how Helen has snuck out, many times, apparently.

Darius checks his pocket watch and then motions for us to move.

We sneak through shadows, beneath the cover of trees, and then into the dark pockets of the castle walls. Helen leads the way, graceful and silent. Darius handles the lock, and we slip through the servants' entrance into darkness.

The cellar is cold and musty. My boots scuff against the uneven floor as Helen leads us to a shelf tucked along the far wall.

She fiddles with one of the wooden slats, and with a soft click, the wall shifts. Stone grinds against stone as a section slides open, revealing a narrow, hidden passage.

We slip through the opening one by one. Helen closes it behind us, then snaps her fingers. A golden flame sparks to life in her palm, casting flickering light over the close, shadowed walls. "This way."

We follow her through the winding maze, the air growing cooler and more oppressive the deeper we go.

At a fork in the path, Helen nods toward a branching corridor. "The dungeons."

Darius peels off without a word, the shadows swallowing him whole as he disappears down the dark hall.

The three of us continue on, up a set of stone stairs, through dusty passages. Every creak and distant tap sends my heart into overdrive.

The passageway tightens as we head up and into the wing where the bedrooms are, forcing us to walk single-file and ease our steps to avoid banging into the surrounding walls.

Lord Hugh will be keeping the ring close. We don't know where he will be, somewhere in the castle, maybe asleep in his bed, but we have to start somewhere and his room is the most obvious place.

If he is sleeping, Helen plans to spell him into a deeper slumber while we search his room—and his fingers. If he's not there, she'll keep watch while we locate the ring with our magic.

Helen stops, motioning for us to wait while she eases open a slender door and slips through into a dark bedroom.

We hold still, barely breathing.

A long moment passes. Then another.

She peeks her head back out and shakes her head. No Hugh. That means it's our turn. We go inside, leaving her in the corridor.

The bedroom is huge and empty. Heavy velvet curtains block the moonlight, and the fireplace is cold.

Bennet takes my hand. "Let's find it."

I nod and reach inward, calling on the thread between us. As always, the magic rushes to meet me—but it's stronger when we're together, sharper edged, like a current flaring with contact and heat and want. I focus through the arousal, drawing on my gift.

A golden thread unfurls in my mind. I follow it, tracing the magic signature: ancient, searing, unbearably bright. A flash behind my eyes, a pulse in my chest. The ring is close.

"It's here," I whisper. "Not in the room, though, but near. It's moving."

Bennet inhales sharply. "He's coming."

I stiffen, eyes wide.

We both spin toward the door—too late.

"I wondered how long it would take you."

I whirl around.

From the shadows, a figure steps forward holding a lantern.

Hugh.

I knew those shadows weren't right.

His white beard is neatly trimmed, his fine robes dark as wine, gleaming with gold thread. His eyes glow faintly in the low light. With stolen magic?

Helen stiffens. "How—?"

"I have more magic than you and your brother combined now, and eyes everywhere. Not to mention, of course, the curse." His gaze lands on Bennet and me. "It's practically a beacon. I picked it up the moment you stepped into the lower halls."

Bennet steps in front of me.

Hugh tuts. "Ah, young love. Messy, isn't it? But also useful."

With a flick of his fingers, half a dozen guards emerge from behind him. Armed.

We're surrounded.

Helen lifts her hands, but before she can use her magic, another spell pulses from Hugh's hand, an invisible force that flings her back against the far wall.

She crumples with a cry.

"Helen!" Bennet moves toward her, but two guards block his path.

"Don't worry. She's not dead. As for the rest of you, well." His eyes land on me. "Let's test the strength of the bond between you, shall we?"

Cold panic floods through me.

Bennet growls low in his throat, but then another invisible force strikes him square in the chest, dropping him to his knees.

"No," I gasp.

A guard yanks me back.

"Lock them up. Keep them separate."

"No!" I struggle, but it's no use. The guards squeeze my arms behind my back with bruising force.

I catch one last glimpse of Bennet's face, twisted with concern, before we're dragged in opposite directions.

Before the door slams shut, Hugh's voice echoes off the stone. "You should've stayed away."

Pain.

It envelops me in cold arms, invades my lungs, infiltrates my pores. It coils around my bones like barbed wire. There's no thought, just the violent, pulsing ache of absence.

I can't breathe. The walls press in, slick with damp. Am I in a cage? It doesn't matter. My own body is the cage now. Every nerve is scrubbed raw, every beat of my heart like a scream.

I don't know where I am. Only that I'm alone.

Time ceases to have meaning. All I know is throbbing agony.

Somewhere, beneath the agony, a whisper stirs. A warmth. Distant. Familiar.

Bennet.

No words, just a sense. A steady presence I didn't know I'd come to rely on. That I've *always* known, in some impossible, terrifying, beautiful way.

Cassie.

I gasp. The pain lurches, then sharpens. My body curls forward on instinct, but then like a flare in the dark, his magic brushes mine like an outstretched hand.

But it's weak. Flickering.

He's hurting too.

"I'm here," I whisper, not sure if I'm speaking out loud or in my head. "I'm here, I'm here."

You have to choose, a voice whispers in the back of my mind. It's not Bennet's voice, it's mine.

Seriously, is it that hard? Oh no, some super-hot genie prince who's great in bed loves me and wants to treat me like his queen for the rest of my life. The voice huffs. *Don't be a dumbass.*

"I don't know how." I somehow manage to grit the words out.

Yes, you do. Stop talking to yourself and do it.

The voice is right. I do know. It's like falling, but the kind where you let go of the edge because you want to. Because you know what's waiting at the bottom isn't a crash. It's him.

I think about everything he is. Not just the danger and mystery. But the way he looks at me like I'm fire and starlight. The way he held me. The way he told me I was his mate like it was both a truth and a vow.

I choose you, I say in my mind. *Bennet, I choose you.*

The bond snaps into place like a door slamming shut and then flinging open.

Magic floods my limbs, hot and wild—but clean. No backlash. No pain. Like a river finally running the right course. Our magic is ours now, aligned. Whole.

And with it, his thoughts and emotions flow into mine.

It's like touching sunlight for the first time. My body still trembles from the pain, but it's fading fast, burned away by the heat of something older and deeper. The moment our magic clicks into place his presence brushes against every corner of my mind. Warm, steady, furious, and tender.

And I know he's getting everything pouring out of me too—the ache, the confusion, the need, the part of me that wants to collapse into him and never let go.

We're really here. Together.

The pain is gone.

I choke on a laugh-sob, half joy, half relief, tears stinging my eyes. *Bennet, I'm here. Damn, I should have done this before. I am an idiot.*

His presence sharpens with the sound of my name. And then—his voice comes through the bond. *You're my idiot.*

I'm definitely grinning in a damp cell in a dungeon like an idiot.

Cass—he killed them. My parents.

My grin drops. *What?*

An image of Bennet floods my thoughts. He's in a dark, cramped room, somewhere above me. Some kind of a storage space. His presence is like a warmth in my midsection. He's leaning against a door, listening to an ifrit guard right outside of it.

Are you reading that creature's thoughts? I ask.

His response is laced with uncertainty. *I think so. My powers. They are more. I think it's the bond.*

I search inside, seeking my own magic. He's right. What used to be a glimmer of flame I could draw on to track objects is now a roaring inferno that I'm not sure I can control. I tamp it back down and focus on Bennet. He's drawing information from the weaker minds around him.

My uncle. It's always been about power. About control. Everything he told me was a lie. He was jealous of my mother who would inherit more than him. He planned their death, the ifrit attack. He asked them to kill his own sister and brother-in-law and fiancée in exchange for power and land. All because he couldn't stand being second in line.

The rush of it hits me in waves—his thoughts, his grief, his fury.

He's not right in the head. He's been planning this for years. He hates Helen because she's part mortal. Thinks she is dirty. I can hear him speaking with her, somewhere below me. When the wedding plans began, he ensured she discovered the truth of her parentage and encouraged her to flee.

He pauses. *I think my senses are more enhanced as well. Hugh and Helen aren't even on the same floor as I am.*

I sniff and glance around my dingy cell. Well. I'm glad I still have my lame human senses because this dungeon stinks like ass.

Bennet's warm chuckle fills my mind. Then he's quiet again, listening.

He says everything he has done is for the realm, but it's mostly about hate and prejudice. He thinks humans are weak. That my parents were fools for choosing to mingle our line with mortals. The reason it is hard for us to conceive is because we need more diversity in our bloodline, but according to him, we should be using the more powerful, darker blood of ifrit.

Horror rolls through him and into me.

He plans on getting the fake Helen with child. He wants his bloodline merged with an ifrit to be all powerful. He's going to use Helen's magic to bond her likeness with the ifrit, forever, and destroy her.

He'll merge her image with an ifrit and control them with the ring, including his own children. Then he will be in charge of all the realm, and the ifrit.

Not if we have anything to say about it. Bennet's thought is a growl.

I rise to my feet slowly, my pulse steady. *What do we do now?*

TWENTY-SEVEN

We get the hell out of here, Bennet says.

Sure. No problem. I'll just conjure a key.

Except . . . I glance at the thick iron bars and rusted lock on the cell door, then down at my hands.

Maybe I can.

The magic in me is different now. Like Bennet said, it's more. Before, it was like a compass needle, pulling toward lost things. Now it's a wildfire just waiting for oxygen. It coils beneath my skin, humming with energy. But I don't know how to shape it, how to aim it. I've never had to do anything like this before.

Bennet reads my thoughts. *I could come to you.*

No. You are surrounded by guards. I'm alone in this cell, probably because they figured there is no need to guard the stupid weak mortal. I can escape, find you, then we can take out your guards together.

You can do it. I can feel it. Bennet's voice in my mind is a caress full of pride and love.

I close my eyes and push my way through it. The bond

pulses bright between us, aiding my magic like he's showing me how to use it.

I've always found things. That's my thing. A missing necklace. A misplaced letter. The path through the dark. The broken piece in the water heater.

I have to find a way out.

I place my palm flat against the cold metal of the door, exhale slowly, and let the magic rise. I picture it weaving into the iron, searching the bars and hinges and age-worn bolts. Like fingers brushing over braille, trying to read its secrets.

No, not the door. The *lock*.

I reach for the lock, not with force, but with focus. The magic inside me recognizes the shape of the lock, understands it on some level I never could before. The shape of it takes form in my mind, and the shape of a *flaw*. Deep inside the mechanism, the metal of the pins thins due to too many cycles of pressure. A tiny crack, nearly invisible.

I scan the cell. The floor is layered in grime and splinters, the corners thick with dust.

My eyes are pulled to a bit of debris near the far wall: a jagged length of rusted wire, no longer than a needle, half-buried in old straw. I scramble over, pry it loose with numb fingers. It's brittle and bent, but just rigid enough.

Back at the door, I slide the wire into the keyhole, guiding it by instinct, tuned to the lock's breaking point. I wiggle the metal, press just right, and—

Click. Then, with a sharp metallic snap, the bolt gives way.

My breath catches. "Holy shit."

You did it. Pride blooms through the bond.

I blink at the door, then down at my hands.

No time to waste. I ease the cell door open, heart pounding, and slip into the corridor beyond. The dungeon air is heavy and damp, thick with stone and silence.

I press onward, the lure of Bennet like a current in my blood. *Hold on. I'm coming.*

Blood roars in my ears, my hands shaking as I slip from shadow to shadow, ducking into alcoves and behind crumbling tapestries.

The bond is a compass, tugging at my chest like a magnet pointing north. *Bennet.* He's up higher. A floor or two. It's like there's a thread wrapped around my ribs, leading me inexorably forward.

My breathing is too loud. I stop for a second, trying to still my racing heart.

Bennet is in my mind, following my steps, staying silent like it will help me stay quiet as well.

Almost there.

The tug in my chest sharpens. So close.

Up here, the halls are narrower. Richer. The stones cleaner, the air colder. I crouch at the corner of a hallway, peeking around—and stop.

Two guards stand outside a wooden door with a heavy latch. Bennet's behind it. No doubt in my mind.

But I can't just waltz up and ask them to step aside.

Excuse me, sorry to interrupt your evil overlord shift, but I need my maybe-boyfriend. Could you scooch over a bit?

Bennet chuckles in the back of my mind. *Maybe-boyfriend?* His incredulity brushes against my senses.

It's not like we've had the whole exclusivity conversation.

His response is dry. *I would think the whole fated mates aspect of our relationship would supersede the need for such a thing, but I am willing to talk if you are.*

Later. I blow him an imaginary kiss and press my back against the wall, heart thudding as I think. I need to get them away. Make them move. Make it believable.

Wait, Bennet says. His voice hums low and steady in my head. *Let me try something.*

There's a pause. A quiet gathering of magic like a breath held beneath the surface.

Then, from inside the room, a loud crash—metal clanging against stone, followed by a snarl of pain and furious muttering.

The guards snap to attention.

"What the hell was that?" one says, hand drifting toward the hilt at his waist.

The other bangs on the door. "Hey! What's going on in there? Lord Hugh said he would be out cold."

More thuds. Something shatters. Then Bennet, voice perfectly pitched with desperation, calls out, "Help! I—I can't breathe—something's wrong—"

The guards look at each other, curse, and one scrambles with the latch while the other reaches for the handle.

It opens and a rush of wind blows out, knocking them back and slamming them into the wall before they crumple to the ground.

I surge forward, passing the motionless guards.

Bennet emerges from the room, a smile lighting his face when his gaze connects with mine. The room is a mess, glass everywhere and a broken stool in the corner, but his eyes burn, fierce and bright.

He hauls me to him, mouth coming down over mine, the kiss savage and wild as the bond burns even brighter between us.

"Wow." When we finally separate, my legs are shaky.

Bennet holds on to my waist, keeping me steady. "We must find Helen. He's starting the ritual now."

The pressure in the air shifts, like the sea pulling back from the shore right before a thundering wave. My breath catches, the hair on my arms standing on end. My magic, still buzzing from the bond, flickers wildly in my gut.

Bennet's hands clench on me. "You feel that?"

"It's like something's trying to suck all the air out of the castle. What is that?"

"Power. The ring."

A chill skates down my spine. The Ring of Solomon. It's like a moon. A gravitational pull, not just of power but of intent. An ancient hunger being woken up. Used. Controlled.

We move, fast and silent. The deeper we go, the colder the air gets and the more the castle around us changes. The walls are no longer decorative or grand, only raw stone and flickering torchlight. Older. Forgotten. A hidden corridor, a stairwell spiraling down, deeper and deeper into the foundations.

The magic pulses again, stronger now, rhythmic, like a heartbeat echoing through stone.

A voice rises with it. Low, but getting louder. Chanting. Each word makes my skin crawl, like the syllables weren't meant to exist outside of nightmares. The energy sharpens like a blade. I grab Bennet's arm and nod toward a heavy door cracked open enough to let a sliver of golden light spill through.

Bennet peers through the crack and I duck into his side to view what's happening inside. A wide, circular chamber stretches out, lit by a ring of fire that dances in unnatural colors, violet, blue, and a sickly green that makes my stomach revolt. Symbols are etched into the floor, glowing beneath a circle of black stone. At the center of it all is Helen.

She's on her knees, bound by chains that shimmer with magic. Her head hangs low, dark hair falling into her face.

Standing above her is Hugh, and next to him, another Helen. *Fake* Helen, draped in a deep purple ceremonial robe.

Circling the chamber like hungry wolves are three smoky ifrit charged with lightning.

Hugh lifts his hands above his head. Darkness swirls around him, drawn in by the magic, wrapping around the false Helen, and then the real one, tying them together.

His voice echoes through the chamber, proud and venomous. "You should be honored, Helen. Despite your half-blooded weakness, you will be the instrument of our victory. Through you, we will become what the old blood only dreamed of. We will transcend."

Helen raises her head, defiant even as her limbs shake. "You mean *you* will. You're using them. Just like you used my parents. Just like you used me and Bennet and everyone."

Hugh sneers. "They were foolish. Weak. Your father allowed you to be born through mortal seed. Your mother clung to peace and treaties instead of domination. I warned them, and they ignored me. So I did what had to be done."

Then his hand sparks with magic and he lifts the flare overhead to strike.

Bennet bursts into the chamber like thunder, magic pulsing off him in waves that crack the stone beneath his feet. "Don't you dare."

Hugh whirls around, the ring in his hand spitting sparks of furious gold.

"I wanted to be like you." Bennet's gaze locks on Hugh. "I thought you loved me. I thought what you taught me meant something."

Hugh's lip curls. "*Love.* You fool. You haven't learned a damn thing from me. You're weak. Powerless. The ifrit understand power. They don't shirk their duty for their feelings. They don't dilute their bloodlines for *love.*"

I sprint to Helen's side while they face off. I grab the chains around real Helen's wrists. They are looped through another chain, attached to the floor. They sting like acid, but I don't let go. I have to get her free.

Bennet stands tall, his eyes burning with the fury of betrayal and grief and barely leashed magic. "You killed my parents for this? Because love made them weak?"

Bennet takes a step forward, and the flames bow away from him. His magic surges around him like a rising storm.

"You don't understand strength. You think it's about domination. About the pursuit of power with no limits. But real strength—real power—is about protection. It's standing in the fire and saying: *I will burn before I let those I love get hurt.* My parents knew this. I pity you, that you don't."

I try to tune out their argument, knowing Bennet isn't just trauma dumping. Thanks to the bond, I know he's giving me time to free his sister. Where is it? Where's the weak link? But these chains are new, and—

"Cassie. Behind you!" Helen screams.

Fake Helen lunges for me.

Time slows, my magic flaring. Of course Hugh let Bennet talk. A distraction while his minion goes for the weak link— me. It's the giants all over again, dammit. My heart hammers, instincts screaming. I need a solution. Where? *Where?*

There. Between the steps of her awkward gait and the angle of her charge is an opening. A narrow, perfect fraction of a second where her weight will shift off balance.

I dive sideways, kicking out and tripping her at the kneecaps. She stumbles, crashing to the ground.

Praise the gods.

"What do you think you are doing?" Hugh's fury boils over.

The ring flares and he throws everything he has at us.

TWENTY-EIGHT

The chamber explodes into motion.

Hugh hurls a column of fire straight at Bennet, the magic laced with shadowy tendrils that twist and snap like vipers.

Bennet catches it with his bare hands, the smoke and fire wrapping around his forearms and vanishing into the air with a hiss.

He snarls, "You'll have to do better than that."

I duck as a smoky ifrit lunges at me, fiery hands slashing the air where my head was a heartbeat ago. I roll to the side.

The ifrit circles me, silent and inhuman. Its eyes are nothing but glowing coals. No thought. No will. Just Hugh's puppet.

"I really hate creepy fire zombies." I stretch out my magic, trying to shove it toward the ifrit. But my power's not built for blasting.

Still, a spark shoots forward—then fizzles uselessly against the creature's shoulder.

Cool. Cool cool cool cool cool.

But then Bennet whips a hand through the air, and the

seemingly useless ember *detonates*, white fire flashing outward. The ifrit stumbles, smoke hissing from the wound.

"That's nifty."

"You're welcome." He flings another blast toward Hugh that sends sparks cascading off the ring's shield.

I dive toward Helen, yanking at her chains. The lock is thick and ironbound, but I push my magic into it, not to break it, but to find where it gives.

And there it is: the tiniest flaw, a catch in the mechanism.

Before I can act, Fake Helen lunges.

I grab a slack length of chain and whip it at her. She ducks and throws lightning.

I lift my arm—and reacting purely on instinct—reach through the bond inside me.

Heat floods me. Not mine. Bennet's.

It flares from my skin in a sharp burst, cracking the lightning midair and flinging it into sizzling sparks.

The fake stumbles back.

Holy hell. That actually worked. I turn to the chains again, letting my seeker magic stretch into them and pull.

The lock snaps.

Helen slumps forward, gasping. "Took you long enough."

"Nice to see you too."

She grabs my arm, eyes flashing molten gold. "He's channeling power through the ring. That's what's sustaining my double. He's not strong enough without it." She grins, feral. "Let's break his toy."

We rise together, Bennet beside us, blood on his temple, fury in his eyes. The ground cracks under Hugh's next blow, and more ifrit rise from the circle. Fake Helen rises once again, moving toward us. There are too many.

Bennet breathes hard next to me. Helen limps closer. The

ifrit close in, surrounding us in a tightening ring of flame and ash.

And Hugh laughs. "You see now? Emotion makes you weak. That's why you'll fall."

I grit my teeth. "No. It's why we're still standing."

But even as the words leave my lips, I know the truth—we're about to go down fighting.

Bennet reaches for me, our fingers entwining. "I love you." His expression is fierce, his love pulsing through our bond.

Then the doors explode open behind us.

Wind roars through the chamber, blowing away the smoke. The fire falters.

My parents charge into the room, flanked by Darius and the others. Magic flares, and in the light, weapons glint and a group of faces glow grim and glorious. Light crashes into the circle like a divine hammer, slamming into Hugh's shield and shattering its outer ring.

The tide turns in an instant.

The chamber erupts into chaos.

Magic explodes in brilliant arcs: gold, blue, violet, and vibrant red. Fire slams against shields. Light sears through shadow.

Mom shields the others with glowing runes. Darius blasts a fiery pulse across the room, clearing a path.

Helen and I press forward through the fray, dodging strikes, countering where we can. But half my focus is on Bennet.

He's standing across from Hugh now. Just the two of them, fire curling in their palms, the floor cracked and blackened beneath their feet.

"You think you can beat me? You weren't trained." Hugh sneers, circling.

"You trained me to be a pawn." Bennet's voice is steady. "I trained myself to be a warrior."

And then he *moves*.

Their magic collides in a thunderclap, raw energy lashing out and sending shockwaves through the room.

Hugh is fast, but Bennet is faster.

He sidesteps a blast of lightning, then slams both palms into the ground. The stone beneath Hugh's feet erupts, forcing him into the air. Bennet follows, rising in a pillar of fire, wings of flame stretching from his back.

"You think you can win?" Hugh's eyes flick to me, to Helen. "You've bonded with a mortal. You're diluted. Impure."

"No," Bennet says. "I'm complete."

Hugh snarls and hurls a spear of molten power.

Bennet catches it midair and snaps it in half. "You were never the strongest. Only the cruelest."

Hugh lunges, the Ring of Solomon burning bright.

Bennet meets him with open hands and closes them around the ring.

Their magic ignites.

It's too much. The power arcs violently, surging up Bennet's arms, through his chest—and then *out*, into the chamber, cracking the air with light. Hugh screams, the sound tearing at the walls.

But it's not enough.

I run, reaching for him. "Bennet!"

I grab his shoulder.

The moment we're connected, the energy changes. I concentrate on the ring. Where's the weakness? Where, where, where? I seek and seek deeper into the ring, the layers of metal, the goddamn atoms of it and there is nothing and *oh, no we're gonna die.*

No.

There.

A fault line buried beneath centuries of misuse and corrupted power.

I guide Bennet's power to it like a key to a lock, and together, we push.

The ring screams and then cracks and then shatters.

Hugh crumples to the floor. Still. Unmoving.

The smoky ifrit around us dissolve, their bodies unraveling into mist. The room is still lit with embers, glowing in the aftermath.

Bennet lands hard, stumbling to one knee.

I bend over him, clutching at him. "You're okay. You're okay."

He nods once, dazed. "I—I didn't know if I could do it."

Helen stands nearby, silent for a long moment, then says softly, "It's over."

Behind us, our allies regroup, helping each other up, brushing off dust. Bruised and bloody but alive. The castle has gone still, the threat broken.

Holy shit. We kicked ass.

TWENTY-NINE

I'm wrapped in a soft oversized shirt from the wardrobe in Bennet's chambers, curled up on a couch near the fire while he leans against the hearth, shirt half-unbuttoned and hair still damp from a bath. He's got a cut on his temple, bruises all over, and fatigue etched into his pores. We both look like we nearly died. Maybe because that's exactly what happened.

But we're alive. We won.

The fire crackles, casting warm light over the stone floor. I let my head rest against the cushions and close my eyes for a moment.

My mind won't stop buzzing.

The aftermath is a strange kind of numb. I keep turning the whole night over in my head, trying to make sense of it. After the battle, everything blurred.

There were others in the dungeon rescued, servants that had been locked up for not complying with Hugh's plans, including Torren, the head guard. Dominic and Lord Wallace were among the prisoners, both bruised and hungry but upright.

We cleared the castle of the lingering ifrit. Most had vanished when Hugh fell, like smoke in the wind. But a few remained, confused and suddenly directionless. Bennet and Helen handled them quickly, banishing the remaining wisps of smoke with magic.

Helen wanted to return to Delores right away. And Mom and Dad are aching to see Jackie and Kevin and Mimi. But we need rest first. Just one night.

Tomorrow, we'll regroup. Head home. Make a plan.

And tonight . . .

I glance at Bennet. He's watching me, that quiet, thoughtful gaze of his, like he knows exactly where my head is even if I haven't said a word.

"You're thinking too loud." He pushes off the fireplace and crossing the room to me.

My lips tug upward. "Sorry."

"You don't have to be." He sits beside me. The heat of him is solid and warm and real. "I keep going over it too."

I lean into him. "We almost didn't win."

His arm wraps around me, a kiss whispering against my hair. "But we did."

I nod. "I know. I didn't think it would feel like this. I thought there would be cheering. Some kind of cinematic music swell."

He huffs a soft laugh. "You want me to hum something dramatic?"

"Only if you simultaneously rip your shirt open."

He glances down at his shirt. "Halfway there."

Despite everything, I laugh. Just a light chuckle. But it's real.

I sag further against him, our physical connection helping the stiffness bleed slowly from my spine.

"We're going to have to explain everything tomorrow. To

everyone. Servants, council members, visiting delegates. Helen wants to go back an hour ago. Your parents too." Tension tightens his body and his emotions seep into me.

I turn my head to look at him. "You're worried."

He swallows. "The bond allows no secrets."

"You think I don't want to stay here with you?"

His gaze narrows on mine. "You . . . you wish to stay here?"

"Don't you have to? You're like, the ruler, or whatever, you and Helen?"

"Well, yes. But—"

"We can go back and visit my family sometimes, right? I mean, we are pretty magical now, together. I bet Helen can show us how to open a portal."

"Of course."

"So what's the problem?"

He slips off the couch and comes to his knees before me. "You would give up your life in the mortal realm, for me?"

I chuckle. "What life? I was raising my siblings, which I don't have to do anymore because they have parents, and doing random side jobs that I hated. Here, I can learn about a whole new world." Excitement slips through me. "A whole new, magical history of art and literature and artifacts. The possibilities are endless."

His hands slide gently into mine. "Cassie, I've lost so much in my life. I was living half a life. And then you freed me from the lamp, threatened me with your stick, and I—I never stood a chance."

My chest tightens, warmth blooming in my ribs.

Then he leans closer, his voice a little steadier. "So. I have no ring," we both wince at that memory, "no speech prepared, and we still smell like demon smoke, but, uh, will you marry me?"

My heart stops in my chest. "Wait. Seriously?"

His head tilts. "Is that a yes?"

My mouth falls open. I shut it. It falls open again. "Isn't this kind of fast?"

He shrugs. "We're fated mates. I think we're already legally, mystically, cosmically bound."

I pretend to consider. "True. And you'll promise to love and honor and take care of all the evil bugs that might come into my presence?"

He nods. "It's a strong foundation for marriage."

"Okay." My mouth stretches across my face. I must be grinning like a lunatic. This must be what bombshells feel like when they're dropped into the *Love Island* villa, ready to cause chaos and drama and revel in it. "Let's get married. But like, in a bit. Like next year or later."

His answering smile could rival the sun.

And then we're kissing.

The pull of the bond hums through my veins, answering his like a heartbeat. It's more than simple want, it's need, sharp and radiant and fused with love.

My fingers find the edges of his jaw, the curve of his neck. He makes a low sound, rumbly and pleased, and deepens the kiss.

Heat unfurls in my chest. In my fingertips. Everywhere.

The bond between us throbs as if it's alive, feeding off our connection and wrapping us tighter together. There's a shimmer under my skin, a golden thrum like sunlight and fire and something ancient, something inevitable.

"Cassie," he whispers against my mouth. "You're everything."

I can't think. I don't want to.

His hands slide under the hem of my shirt, warm against my waist. I shiver, not from cold but from the thrill of his touch. It's electric but familiar. Safe. Like coming home.

I tug his shirt over his head and he lifts mine in return. Skin meets skin, and the bond flares even brighter between us. The magic is wild and exultant, glittering through every nerve.

He scoops me up in his arms and carries me across the room. We fall back into the bed, wrapped in each other.

His hands are everywhere, tracing my skin like he's learning me all over again. His mouth follows, brushing over my collarbone, down the slope of my shoulder. His lips are warm, tasting of jasmine and spice, the ghost of laughter still lingering in his breath.

I sink into him, fingers threading through his hair, tugging him closer. Every kiss, every touch, ignites a sensation deeper than heat. It's like pressing against the edges of a universe built just for us.

He murmurs my name like a prayer.

I answer it with a sigh, with a gasp, with my whole body.

When he slides into me, we still, savoring the connection for a long minute. Then we're moving, together, like we always have. Like we always will.

The bond unfurls between us like a living thing, raw and radiant, a shimmering thread connecting nerve to nerve, thought to thought, soul to soul. He surrounds me, and not just in body. Our connection intensifies with every movement, in the way his breath catches, the way his hands tremble against my hips, the rush of love blooming beneath his ribs, the awe, the near-disbelief that this is real, that I am his and he is mine.

My chest aches with the sheer fullness of it all, our emotions mirroring each other and rushing back and forth, intensifying. Each touch drives the breath from my lungs and fills me up in the same instant. We're open to each other in a way that defies language. No shields. No fear.

His forehead rests against mine, and our rhythm is its own

spell, old and sacred, as if the universe built us and brought us to this moment in time. It was inevitable.

My fingers dig into his back.

Pleasure builds, along with something quieter. A tether that stretches across this world and the next.

When release finally crashes through us, it's not a firestorm—it's a homecoming.

A breaking and a healing all at once.

Breathless and tangled beneath the sheets, he traces slow circles on my back. "You still want to wait until next year?"

I shift like I'm going to get out of bed. "Does your kingdom have one of those drive-through wedding chapels?"

He laughs, warm and low, and pulls me back into bed.

The afternoon sun slants through my bedroom window, soft and golden, catching on the floating dust motes like they're little bits of magic still hanging in the air.

I sit cross-legged on my bed, Bennet beside me, half a duffel bag packed with books and sketchpads between us.

He turns a little beaded keychain over in his hand. "You want to take this?"

The metal charm dangling from his fingers is shaped like a saxophone, worn smooth from time.

I shrug. "Maybe. It's kind of silly. I bought it after a Mardi Gras parade when I got lost and found my way back by following the sound of a jazz band. I was maybe nine?"

"The first time you used your magic, perhaps?" He turns the keychain over once more, thoughtful. "That's not silly."

I pause, struck by the idea. Was it? And how did he know? How does he just . . . *get* me? How does he understand it's not just the memory, but the weight of it? "I want a little piece of this place with me."

He sets the keychain down gently on the nightstand, like it's precious. "Then we take it with us. All of it. The silly and the sacred."

Downstairs, Mimi and Jackie are making cookies, the scents of sugar and vanilla drifting up the stairs. Mom and Dad are down there playing board games with Kevin at the dining table.

The sound of their antics makes my heart swell. Jackie's laughter is stronger now. *She's* stronger. Color in her cheeks, energy in her voice. It's like someone turned the lights back on inside her.

Nostalgia hits me right in the gut. I'm going to miss this.

Bennet turns toward me, propping his chin on one hand. "It's a good home."

Of course he knows exactly how I feel.

"It was. It is." I glance around the room—my cracked mirror, the posters from high school, the shelf of books now half empty. "But I'm ready for something new. With you."

His hand finds mine. "We don't have to leave right away."

"I know. But I want to." I exhale, letting the tension go with it. "This place, it held me together when I was young, then I held it together when my parents were gone. But now I can let go, breathe deeper somewhere else."

He squeezes my fingers. "Wherever you breathe, I'll be there."

"God, you're cheesy."

"For you? Tragically."

We both laugh, and I lean my head on his shoulder. For a few seconds, the house wraps around us in peaceful silence, the kind that comes after a storm.

A few minutes later, I've shoved all I can into a couple bags,

Bennet slings one of the heavier ones over his shoulder like it's nothing, and I loop my arms through the handles of the last one. My room is both too full and too empty.

I've packed most of the things I want to bring. I can always come back later. I will come back later. This isn't goodbye, it's only see you later, and yet moving to another dimension sure does have a ring of finality to it.

We head downstairs, and right as we set our bags by the door, someone knocks.

I glance over at Bennet. Who could that be?

He opens the door, and Richard waltzes in. "Anyone order a ridiculously handsome witch with impeccable timing?" He's wearing a velvet blazer that sparkles like it's been dipped in sequins.

"You total dick." The fury hits so fast I'm moving before the last word exits my mouth. Bennet's arm is across my middle, holding me back. "You knew. You got them into Aetheria—my parents—and you didn't think maybe, I don't know, leaving a backup plan might be smart? Or maybe telling their children so we wouldn't spend years thinking they were dead? Wondering if they abandoned us? Watching Jackie waste away with no answers?" My voice climbs. "We didn't even get a note!"

Richard blinks, expression schooled into something halfway between regret and theatrical pity. "I would like to remind you how useful my hex bags were, if you're considering who to include in your wedding party."

Is he for real right now? "Yeah, I know. The stupid hex bags were good. They warded off the dark magic. Great job. But that doesn't erase the fact that you still acted like a complete sociopath."

He waves a hand, unbothered. "Well, sure. And they also helped bring the right person in."

I blink. "Wait. What?"

He inspects his nails. "I may have added a little something. Nothing too invasive! Just a wee enchantment to amplify connections, open paths, light little sparks if the timing was right."

My mouth pops open. "You meddled."

"Darling, I'm a witch. Meddling is in the job description. Besides, it was nothing that dramatic. I was a mere facilitator. You're the one who fell in love. I just made sure the path was lit." Richard grins. "How else would you have found your soulmate who lived in another realm? How else was he going to show up at your door to teach Jackie how to access powers no one has seen this side of the veil in centuries? How else were you going to be there to let him in? Your parents had to leave, he had to come here, and you had to go there. It's all very circular, you see." He tips his head, enigmatic. "Even fate needs a nudge sometimes."

My mind is exploding. Is he suggesting all of this had to happen for me and Bennet to meet? My parents had to go to Aetheria and join their band of misfits to be in the right place at the right time? But why? "Why do you even care so much?"

He offers a sly smile. "Let's just say your line and mine have crossed paths before. Once or twice. Or even many times." His eyes gleam, a flicker of something ancient beneath the glamour. "You could call it ancestral interest."

My brain short-circuits for a second. "You're what, like my great-great-grand-djinn?"

He winks. "Oh, please, I'm far too young-looking for that."

The light bulb goes off in Bennet's head—which means it's lighting up in mine too. "That's why you said you're welcome, before," he says. "When we first met."

And that's also why he kept stealing my hairbrush when he stayed with us. He was using my hair in the hex bags for his . . . love spell?

"If you ever need a place to stay in Aetheria, our door is always open," Bennet adds. "And I would be honored to have you in my wedding party."

Richard tsks. "You kids. You're going to make me feel things." He reaches into his coat pocket. "Speaking of sentimentality." He pulls out a delicate gold ring, dangling from a familiar chain.

Bennet freezes. His gaze drops to the ring, and for a moment, he doesn't move.

"I believe this belongs to you. Even the swamp witches know when it's time to return what matters."

Bennet takes it, fingers curling around the chain like it might disappear. "Thank you."

Richard waves a hand in front of his face. "Don't make me cry. It'll ruin my eyeliner." His sigh is cinema-worthy. "Well. I'm off, children." He sashays to the front door.

As soon as Richard disappears, Bennet grabs my hand and pulls me into him.

His mouth captures mine in a kiss that's become familiar, but never ordinary. It burns through me like wildfire, deeper than our first kiss, richer than all the ones that followed. Like he's trying to memorize the shape of this moment, and I am too.

When we finally break apart, breathless and buzzing, he catches my left hand and lifts it between us, inspecting it like it's an interesting puzzle.

"What are you doing?"

"Measuring your ring finger, to see if I'll need to have my mother's ring resized."

My breath catches. My chest aches with joy, and grief. I found my parents, but his are still gone.

He brushes a kiss over my ring finger. "She left it for me.

With the hope that I'd find something real. A love as true as her and my father's. I would say I succeeded."

I press my forehead to his. "You're going to make me cry before we even wish everyone farewell."

"Then let's say goodbye fast," he whispers against my lips.

"Mom?" I call out. "Everyone—we're leaving."

They emerge from the kitchen. Jackie's wearing one of my old sweatshirts. Kevin trails her, hands shoved in his pockets. Mimi's behind them, eyes already glassy. Mom has her arm looped through Dad's.

"So," I blink back the emotions threatening to leak out of my eyes, "this is it."

Jackie sighs. "It's so cray you're about to step into a magical portal and leave reality behind for like, ever."

Bennet raises an eyebrow. "We're coming back. And you can come visit us too."

"I know. But who's going to grill me with fifty questions about my daily caloric intake and chores and homework and sleep patterns?"

I smile and pull Jackie into a hug, then Kevin joins, awkward and tangled. "You've got each other. And Mom and Dad. You don't need me hovering anymore."

Jackie's voice is muffled in my shoulder. "Doesn't mean I don't want you hovering."

I give them both a squeeze before I pull away and turn to Mimi.

She opens her arms. "Look at you. Wandering off with a djinn prince. I always knew you'd be the exciting one despite the past few years ignoring my advice."

I laugh.

Mom is next, cupping my face like she used to when I was little. "I'm so proud of how you held everything together."

My throat tightens. "I didn't always do a great job."

"You did what no one else could," she says simply. "Now go. Build something for yourself."

Dad pulls me into a crushing hug. "I'll fix the house. So when you visit, there will be hot water and no flickering lights."

I blink hard. "Thanks, Dad."

"Wait!" Kevin runs into the kitchen, then returns with a paper grocery bag, passing it to Bennet.

Bennet peers inside the top. "What is this?"

Jackie puts a hand on her hip. "Just some stuff we put together that you will definitely need in Aetheria. Hot sauce, peanut butter cups, sour gummies, bleach, penicillin, oh, and toilet paper."

Bennet chuckles. "This is the weirdest care package I've ever received."

I take his hand. "Welcome to the family."

There's laughter, a second round of hugs from everyone for Bennet and myself, and a few more quiet promises.

I glance at each of them one more time, heart full, chest tight, soul steady. "See you soon."

And then Bennet and I head through the door side by side, leaving one home behind to return to another.

EPILOGUE

The castle is brighter than it used to be.

Maybe it's the weather, the spring sun pouring through the arched windows, or the fact that it's no longer full of secrets and ifrit and traitorous uncles. Or maybe it's just me, finally exhaling after months of holding my breath and years of trying to stay afloat.

I walk through the east wing with a basket tucked under one arm, the corridor warm with light and the scent of blooming jasmine from the gardens below. Bennet's voice echoes distantly from the council chamber. He's in there with Helen and two advisors, probably debating trade routes or ceremonial titles.

He's good at it. Charming and diplomatic when he wants to be. Dangerous when he has to be. And underneath it all, still mine.

We're not married yet. Bennet's been pressing me for a date, but I don't even want to think about it until after Helen and Delores tie the knot in a few days.

Delores has been overseeing flower arrangements and

security with equal levels of intensity. Helen, for her part, won't stop smiling, and it's the good happy kind, not the baring of teeth before she throws herself into combat kind.

I round the corner and duck into a quiet, dusty chamber off the main library. My basket lands with a soft thump on a table, and I pull out scrolls and half-crumbling volumes, brushing the edges delicately.

This is what I do now. Mostly. I spend my early mornings training with Bennet and the guards and learning to fight and use my increased levels of magic. Not that we're expecting any battles, but it's good to be prepared and it's fun. Especially when Bennet pins me down.

The Aetherians have started calling me "the prince's betrothed," which is weird. I mean, I have a name. But I've found a more comfortable title for myself: curator. I'm piecing together the kingdom's lost art history, tracking ancient artifacts, decoding forgotten stories etched in broken mosaics and fractured murals. I've even found evidence of early magical tools that may predate the Ring of Solomon.

That discovery nearly gave Bennet an aneurysm. He now checks in on me whenever I've been "too quiet."

I love it here. Not just the magic or the castles or the endless skies, but the sense that my life is mine now. That I'm building something new, instead of merely surviving day by day. That I'm not alone.

The door creaks open behind me and I don't have to turn to know who it is.

"I brought lunch," Bennet says, his voice warm. "Also, Helen says if you don't show up for dress fittings soon, she's going to portal into your room and personally zip you into something sparkly."

I chuckle. "Terrifying."

"She means it."

I look over my shoulder at him, leaning in the doorway, holding a basket of food, hair tousled, eyes bright. His sleeves are rolled up and his tie is loose.

"You good?" I ask.

"Better now." He crosses the room and drops a kiss to the top of my head, setting lunch on the table, then peers over my shoulder at the dusty scroll I'm unfurling. "That looks cursed."

"It's a map." I reach into the basket, pulling out a square item wrapped in linen. Mmm. Sandwich. "To a vault of lost sculptures, probably. Maybe cursed and valuable."

"Perfect."

I take a bite of food and chew. "You sure you're okay with me being the weird history geek in the tower while you help run the kingdom?"

"As long as the weird history geek marries me eventually, I don't care where she lives."

I grin. "Deal."

Outside, bells chime, signaling the hour. In a few days, we'll be celebrating Helen and Delores with firelight and feasts. In a few months, maybe it'll be our turn. But right now, I have a dusty scroll, a castle to explore, and a prince who feeds me.

Turns out, happily ever afters aren't so bad after all.

Especially when he kisses me like this.

Bennet brushes a crumb from the corner of my mouth with his thumb, his touch lingering. "You've got ink on your face."

"Occupational hazard."

He leans closer. "I like you like this, smelling of parchment and ham."

"You're such a nerd." My breath catches as his mouth finds the hollow beneath my ear. I set the food on the table away from the scrolls.

"And you're mine," he says against my skin. His hands slide

around my waist, pulling me into his lap as I laugh, startled and breathless.

The table creaks behind us, scrolls and sandwich forgotten as his lips find mine, the kiss starting slow but deepening quickly, like he's trying to memorize every inch of me all over again. My fingers tangle in his shirt, tugging him closer.

"I thought you had meetings," I murmur between kisses.

"I canceled them," he says, voice rough with affection. "For research purposes."

I arch an eyebrow. "Oh? What kind of research?"

His grin is wicked. "Extensive. Hands-on. Involves a very thorough exploration of my fiancée."

"Well, as a scholar," I feign seriousness even as he lifts me onto the table, "I feel obligated to assist."

Outside, the bells keep chiming, and the sun slants golden through the windows. Somewhere down the hall, Helen is probably barking orders about seating arrangements.

But here, in this moment, it's only us.

No rituals. No war. No looming shadows.

Just magic. And love. And a future that is full of promise, humor, and each other.

The End

ALSO BY MARY FRAME

Imperfect Series:

Imperfect Chemistry

Imperfectly Criminal

Practically Imperfect

Picture Imperfect

Imperfect Strangers

Imperfectly Delicious

The Dorky Duet (Plus a companion novel!)

Ridorkulous

Geektastic

Nerdelicious

Time after Time Series:

Time of My Life

If I Could Turn Back Time

Castle Cove Mystery Series

Fake It to the Limit

Too Much Crime on My Hands

You're the Con That I Want

Fox Family Series

Between a Fox and a Hard Place

The Fox and the Rebound

Another Fox Bites the Dust

Some Like It Fox

For Fox Sake

Stand Alone Books

Bewitched By the Djinn

Coming October, 2025

About the Author

Go to my website to sign up for the newsletter and purchase books directly with discounts and exclusives!
www.maryframe.com

Mary Frame writes romantic comedies with quirky characters, steamy moments, and banter that will make you blush and snort-laugh at the same time. She's a full time mom with a full time job and has no idea how she manages to write novels, but it probably helps that she's a dedicated introvert. She doesn't enjoy writing about herself in third person, but she does enjoy reading, writing, dancing, and damaging the ear drums of her co-workers when she randomly decides to sing to them.

She LOVES hearing from readers and will not only respond but likely begin stalking them while tossing out hearts and flowers and rainbows! If that doesn't creep you out, e-mail her at:
maryframeauthor@gmail.com